LOREDANA

ALSO BY LAURO MARTINES

Non-fiction

April Blood: Florence and the Plot Against the Medici

Power and Imagination: City-States in Renaissance Italy

Strong Words: Writing and Social Strain in the Italian Renaissance

An Italian Renaissance Sextet: Six Tales in Historical Context

The Social World of the Florentine Humanists

Lawyers and Statecraft in Renaissance Florence

Violence and Civil Disorder in Italian Cities, 1200–1500

(editor)

Not in God's Image: Women in History from the Greeks to the Victorians

(with Julia O'Faolain)

Society and History in English Renaissance Verse

LOREDANA

A Venetian Tale

Lauro Martines

Thomas Dunne Books
St. Martin's Press ✠ New York

For my agent, Kay McCauley
And again for Julia O'Faolain

Let the upper streets be for the use only of the
nobility, the lower streets for carts, pack animals
and the common people . . . The city should be
built near the sea or a big river, so that the filth
can be washed away.

Leonardo da Vinci, *Notebooks* (a new city)

Any city, however small, is really two cities, one
for the poor and the other for the rich.

Plato, *The Republic*

Entrée

Of this love story and political tale, belonging to the sixteenth century, only a single manuscript exists. How it came out of Italy cannot be told here, because the transaction was probably shady. Italian law bars the export of the nation's old masters and historical papers, unless they have first been vetted by the Ministry of Culture. The volume in question, however, would not have been approved for export: it includes a major run of state papers, all taken from Venetian government archives in the 1690s. The collection then passed quickly to a great family, and remained in their library for three centuries, until a year ago, when needy descendants secretly sold and spirited all their historic papers out of the country.

The form of the tale is unusual. It reaches us as a composite of documents, assembled around 1700 by a priest and archivist, Fra Benedict Loredan. Springing from the Loredan lineage, like Loredana herself, he had heard the old story, and resolved to get at the true account by trawling through family and archival records. In the course of his researches, he took a surprising turn. Selecting complete documents or key passages, he decided to let the voices of the protagonists speak for themselves, and had no qualms about pilfering original records or using scissors and paste. With an eye to the shape of the unfolding tale, he also broke up the flow of testimony by moving parts around, or cutting and splicing as he saw fit. Thanks to his friar's holy vows and archival expertise, he must have had free access to all documents.

I surmise that his theft of state papers was driven by his descent from the ancestral house at the heart of the tale. He felt, perhaps, that he was doing little more than retrieving family honour and property. And the better to seal his secret, or to cover his tracks, he bound the documents together by making a fine use of needle and thread.

The codex, however – if it may be so called – requires a few preliminary words. In piecing it together, Fra Benedict became so fixated on the story that he took a rich background entirely for granted. He was still close enough to it to do so. The documents, therefore, smack of something strange. And modern readers are likely to be daunted when they learn that Venice in its great day was a two-tiered city: the city of the sun and the shaded or shadowy city below, one looming above the other. In emergencies, the Republic of Venice, la Serenissima, could turn itself into a police state. The use of torture was common, as it was throughout Europe. Capital punishment was turned into theatre: the occasion for grand educational spectacle. Most people had no proper family or surnames. And I could go on citing many another oddity – such as the daily use of a language of bells, municipal trumpets and coats of arms – with a view to preparing the reader of this tale for entry into a world different from our own.

The question naturally arises, can we trust the documents collected in the priest's codex? Everything about them turns out to be reliable: the paper and watermarks; the harsh, acidic ink; the sixteenth-century script; names and dates; not to mention mores, official procedures and the principal historical facts. Venetians were superior record keepers. Thanks to the scale of their shipping and overseas trade, they were in the daily habit of putting pen to paper.

All written history is a mosaic. Once a historian has combed through a variety of sources, he constructs an account with something like a beginning, a middle and an end. It involves descriptions, statements, hunches and stretches of analysis. But the resulting picture has to be reconstituted by the reader's imagination, as he or she, turning pages, moves through the narrative. In this sense, every reader of history is a historian.

For all his labours on the text of Loredana *(although he left it nameless), Fra Benedict's words turn up only in interpolations [bracketed thus] and only to list the name of the given archival source or the year of the event. His voice is nowhere in the narrative. We are offered, instead, the mosaic itself – an affair of raw testimonials. Each document is a part of the whole tale, with the pieces strung together so as to give us the sense, now and again, that we are being borne through city streets and, in effect, through a whole society.*

Curiously, too, as if seeking to fix the many shards of a shattered vase, Benedict Loredan numbered each document as he sewed it into his collection, thereby giving the movement of events a particular order. So that just here, in this hard feature, is where we may detect his personal stamp.

I undertook to edit and translate the tale because I was astonished by it, by Loredana's character, and by the tenacity of the young Orso, her lover. In working with the codex, I also edged my way towards a strange reason for admiring Benedict.

The so-called 'Myth of Venice' refers to the history of a wise, long-lasting, and serene republic, full of justice, moderation, wonderful rituals and beauty. This myth is trampled by the story of Loredana and Orso – the work, really, of its compiler. Yet I have not come to love Venice any the less. In some ways, disturbingly, the story has made me more ready to accept our 'fallen lot'. And hence, for having salvaged it, Friar Benedict – I passionately feel – deserves our worldly benedictions.

In the quest for something of radiant value, we often turn Renaissance Venice and Florence into glorious historical plateaus – imaginary places where justification for the human animal is more easily found. We desperately need such places, of course, and yet they are an escape. I suppose I want to say that we should have the grit to stop transforming the inadequate present into a distant golden age. Better to grapple more honestly with our inglorious world.

Lauro Martines

Archives of the Tale

Italy in the 1520s.

The Renaissance is in full swing, and so too are the banners of dark forces. German, Spanish, French and Swiss soldiers occupy parts of the peninsula. Anxiety and melancholy course through the life and letters of Italian princes and noblemen. The Church has long been under the rule of popes who sell its graces and offices while also heaping dignities on relatives and friends, and reserving major appointments for the favourites of great lords and political elites. In Germany, Martin Luther and his princely supporters are having little trouble shattering the unity of the Catholic Church, and Protestant heresy has already seeped into the Italian peninsula.

The aristocratic Republic of Venice is the leading Italian state. In Tuscany, the last Florentine Republic, cherishing open political debate, is fighting desperately to avoid the despotic return of the Medici house. Farther south, the Papal State straddles central Italy, and Rome is the city of Pope Clement VII. Up north, the powerful Duchy of Milan is the contested prize in the fierce rivalry between the King of France and the German–Spanish Habsburg Emperor, Charles V, who also rules the Kingdom of Naples in the far south.

Large parts of Italy, in short, have been turned into battlefields for ravaging foreign armies. Yet daily life appears to go on as before, chiefly in the pursuit of local concerns. The great questions remain the business of rulers.

Vendramin, the following diarist, was born into one of Venice's fore-most families.

1. [Pietro Vendramin, extract from his DIARY]:

xii September [1529] . . . The appointed time was yesterday at the sixth hour. The Ten [*Venice's secret political police*] had the perfumer and counterfeiter Sardesco rowed to the Rialto. A great crowd waited for him. It was a sunny day. The town criers, trumpets blaring, came first. When the executioner's party arrived at the square of silence, a goldsmith melted down the counterfeit ducats. Holding him down, constables then forced Sardesco's mouth open with tongs. The exec-utioner poured a fine stream of red lead into the hole of his mouth. My God. His feet jerked and kicked. People pulled back. Someone cried, *Look*. The forger's hands like claws poked up once, sharply. His eyes were wide open. And the crowd also, me too, we were all eyes. No sounds came out of him, not even a cough. He just went straight and stiff and died right there on his back.

I say, would to God that others would learn from this lesson. Amen. Amen.

Afterwards we needed a glass of wine. I was with Jacopo [*Loredan*]. We also wanted to pick up the gossip. So into the Golden Falcon we went with a few foreign merchants. One told us that twenty months ago in Milan a priest was caught at the same game, though his trick was to debase silver. Well he paid for it. A cage was lowered from the high windows of the government palazzo. He was inside, strung upside down. It took him two days to stop moving. On the third he died. But a Milan merchant, who was sitting nearby, overheard the story. No sir, he corrected. It hadn't been quite like that. There was more: the priest had also sullied himself with murder. He had helped a noble lady to kill her husband – she, his parishioner and fornicator. They used poison. Without the husband they could more safely and more often become the beast with two backs, and they burned to do so. Well in the end they didn't burn. The priest went into the cage and she lost her head on a sharp blade.

The second of the following missives was in code, with numbers representing letters and capital letters standing for certain words. Code was common in Renaissance Italy, especially in diplomacy and in communication between political exiles.

2. [Bernardo Loredan, LETTER]:

In dei nomine.

Dear Pandolfo, I beg you to reply at once. Is it true that the friar is in these parts? In God's name, what does he look like? I need an exact description. Christ have you. Venice. xviii Septembris [1529]. Bernardo

3. [Pandolfo, surname unknown, LETTER in code]:

To Bernardo Loredan in Venice.

Esteemed Bernardo, the worst has happened. Another Judas has surfaced and the kiss is on its way. I have the proof. Take heed. There is no time for details. I pray this warning reaches you first, before you hear in Council. In Christ. Vicenza. xix Sept. 1529. Pandolfo

The next entry, a religious confession, introduces the story's chief personage. Penitential confessions were, of course, spoken directly to the confessor; but in the most exceptional circumstances, they might be set down in writing.

Since Loredana's confession runs on – she used few paragraphs or full stops – some paragraphing and punctuation marks have been added. But her use of the comma as full stop has been let stand.

4. [Loredana Loredan Contarini, CONFESSION]:

Honoured father Clemence pray please bless me for I have sinned.

You do not know me and you've never even seen me because I need a confessor who doesn't know me, so please read on and I ask you to forgive me for coming to you this way with no warning, but you do know fra Orso, he told me so. This confession rolled up together with his will be put into your hands by my cousin and dear friend sister Polissena Giustiniani, and after you read all I write I pray you'll want to talk to me and be so kind as to tell sister Polissena when I can see you.

Here at once at the beginning I have to say that I hope you'll be able to release me from my deep sins. The lady called madonna X in fra Orso's confession is me and my confession should be read next to his by the same servant of Christ, you'll see why. With all my heart I thank you truly.

Orso gave me his confession before he went into hiding, and he wanted me to read it before I give it to you but he also wanted me not to tell you who I am, only I decided that for you not to know isn't right, I'm trapped in the same sin with him so that we're almost one and this should be known too so you can see what truly happened. I have found in fra Orso's confession the courage to write down my own frightening story, *rendering an account*, as preachers call it, and to confess all the things I did that were weighed down with shame and sin a long time ago, including all the brute and ugly words. These were loaded with sin. I tremble holding this writing pen as I start to remember some of the things I'll have to tell about, my God. There are too many deeds which I never confessed and you'll see why, but now all must be brought out and seen so as to save myself and to help save Orso if possible. I think women never write more than a few words or a page at a time, maybe only religious women write more, but I'm writing this confession down here because I couldn't tell it or write it in front of you, not in front of anyone. Too many shames and low acts are going to come out, and I couldn't even bear to be near someone reading it and then looking at me – that no. But now as I get started I think I don't know where to begin because I have to tell you about all my life the way fra Orso told about his. That was the right thing to do, it brings out everything, so I'll give names first and next tell about my family.

I am Loredana Loredan of the upper city, the widow of Marco di Domenico Contarini and daughter of Antonio di Francesco Loredan, names that tell a whole story. I won't say anything about my childhood – I can't remember anything sinful there because I was brought up with many eyes always on me, with a nurse and maid-servants and other women and my mother always close by, and we went to church once-weekly at least. There was also a great pile of needlework to get at all the time and you don't get into trouble doing that. My two brothers died when they were little, then death took my doting mother when I was eleven, a terrible thing which left me at home with my sister Quirina who was two years older and died last spring. Our father sier Antonio did not marry again because he was always too busy at the Palace and loved it too much, you can imagine, with all their big affairs there. Oh, and we also heard, heaven knows how, that he had a woman in the lower city – yes.

Now into the important things. My sister Quirina was married at nearly sixteen to a gentleman from the Mocenigo house but then it came out that she had an impediment, that's what they called it, which I suppose somebody touched (you couldn't see it). I mean an impediment in her parts for having children, and she was examined by doctors who said it was true, so the poor thing was considered not to have married at all and had to come back home to us. There she was then, married but not married and just plain Quirina again. Well what a burning shame that was for our family and how ugly that the scandal was all about that impedimented part. We were too ridiculous and lost honour at the Palace, so we were stone quiet about the disgrace as if trying to keep it a secret. But how could you good heavens with names like Mocenigo and Loredan? You might as well deny the stars. The whole city knew and prated about it, enemies were paying us back, they whispered rimes, they sang ditties, people laughed behind our backs and this was a knife in my heart because I was also ready for marriage. Remember I was fourteen years old at the time so I did worry extremely, I was afraid and cross too, I couldn't sleep at night, I had nightmares and who could I talk to? My mother was dead and my aunts – you can't count on your aunts, they had their own daughters and worries. Besides, they felt the ugly shame too, they felt it most definitely, and my father wouldn't talk about it because he was too angry about the laughter he knew was out there. Anyhow he offered a large dowry for me but he always meant to do that, good heavens it was expected, and though I was considered to be beautiful and fine and I was also in perfect health and we are a great family always in the top offices, I wasn't married till I was nearly nineteen! Which in families like mine is old and a disgrace, but partly too I think to tell the truth my father wanted to keep me at home. He did sacrifice me a bit, Quirina was too pious for him and she unsettled him and wouldn't go into a convent, though he often said he could force her into one. After her great shame and the ongoing scandal she took to praying all the time and was full of talk about Saint Ursula and Saint Barbara and we were worried that she would throw herself out of a top window to make a show of her virginity, like the fifteen-year-old virgin Saint Margaret of Antioch.

Before I tell about my marriage to Marco of the Contarini family, God rest his tormented soul, I want to get in some things that happened before that. My early life is as clean paper, no writing on it because I was brought up like every Venetian girl of the upper city to let all honour and virtue be in our white-as-snow chastity, in the special parts where poor Quirina had her impediment. How else can I say this if I'm being truthful? Families talk about honour, priests talk about virtue and giving alms and doing what is right, but for girls all such talk comes down to keeping those parts (the treasure of our bodies) away from every man except your husband when you get married. We look up to take orders and down to guard virtue, and you'll come to see why I seem cross about this. Why do you think that unmarried girls in Venice go around so covered up that visiting Germans and other foreigners can't make out how we can even see the ground to walk along the streets? Well, but you know this better than I do and yet I have to say it. We wrap ourselves up as if we are covering and protecting our Saint Mark's treasury, our chastity, and so my idea of what it was to be good was first about the chaste parts, everything else came after that, like hearing mass on Sundays, making donations at church and maybe giving charity to fallen noble families or even to poor people from the lower city, though I wonder if you know that only older ladies ever go down there unaccompanied, not young or unmarried ones.

Our father brought in nuns to teach Quirina and me to read and write, and one of our aunts who loved numbers was very good at teaching us to cast accounts. This was something special and I took to it with glee, but as to reading, we read mostly religious things like *The Flower of Virtue* and *The Mirror of the Cross*, and also a few things about good conduct and then later on some safe tales and poetry. I think I'm telling you all this to say that to be good added up like a row of numbers to something as narrow as we were meant to keep our parts for having children. Even then I asked myself, is that all they mean by preachy words like virtue and chastity? I know my talk about narrow parts is low but I'm still bitter about these things because later, after my evil marriage and after I started really thinking, I began to see little by little how girls are kept ignorant and how innocent and unready they are for anything in the world except sewing and looking well and gossiping and giving orders to servants and being told exactly what to do. Why did they do this to us? Girls need to know things too. I didn't know enough then to be cross with anyone and I was too afraid of my father, too respectful (they come to the same thing) to ask questions. But the thought comes to me here that you may think I got these notions from fra Orso. No, we never talked about such things, never. We've had so little time together dear God that I want to break down here in a passion of tears. I have to stop a while.

I'm going to write down next a shameful happening in my life which tells you exactly what I mean about being innocent and not ready, and anyway the beginning of sin can be in innocence. Quirina and I used to go to confession on Saturdays about once every six or seven weeks, and until my mother died we went with her and a maid, then we used to go with our father sier Antonio and later with two maids because father got to be too busy. I suppose the priest was waiting for that, for us to come to him with servants and no one else because one Saturday about a year after Quirina's impediment (yes it must have been a year or a little more) my turn came to confess, and you know the things unmarried girls that age are likely to confess, mostly trivia about being cross with someone or resenting something too much. So all swathed nearly to the eyes, with wrappings and a headdress and such for girls of my sort, I stepped up to the usual place and kneeled down and started talking. It was a quiet day and there was no one else about in that part of the church aside from Quirina and our two maids all standing behind me at some distance. And here's the point. I was telling the priest I don't know what in my confession when all of a sudden without saying anything or so much as making a sound father Ludovico, that was his name, put a thing in front of my eyes such as I'd never seen before in all my life. It was straight and pointing right at me. I was so frightened that my throat closed up like a fist. I tried to make a noise, I think I wanted to shout and say NO, but no sound came out, I was still kneeling remember, and as quick as a lizard he put it against my hands which I'd been holding up pressed together in front of me in prayer and it squirted on them and over the front of me. I don't know where it came from but the thing had been so close to my face that I saw the veins and ridging and small eye. Then he growled, *Now go, eh eh, and if you tell anyone there'll be a scandal, and you don't want any more scandals in your family do you?* He was pushing and hiding his object down under his loose cassock between hairy legs, biting his lip and scowling, and he looked as if he was scolding someone. It was all a violent slap on the face and I got up confused or cross, no, I'm adding that now. It happened so fast there was no time to be cross. I was stunned and frightened and I pulled my cloak tightly around me to hide his beastly liquid and rushed home with Quirina and the maids trailing behind, I had to wash that pasty stuff off me and get it off my cloak, and I felt my hands were stained and I hated that cloak evermore because I thought of it as shameful and I can still see myself rubbing away at the foul stains with cold water.

Pious Quirina and the maids never knew what happened, I didn't say anything to anyone but I told Quirina I wasn't going back ever to confession to that beast father Ludovico. I didn't call him a beast to her, I simply said that I hated the way he treated me, that he had terrible smells (which was true) and that I was going to find another confessor. She accused me of being too wedded to this world (what did smells matter?) but in the end she followed me to another neighbouring church and you can be sure that from then on I was chary of priests, I thought about that man's base action for a long time and about what I ought to have done but still I kept quiet about it, scandal frightened me too much. At fifteen I had to think of marriage and my prospects, what choice had I? Who would I be married to, when oh Lord when, that's all I knew, that's the way I was brought up, and I couldn't go to my father with a disgusting story about a priest poking his member into my face, besides, what could he have done about it, got the man put out of the parish or even the city? And how keep it quiet? Look, the harm had been done, as quick as you please that priest father Ludovico had filled me with fear and secret shame. I told my cousin Polissena about it, the one you'll have met, who was already in the convent of San Zaccaria and she was taken aback but her advice was for me to be silent. The Quirina scandal was still on everybody's tongue. That father Ludovico had certainly known how to do his deed and she said that talking about it would do our family and me no good, that there was much worse about, like boys and priests coupling. I had to ask her what this meant and I was amazed by her answer, for some reason she always knew more things than I did, more about what went on in the world even though she was in a convent.

That deed by father Ludovico which naturally I never confessed (how could I tell one priest that sort of thing about another priest?) taught me to hold my tongue about things. You go on as if nothing happened otherwise you make things worse for yourself and your family, but then much later when it was too late alas I found that little by little this was the beginning of rot because it was the way to store up evil things, unconfessed sin, and that stored-up sin could turn into fear or shame of a kind that became nearly interesting, a fear that interested you. Do you know what I mean? If I had denounced father Ludovico (but then what about the resulting scandal? Why would he hold his tongue? And surely he'd lie about things), maybe I'd have got his low deed out of myself for ever but instead I brooded about it and the memory of that veined thing kept slipping back into my thoughts.

But thank God I had many other thoughts too, I was reading more and seeing more people. At parties with my cousins and their friends the men stared at me, and we danced and there was sometimes a secret squeezing of hands, especially with the handsome young men who dared to squeeze, but we didn't say much at all because my father and aunts were always very close by and also there was no point in it when you're waiting for your father to pick a husband for you and you have no idea of who that's going to be. Still I regretted not being able to see some of those faces more than twice in a year and I was ashamed of the stupid things I said when we did utter a few words. It was childish talk, but I *was* a child and so were all the other girls I knew, except for Polissena who was in a convent and three years older than me.

There were a few stories naturally, not important or I'd write them down but I'll tell you about one so you can see the way things were at that time. A red-headed young gentleman, very bold, the distant cousin of a cousin, tried four times to hand me a secret letter, once in church as I was leaving with Quirina and the servants, but I wouldn't touch it and I turned away from him. I heard he was a good man and maybe he was, but it wasn't honest to hand me letters, I knew this because I knew about the trick, we had been warned about it many times. Never accept letters. A letter to a young woman can only be a danger and dishonest, so we were never to accept one because it had to be a trap laid against chastity. Then I heard that the red gentleman had wanted me in marriage and that his family sent word to my father through another family, but sier Antonio wanted nothing to do with them, they were not of the right sort at the Palace, yet he never mentioned this to me and I only heard about it the next year from Polissena, and for all I know there were other interested families too but it was none of my business was it? Think of it, what did I know in those days, so how could I have anything to say about something as important as getting married?

Listen father Clemence, I'm now ready to talk about my marriage and my dead husband Marco di Domenico Contarini who drowned more than fifteen years ago. It was a strange drowning, but first I have to tell you about the things that led up to it. Since the Contarinis and Loredans are counted among the greatest houses in Venice, a marriage between them cannot be a small thing. There was I eighteen or nearly nineteen and with a magnificent dowry, not just cash and houses and market rents, but farms and woodland too, also good-looking and with the most glorious smile in Venice (everyone said), when my father sier Antonio finally turned up the perfect match for me. As nearly all girls marry at fifteen and sixteen, I thought it was time and more than time, in fact a horrid embarrassment too considering the impediment scandal or maybe because of it. Actually I'd never seen him before but Marco the match looked as if he'd come out of a panel by the dreaming Giorgione, he was so wonderful-looking, a vision from heaven, and everyone seeing us together said that we looked as if we'd come out of paradise and that by comparison everybody else looked plain and dull. All the bells of Venice rang out, and you can picture the wedding parties, the crowds of relatives and friends and heaps of gifts, but don't worry, I'm not going to tell you about all this, you know what happens when families like that have a marriage. Besides, our sin (mine and Marco's) wasn't in those things.

5. [Vendramin, DIARY]:

xxii September [1529]. It happened at dawn today. I must get this right. The night-watch pounced on three men in the lower city. One got away. Minutes later the other two were dead. A mystery. These tidings come to me from a witness at the Palace. The [*Council of*] Ten were called in, and this afternoon they put out a secret and strange order. All guardsmen are to observe it strictly. Any man hereafter arrested in lower Venice is at once to be grabbed by the throat. Grabbed, tightly held and not allowed to swallow. Not till his jaws have been wrenched open and fingers thrust into his mouth to search for hidden poisons.

How can a poison be hidden in the mouth?

xxiii [*September*]. Rumours do the rounds about a sect of conspirators. They hate the nobility. Venice has not heard the like for over a century. The Ten advertise nothing. Cousin Alberto says the Palace is a hive of meetings, of rushed comings and goings. Patrols scour the Grand Canal. Tomorrow a new company of soldiers arrives in the upper city.

I went fishing at dawn. Beautiful light. Got four lovely mullet. The [*crossbow*] shots were well placed.

xxiv [*September*]. The night-watch arrested a certain Nicolo Baron, the man who got away two days ago. He was hiding under the main altar of a church in the lower city. Everyone believes he was betrayed. Three guardsmen edged their way up to him. Maybe he was asleep. Taking him by surprise, they grabbed his throat. He had no chance to swallow. When they prised his mouth open they found a tied-up segment of sheep gut. Wait. It was filled with an odd substance. He was rushed to the Ten. The substance was poison. He lost his last chance by not biting into it. Or so they say.

We live on a supper of mad rumours. The Ten release no facts. This is policy. Rumours they say worry the innocent but scare and confuse the guilty.

Coming home three hours ago, I noticed a hush along the Grand Canal. Guardsmen were stopping boats. Looking through papers and scrutinising faces. Some gondoliers looked worried. I wonder if the trouble started with heretics. Germans?

Friar Orso's confession begins here, and again the question of why he put it into writing is fully answered.
6. [Fra Orso Veneto, CONFESSION]:
   In the name of God and all the choirs of heaven.
   My dear Father Clemence, pray bless me for I have sinned. I believe in miracles, and here is my proof.
   Crossing the river in Florence one morning, years ago when I was twelve, I turned to draw away from an outburst of cries. Suddenly, as if thrown out of a shop, a falling man knocked me over into the street and partly under a cart. There were many witnesses. As I lay on the ground, one of the wheels of a cart, laden with building stone, rolled over my face. Then the miracle: I felt a blow, I stood up, and hours later one cheek went blue. But after four days the bruise was no more. Therefore, Father Clemence, perform a miracle: release me from the chains of the devil.
   I am seizing two days to prepare a confession in writing. This will surprise you, all the more so when you learn that these words are destined first for a lady here known as madonna X and will reach you by the hands of a third party. The reasons for all this will emerge. To protect her to the utmost, I refrain from naming her; and knowing you, I believe that you will understand. She has the right to confess her sins in her own time.
   Now I must hurry with this. You should have it in spoken words, naturally, but I cannot get to you. All exit points are blocked and the main streets and waterways teem with guardsmen. Above and below, the city is an armed camp, but you may already have heard.

Listen, Father Clemence, if I am to feel horror at my misdeeds, and if you are to give me your absolution and blessing in the light of true knowledge, I must comb through my past, looking to catch every high passion and secret, in search of what made me. Am I being too thorough? This is the Florentine way and, as you know, I was brought up in Florence. Here and now, therefore, I shall try to live my life over again, such as I know and remember it, by rehearsing its primary facts. The Council of Ten have a mandate out for my arrest. Why they are seeking me is what this confession is about. You will read things that I have never told you.

I start with the tale of a girl, an event of unspeakable sorrow that comes back to me now out of my Bologna years. It belongs at the head of this confession. I need it here as a devotional icon against the Council of Ten and the tyranny of the upper city, this memory of a girl who met a fiery death in Bologna, burned alive for infanticide, two weeks before my first journey to Venice. Her face is branded on my eyelids.

The friar assigned to hear the condemned girl's confession had been unable to calm the disturbed creature. I went to him and made so warm a plea that he was pleased to get the authority for me to replace him. We then made our way to the prison to see her. She was a scrawny girl who, like most people of her sort, had no family name. She was called Betta simply, and her father was Nuccio, a moutaineer; so she was Betta di Nuccio. When we stepped into her cell, I found her tormented and agitated. Her body was in spasms and her eyes saw nothing as she gibbered and wept and beat the air. She was terrified of fire and death – that much was plain. There were gaps in her mouth where she had lost teeth, her filthy blonde hair was a weedy tangle, and she

stank unbearably. Telling the guards what I wanted, I had a
tub of hot water brought into the cell and her rags and torn
sandals stripped off. She had no idea of what was happening.
With the help of two of the guards, I managed to get her
into the tub. Then I held her face firmly between both hands
and looked unflinchingly into her eyes as I prayed into her
face and urged her to stop ranting. At long last she began
to quiet down, though I went on holding her head and kept
her eyes locked into mine. I forgot myself utterly, just as I
would in the desert later on, and was somehow able to enter
into that wretched girl's mind. We tied a warm coverlet
around her, and after two or three hours, she was able to tell
me her story.

At thirteen, to get away from her brutal, widowed father,
Betta fled from their mountain shack with a traveller who
took her into Bologna where they lived together for several
months. Made pregnant, she was soon cursed, kicked and put
out in the street. Having nowhere else to go, she found her
way back to the mountains and there, under a reign of beat-
ings from Nuccio, her father, she gave birth to a male infant.
Spurred on by him and seeking his approval, she stifled the
infant, whereupon Nuccio suddenly turned and denounced
her. Betta was arrested, taken to Bologna, tried and convicted.
When questioned, she brought out her terror of her father
and said that she had stifled the baby because he had pressed
her to do so, but no one would believe her because he, after
all, had been the one to accuse her.

That face of hers, as she spoke, oh my God – a picture of
pain, terror and confusion. Betta wanted to understand her
father's cruelty, but did not know how to voice the wish. She
wanted forgiveness, but did not know how to ask for it. She
wanted to be understood, but did not know how to give

words to her desire. She wanted to pray to God and call for His help, but knew not how to do this either, because she had none but the most primitive religious and moral sense.

Was Betta lying cravenly, hoping to escape the flames by incriminating her father? She had not the wits nor possession of self to do such a thing. I looked into that child's face for the better part of five hours. She was only thirteen, though the judge declared that she was fifteen so as to make his sentence seem less harsh. I held her close; I studied her; and once she came out of that tub, I could smell the truth in her. If she was a liar, then every one of us is a liar a hundred thousand times. No, she was telling the truth. But since nothing could be done to save her from her fiery death, I could only seek to stay near her to the bloody end. When she was hauled through Bologna for all to see, with the carcass of her dead infant tied around her neck, I walked alongside her cart as she was screamed at with insults or pelted with rotten fruit. But among the thousands who stood by and watched, I was told that most faces were silent and frightened. Betta's eyes were fixed on me as she went through that ordeal. She had confessed; she had most woefully repented; I had given her absolution; and I made her believe that she would see God. I also got her to believe that being first overcome by the fire's smoke, she would be spared most of the burning pain. But there, alas, I was cruelly wrong. The executioner saw to it that his work wrapped her in flames. Her screams cut through that ghastly licking of tongues. I saw her hair take fire and her skin turn crimson, brown, black; and the little corpse was a cinder on her breast.

Tell me, Father Clemence, do we live by the law of the old Jews, an eye for an eye? I thought Jesus came to us with a message of love and mercy. Could Betta's screams raise her infant up from the dead? All upper cities, all authorities and all important men are responsible for what Bologna did to that thirteen-year-old infanticide, who was brought up as a near-animal, knowing nothing of the world and almost nothing about the difference between right and wrong. It is enough to make one curse all the powers of this world.

With Betta's tale at the head of this confession, I am able to go back to my beginnings, but I must hurry.

I have reason to think that I was born in Venice in 1501, the natural son . . . No, forget the first years. The point is to look for the nodes in a raking comb, and Florence was the true beginning. Seven I was, and from the remote country, so how can I ever forget my first view of the gigantic walls of Florence? I was mounted behind a stranger, gripping his belt, and as we descended into that river valley from the northern hills, I saw the walls and a great floating dome in the middle. A ribbon of silvery water cut through the city. Once inside the walls, we passed straightaway into an onslaught of people, mules, carts, cries, shouts, bells, foreign dress, foreign voices and foreign smells. We crossed the river and came to a large building, where I was deposited in the household of messer Andrea di Zanobi de' Bardi, the head of an old family. They were in need of cash, and my board with lodging was to bring them a good yearly purse out of Venice, so they took me in as a kind of distant cousin. I spent six years with them – with the father messer Andrea, his mother monna Lucrezia, his wife monna Alessandra, their two older boys Piero and Zanobi, and their two small daughters (but older than me) Vanna and Primavera. I was the little one.

Let me offer these particulars, Father Clemence. I wind back to an ancient cry.

My early impressions force me to reach out and feel around for words. What *were* my first feelings in Florence? I was afraid. I was shy. I was watchful. My skin rippled. I had great trouble understanding the Bardis, and every time I opened my mouth to talk, even just to say yes or no or please — they taught me to say please — they all laughed at my ridiculous sounds. I was mystified. At first I thought there was something wrong with my mouth, and secretly I used to run my fingers over it and feel the shape of my tongue.

Messer Andrea said that I would be treated just as the other children were. My only obligations were to learn my lessons and to do quickly and silently whatever I was told to do. Tutorials were a short walk away, in the house of a notary, ser Ugo di ser Bindo Bindi, who took in groups of three or four boys, to teach them grammar and arithmetic.

Ser Ugo's house and the busy street outside his door became Florence for me — that talky, cunning, cruel city. There is where I learned to fend for myself with the likes of boys from the Soderini, Capponi and Guicciardini families. Two of them were a big, tough, bullying sort. That was Florence, and being sent to live there was like a dunking in freezing water. For if at home my funny way of talking was worth a laugh, around ser Ugo's house it was scorned, and I was called lout, lousy foreigner, animal, peasant and braying ass. As a result, my speech changed, I was told, with miraculous speed, and I came to sound exactly like a Florentine. The new sounds soon came as naturally to my mouth as the smells of Florence to my nose — of wet stone, bread, leather, fennel, honeyed confections, incense, the muddy Arno and the odd, leafy smell of heavy woollen cloth. Above me, in the sky, there was a new great pealing of bells, a sound which I had not known in the countryside near Venice.

In picking through my years in the Bardi house, I look for the things that affected me. Not, therefore, the patriotic display so beloved by Florentines – the festivities for the holiday of the city's holy patron, Saint John, when all tradesmen display their prize goods in the streets and all knights and public officials parade through Florence, splendidly dressed. No, I was struck by something else, and I must have seen it for the first time when I was about nine and had just crossed the river, to the main part of the city, with two older boys. Hearing trumpets and seeing a slow procession, we came suddenly face to face with the public flogging and mutilation of a poor wretch being led to the gallows. His agonised cries came over me like blows. It was a spectacle of blood and I shuddered at the sight. Retching with pity for the man, I raced back across the Old Bridge and home in tears.

Being an obedient child, I was beaten no more than three or four times by messer Andrea – very little compared to what other boys in Florence got. Looking round, I often saw bruised arms and cheeks. On Saturdays, in my first year or so with the Bardis, I used to be bathed with the sisters, Primavera and Vanna, and our hair was washed down and dried with special towels. But even when we were no longer bathed together, they went on calling me their handsome little bear [il bel Orsino] and they would kiss me and dress me up sometimes like a girl, cladding me in their own gowns and capes. They protected me – how I loved them! – and this redeemed the nastiness around ser Ugo's house, where the most painful incident occurred when I was about eleven.

I had warned the Bardis and especially monna Alessandra, whom I liked very much, that the Soderini boy, the pimply Vettorio, was a torment in always aiming hard kicks at my legs, elbowing me out of the way, spitting or calling me beastly names. She had answered by saying that I should do everything to avoid him and in any case resign myself. His father was a big man in government, and that's just the way life was. The Bardis therefore were not too surprised, though they were appalled, when I came home one day spangled with blood. Outside ser Ugo's house, Vettorio had come up to me, as I was kneeling down to pull up a stocking, and farted directly into my face, whereupon I called him a swine. I thought that had settled things, but suddenly he flipped off one of his shoes and struck me across the face with it. My nose spilled blood and the next few moments were a blur of passion. I threw myself on him, and as we fell and rolled in the street, I hit out at his horrid face again and again with every bit of my strength. Ser Ugo must have been called, for he was suddenly there, pulling us apart, and now Vettorio's nose was also gushing blood. We were both spattered with it.

This fight earned me a beating from messer Andrea, who also apologised to Vettorio's father, and then for some time I was accompanied to my Latin lessons. Vettorio and I thereafter avoided each other. At about this time I also got a glimpse one afternoon of the undressed monna Alessandra, the lady of the house. I had gone upstairs and as I passed a bedchamber door, which had been left ajar, I pushed it open and looked in. At that moment she was in the act of standing up in the bathtub, in nothing but her flesh, while Nelda our servant handed her a body towel. For a flashing moment I saw monna Alessandra's large breasts tumbling about, and saw that she had a rich tail of dark hair under her belly. I drew back instantly and sneaked downstairs to conceal myself behind a great chest. I did not want to see, nor did I want the image of her daughter Primavera, which now came hard at me. I had heard too many jokes from older boys about hot women and widows, about their stinkpots, liquids, big holes, itchy backsides, unruly flesh, and about how their wool was always ready for beating, their land ready for ploughing. How could flesh be unruly, I wondered.

Remember, Father Clemence, the nodes in the comb.

My memory spirals back to an incident that took place shortly before I left messer Andrea's house. I was nearly thirteen and Primavera was fourteen. Everything about her pleased me, so I used to stare at her slyly and she, I think enjoying it, sometimes returned the stare. We had been in the country and on the last day there saw a glossy black horse mounting a mare. Back in Florence on the next day, as Primavera and I stood alone for a minute or so near the head of the dark staircase, after supper, she took hold of my left hand and suddenly thrust it up under her skirts, planting it between her thighs. My hand sank into a firm bold softness, hot in hair and sweat, and at once she yanked it out again, pressed it glancingly to her nose, then quickly pushed it up against my own nose to smell. Then she fled. Astounded, I kept pressing my hand to my nose, assailed by pleasure, fear and shame. I wanted to go after her to smell all of her, but I was fixed with fright.

The next day, and for ever after, she was changed. She kept away from me, acted as if nothing had happened, and no longer caught my eye. Had I dreamed it all? I felt coldly cast aside. She had suddenly taken me into a new world, but now there I was alone. The memory of that soft, firm undergrowth long haunted me and it was years before I could bring it out in confession. It was at once too delectable and too shameful. I didn't want to give it up. At night my complicitous hand seemed to shine with promises and the odour of happiness.

It was as if Primavera had passed some of her delectable essence to my hand and me.

Father Clemence, the tone here must strike you as unworthy, but it will be vindicated as I move deeper into my tangle of reasoning. And if this flow of words, coming forth in the shadow of the Council of Ten, seems too serene, the explanation goes back to my stay in the Syrian desert, where I was taught the secret of composure. I will tell you about this.

The next document was filched from the archives of the Venetian secret police, the fearsome Council of Ten. So powerful that they could suspend debate in the Senate, arrest noblemen at will, and even depose or execute the head of state (the Doge), the Ten served in office for one year and were usually recruited from the ranks of the leading aristocrats.

7. [Council of Ten, PROCEEDINGS]:

24 September. Anno domini nostri 1529. Punctilio: the Ten wore masks.

Accused: Nicolo Baron. Cloth merchant, fifty-two years old, Venetian, inhabitant of the lower city, in Canareggio, parish of San Giobbe.

Testimony . . . [*Deletions*]

Ten: Mr Cloth Merchant, we now want to ask you about the small sausage of poison at the back of your mouth – or was it under your tongue? – where did it come from?

Baron: My lords, I got it from our late confrère, the apothecary Giasone Biondi.

Ten: Yes, but there was something special about that poison. Biondi did not concoct it himself, did he?

Baron: No, my lords. He said it had reached him from the East.

Ten: The East? When and how?

Baron: I once heard him say that it came across the desert, from the shores of the Black Sea.

Ten: Who brought it into Venice and from whom did he buy it?

Baron: My lords, I don't know, forgive me. He was not the sort of man to talk about such things.

Ten: Are you telling us that you and your associates were willing to stuff a deadly poison into your mouths, though knowing nothing about it?

Baron: We knew it was fatal, my lords . . . anyway, we believed it was, and that was enough for us. And . . . and since it was a question of biting into the tiny sack, swallowing and dying, what else did we need to know?

Ten: Beware prisoner, we ask the questions here . . . So, in your dark catechism, it was a fair and just and pretty thing, was it, for people to be hauling secret loads of poison into Venice? And to be stuffing it into their gullets?

Baron: My lords, I don't know how to answer . . . It was not a matter of loads. You couldn't say we were selling poison. Each of us had just enough . . . enough for himself.

Ten: Listen, Nicolo Baron. You, a church-warden in the lower city, you pass yourself off as a good man, yet you never wondered about the evils of slyly transporting dangerous substances into Venice, not to mention taking your own life?

Baron: My lords, I think every apothecary in Venice stocks poisons.

Ten: Not at all! Only certain registered dispensers have that right, and all are under the eye of the foreign-goods magistracy. So let us see now: suicide, contraband goods, poisons. This alone, in every one of you, was enough to mark you out as criminals, was it not?

Baron: Yes, my lords . . . But it was all for a higher good.

Ten: A higher good? Well there, just there, is all your treason and villainy. You and the others in your secret society cut yourselves away from Venice and spurned all authority. You set up your own clandestine community, and then . . . then you purported to speak from conscience and to speak for *all* of us, for the whole of Venice. Yet you did so from outside it, in the dark and by hatching plots. Does that strike you as anything but criminal?

Baron: No, my lords . . .

Ten: This is why we are going to call for your execution.

Baron: But my lords, apart from our own discussions, and the search for ways of approaching and talking to you, the nobility, we saw no other way to heal the illness that is the lower city.

Ten: Heal, did you say? The disease was all in you and your associates, and we are the physicians here.

[*Deletions . . . Later in the day*]

Condition of the prisoner, Nicolo Baron. In some pain at the wrists. Otherwise calm and cooperative.

Ten: Prisoner, your broken wrists are the price of your refusal to admit something we already knew. We know other things as well, so beware. Now then, for the third time, how many of you are there in this conventicle of yours?

Baron: My lords . . . I knew only the other four men in my conventicle, as you call it. We were five in all. I knew no others, and I don't know how many other circles or groups of five there are . . . If I said six or seven others, that would mean about thirty to thirty-five men in all, but I don't really know.

Ten: Listen to us, *signor* Cloth Merchant. The grim reaper is at your back and almost on top of you. Why make things more terrifying for yourself? We have no desire to put you through torture again, but there are things we must know.

Do you understand? You've given us the names of four men. Two are dead by their own hand and the other two have disappeared. That gives us only two names among the living. Think about it. Either you hawk up more names, or we pass to a desperate measure. We could have your eyes burned out.

Baron: I beseech you to believe me, my lords. Think of the way we used poison, please think about it. We were afraid of being betrayed. Secrecy was everything. Each of us recognised only the other men in his circle, no other. So no member could betray more than five men, himself included. The damage to us stopped there.

Ten: Then how did you communicate with your other fives or groups of five? You must have been in touch with them. There had to be messages, instructions, questions, clarifications. This gives you the lie. After all, was there one conspiracy or a dozen?

Baron: My lords . . . one, I suppose.

Ten: You suppose! Then that means that you had converse with other groups and therefore, by God, you were privy to more names.

Baron: My lords, no. I cannot tell you what I don't know. But maybe one of the others was privy to more. I mean one of the other men in my circle . . . Gasparo? But he's dead. He took his poison.

[*Deletions . . . 25 September. Baron had been branded in the eyes and blinded*]

Ten: What were the true aims of your sect, your – what did you call it? – your Third City?

Baron: Again, my lords, we were a religious group, we prayed together, we meditated, we talked about the lower city.

Ten: Nothing more than a little prayer and discussion group, eh? Is that why you crept around in secrecy, with poison in your gullets?

Baron: We . . . we talked about renewal.

Ten: Give us the details, the dark programme for which you were all ready to die.

Baron: We talked about the renewal of two-tiered Venice.

Ten: What sort of a renewal? Details! Spit them out!

Baron: We want . . . we wanted a better Venice.

Ten: God give us patience! Your wrists are no better than the snapped wings of a chicken, and your eyes, have they not suffered enough? Do we have to get at other parts of your body? What kind of a better Venice? A Grand Canal flowing with wine? A Venice for the likes of Martin Luther and stinking Anabaptists? Speak, out with your programme!

Baron [*Here the prisoner suddenly blurted out*]: It's unhealthy and horrid to live in the dark. We want more sun for the dank and black streets of the under city. More of God's light and warmth.

[*Disorder erupted among the Ten and their observers*]

Ten: Silence, scoundrel! Do not muddle things. God does not come into this unless we bring Him in to curse you. Try again. Tell us. You want more sun for the lower city. Good. And how did you intend to get it?

Baron: By getting you . . . [*coughing*] by getting the nobility to agree to turn the two tiers back into one.

Ten: Fascinating! Let's understand, please. You were going to talk us into a simple rearranging of the two cities. We were to shift the sunlight around by making a few changes. Was that the way? No sir. No, no, no, and no. That was not the way. Your plans were to flatten the upper city, to tear it down stone by stone, and to rob and murder the nobility.

Baron: No, my lords . . .

Ten: Yes, Master Merchant, and there was no God or religion in your plans. It was all sword and fire, death, treason and rebellion, and by Christ you are all going to pay for your bloody vision.

8. [Loredana, CONFESSION]:

My aunts and older female cousins, aunt Marina Vendramin especially, told me about what would happen in the dark on the night I married and on the nights after that. Many times Marina Vendramin also told me not to be afraid, that Marco was a man who loved books and had fine manners thanks to having been at the courts of Milan and Mantua. I don't want to be a gossip and drag this confession out into something long but I have to try to write down all the things that'll tell against me.

We were married and nothing happened the first night or the second and third nights and so on for many nights. Marco sat around reading books and receiving visitors, playing his lute and going out to see his friends and then at night he'd undress fast and get into bed fast and keep to his side of the bed and go soundly to sleep. After a week I went back to my father's house in the usual custom for a few days and my Vendramin aunt didn't ask me anything about the first night or the other nights because she just supposed, I could see it in her face, that the expected things were happening and also I put on a good face. I said nothing but part of me felt relieved – I didn't have to be afraid and it didn't seem to matter very much after only a week, and also I didn't want to worry anyone because that might start them prating again and lead to stories, and scandal had already bruised my life.

Next you have to know why the days and weeks came and went so easily without my getting to know any of the deeds or acts of the marriage night. Marco had his own palazzo, his father had died leaving the biggest one to him but his two brothers had large houses too and they, those two, lived together. Marco was the eldest son even though he had delayed getting married, so he had also inherited the big villa and lands out at Asolo from his grandfather, and because we were married in June he could take me out to the villa in July and simply deposit and almost lock me up there. Since as a girl I was expected to be obedient body and soul to my husband, I was obedient and I even strained to obey him with my soul. My father but mostly aunt Marina and my other aunts never tired of preaching this to me. *Your husband is like God on earth for you, pay heed to him with utmost care, take in his every word, do nothing to displease him, be loyal, never speak ill of him for you are reflected in his shame and glory, if he's nasty or troublesome pray for him and yourself. Most of all obey obey*, so I obeyed. I'm not about to talk against obedience, I believe in it most strongly but it can go wrong in some cases as you'll see, that's all. Anyhow there were other things too in the picture. Marco of course had his own servants, a husband and wife who were with us in Venice and in the country and I wasn't permitted to bring in my own maids, and those two servants of his were nearly my jailers, well not quite, but if there was blame to be spooned out I always got it and I felt they were spying on me, all their loyalty was to Marco, we were all loyal to Marco, and what I'm trying to say here is that I was being kept away from the people I'd known all my life, that's the way Marco was arranging our life together, that's why he kept us in the country at Asolo for so long that first summer, on top of which later on he was very jealous about anyone who came to our house in Venice and I'm certainly not talking about just men because he brought in his own men friends and people all the time. Also remember that I had no brothers to visit me, that I couldn't ever have talked about my secret fears to my sister the pious Quirina and though once in a while I saw my father sier Antonio, his visits were never for more than a half-hour or so, he had too many things to do and people to see at the Palace, and when I did see him he arrived with *his* worries. Besides, when any of my relatives came to the house my husband Marco was always right there as if stuck to me so how could I say anything against him? When you are as obedient as I was you don't complain to your father about the handsome husband he picked for you and whom you are supposed to half-worship. What am I trying to say? It's this, Marco was doing nothing at all about his conjugal duties as they are called, nothing to try to have a family, so I thought, well I'll just wait and see what happens.

Father Clemence this quill is hurting my hand so I'll have to stop for a little.

The fear of scandal and of my saying the wrong thing always nagged at me, yet I also began to worry even more. You understand that the reason I'm bringing out all these things as if I were setting a table is so you'll grasp what came afterwards and be able to give me absolution, as I pray Christ and Mary you will, because a lot did come afterwards, too much. I am weighed down with shame over what I did and felt and said and didn't say and do in those days. If only I had confessed then and said something at the very start of things to my aunts about what was happening (or not happening). But before I knew it, before I could even begin to see these things myself, it was too late, because from the very beginning Marco did what newly married men are never supposed to do, and he did it all the time, he started to bring his male friends to the house at all hours for meals and to play music and chess and talk and read poetry and other things. After lunch I would always withdraw to our bedchamber. Ours? Ha, that's a laugh because he usually slept in another room, his favourite one with all the pictures and hangings, and when he did get into our bed, or should I say my bed, he never touched any part of me, can you believe it, not my hands or a strand of my hair. If he spent a night there he'd sleep as far away from me as possible and turn away as if he was afraid I might try to lay a hand on him or as if he didn't like looking at me or my bare skin, though I can tell you I kept it well covered up.

Back to that first summer in the country, Marco's dearest friend at that time (they were always together and I'll give you his name because he's also dead) was Agostino Barbarigo, a man with big hands and a rough as if unfinished but not ugly face. His name alone tells you that he came from one of the grand houses, he was one of us, and he was older than Marco, say about forty, and remember that I was not quite nineteen and Marco was twenty-seven, so also to the good was the fact that my father had married me to a young man, yet another reason for me not to pule or complain. Well Agostino Barbarigo liked Marco very much, I'd say he was devoted to him, real devotion. Listen, their voices once floated up to me through an open window, this was out at Asolo, they didn't know I was there, and I heard Agostino say to my husband as if he was reading a poem, *you of the gorgeous locks and face of an angel.* Maybe I should write it like in poetry,

You of the gorgeous locks
And face of an angel

How I remember those words, like the beginning of a dangerous prayer, because they gave me a start and seemed very odd and wrong, so it's not a surprise that Agostino used to stare at Marco all the time, and Marco loved being gaped at by Big Hands Agostino, he blossomed in that adoring look. I could see it all at table, they didn't hide it, they were like two lovers in a made-up story, one in *The Hundred Tales*. Many times I tried to slip into their conversations but couldn't no matter how hard I tried because they'd be talking about poets I never heard of like Cavalcanti or Ovid, and of course where are you without Latin? They were pleasant to me, very pleasant, I couldn't complain about that, but I was shut out of their talks and I took to leaving them all alone to themselves.

9. [Orso, CONFESSION]:

Before I leave the Bardi family, I want to say that by the age of twelve I knew already that Florence was two cities. My sense of this came from being told – boys were often told – not to wander out towards the great walls into the dangerous neighbourhoods of the workers and the poor, as we might be robbed or beaten up. I associated poor people with shame, ugliness and dark doings, and with the mournful trumpets of the city heralds, the trumpeters of the lessons of blood and inhuman pain.

Then came an earthquake. Before I reached my thirteenth year, I was removed from the Bardi family and put into the friary of Santa Maria Novella. All at once I passed from women and boys to men; from girls to bearded figures; from friendly to enemy space; from happy smells to stale stench; from warmth to cold; laughter to prayer; and from soft cloth to rough woollens and the rich, heavy, lumpy, tepid food of convents.

Years before, when whisked away from a farm near Venice, I had wept without end – a right sniveller. But this time there could be no tears, save for the moment when I said adieu to Primavera and Vanna. And though I embraced them tenderly, I had an inconsolable feeling of finality. Nor could there be any bawling and clinging to monna Alessandra, though I wanted that most desperately. Messer Andrea took me aside and explained. My guardians in Venice had decided that, being a good Latinist, I should in due course become a priest, a friar in the Dominican Order, and that I should devote myself to the Cross and to prayer for their salvation and the salvation of others. I would be well looked after. I should be grateful. There was good money, Venetian ducats, for my education and all my cares. I should thank God that my lot was such a fortunate one.

Pray for *their* salvation? Who were they? Men or women? When would they show their faces? When would they have a name? How could I pray for the unknown? Could I school myself to do so?

The shock of my entry into Santa Maria Novella as a boy friar blunted my first impressions of the convent. An oily, clutching, physical emptiness in my stomach – fear – sucked at my innards. I closed up like some animals to protect myself. The cold stone everywhere, images of the kneeling Saint Dominic, coiling Crucifixions, cowled figures with pungent smells, long corridors that caught the clatter of shoes or the shuffling of sandals, the odour of ancient urine, a great cloister, and the noisy taking of food in a vaulted hall: these and the pre-dawn hours of prayer are stamped on the memory of my daily life then. What could I do but pray, study or cry myself quietly to sleep in the first cell

beside the rooms of the prior of the convent, Dominus
Lanfredino degli Adimari, *utriusque iuris doctor*? A kind but
strict man (had my guardians inspected the place?), he had
immediately taken me under his wing and set out in detail
all the house rules, as well as my tasks, my hours of prayer
and study, my expected conduct, and the warning that I was
to avoid every manner of close friendship. I was never to
enter any but my own cell, nor ever receive anyone in mine.
I guessed that we were back to unruly flesh, in this case the
flesh of men in holy orders. In fact, in view of smells, food-
crusted beards, dank woollens and the gloom of the place,
the mere notion of any such flesh repelled me. I longed to
be pure spirit.

In our second or third conversation, messer Lanfredino
warned me about two friars in particular. Knowing them
well, he said that they would flatter and talk to me sweetly,
but that their true aim would be to kiss and touch me. I
was astonished. Then, in time, as predicted, one of them,
Fra Benedetto, a ruddy-faced man with a beading of fat
across the back of his neck, began to whisper that he wanted
to dandle me on his knees. I dodged him more nimbly
than I had dodged Vettorio. But the more persistent of the
two, Fra Timoteo, an old female-like presence with pouting
lips and runny eyes, called me *il bel Orsino*. Imagine my
amazement. Time and again he tried to offer me money,
sweets, flattery and advice. Several times he grabbed at me,
but I pushed him away and made enough noise to make
him clear off. In the end, Timoteo and Benedetto were
each condemned to spend two months on bread and water
in the convent's locked cells. Though regretting the action,
I would have repeated my complaints.

In reconsidering what I have just written, I see that I

was proud and self-righteous. Bear in mind, however, that I was thirteen years old. I was lonely, dreadfully so. I had been moved around mysteriously. And cloisters, as you know, are sometimes dens of emotional squalor. What would have been easier and more natural than for me at that age to seek out another boy or the tenderness of an older man? I must at times have longed for this, but I was too angry, too frightened, too fond of my memory of the Bardi sisters. Oh, the sweetness of that. They were the light, every kind of light – sun, stars, bonfires, candles – in the happiest of my dreams. They were my need, not a burly old stinker or a wily woman-like friar.

Under the ubiquitous shadow of the prior, messer Lanfredino, I was also driven by a sense of religious purpose, and this was now entwined with the question of who I was, whence I had come, what I was to become, and the stain of being a bastard. To find God was to seek my true and highest self. My bastardy had been only of late revealed to me – I had signed documents. For if I was to take holy orders, the stain of my illegitimacy would have to be expunged and those papers, the prior assured me, were being prepared in Rome. Very well, but then who would my father and mother turn out to be? Messer Lanfredino did not say, and when I inquired, he raised a finger to his lips and said that if ever I had to know, I would, but that my name in any case would remain Orso Veneto. For a long time I wanted to call myself Orso Oveneto, a name swallowed up by the four O's. Oh Oh Oh Oh! But Oh could be uttered in joy or despair.

At fifteen I found the way to spend two hours, now and then, away from the friary. The spectacle of public mutilation and execution, staged along the main streets of Florence, had never ceased to trouble me. With messer Lanfredino's friendly ties, I was able to join the Confraternity of Saint Mary's Mercy, with its seat near the main government square. Now I came into touch with those who were about to die. The office of the confraternity was to bring prayers and comfort to all convicts, men or women, on their way to execution. We would push to the head of the bloody procession, to pray for the soul of the condemned, who was usually racked by such crazy-eyed terror that all our first efforts went into a struggle to catch the poor creature's attention.

We flagged painted images of the Madonna and the bleeding Christ before the eyes of the condemned, to show them how much the Son of God Himself had suffered and to promise the solace of Mary, as they were dragged up the executioner's ladder. The occasion was nearly always too much for me, and just before the dreadful moment of killing I would hurry away from the scene, too shaken and tearful to witness the choking or gush of blood, the gasps, the spewing out of excrement and urine, and the contorted, exploding face.

In the worst of cases, there were no fluids, only the engulfing smell of burning blood, as in the case of my first Betta. One was a dark-haired Florentine. Like the unhappy girl from Bologna, she was forced to wear a necklace of shame and evil destiny, the body of her dead infant – a sight to make stones weep. Was she even fourteen years old? In a stew of fear, I watched her as she was thrust into a small straw hut which had been especially constructed for her. The executioner then set fire to it. Prayers swept through the woeful watchful crowd, who seemed to twist and turn with the dancing flames. They were not against her. In other cases, again, bulky men condemned to be hanged collapsed into howling infantile spasms, while at the very gibbet small, hard-faced women stared fixedly out and appeared to feel nothing, as if already departed from their bodies. Among the gathered throng, children gaped, as their elders cursed, shouted, moaned, laughed and pulled at each other or poked at the air.

I got on with my religious studies – scripture, the early Church fathers, homilies, Saint Thomas, Cicero, Tacitus and Aristotle. Dante was for light reading. Messer Lanfredino, a trained canonist, was not only the prior but also the best teacher in the house. His examples were luminous, his similes concrete, and his explanations as clear as fresh water. I liked him increasingly, and one day, foolishly, I asked if it meant much to him to be descended, as he was, from the Adimari family, a distinguished old Florentine lineage. Looking at me in amazement, he replied that my question was so stupid and vain that I deserved a beating. Then he walked away from me. The next day he explained.

After three years at Santa Maria Novella I had learned nothing, he declared. Old blood was no better than old dung, indeed it was not as noble because dung may produce new fruits and flowers. But the old families now, Venetians as well as Florentines, were made up of sycophants and money-grubbers. They kissed the arses of the powerful. They bought and sold Christ, and turned the Church into merchandise. They worshipped not the Lord but place and rank, as attested to by the routines of their daily lives. This was not the way. You had to remake yourself in spirit, and spirit was compassion, kindness, modesty and courtesy. Christ was the model, but it was all very simple: it came down to having a heart that could reach out to others, a good heart. All the rest was death and clay. Our cities had lost their soul. I, Orso, should put away all worldly ideas. And he ended by quoting a couplet, urging me to spend the rest of the year thinking about it:

> Riches, place and worldly honours
> Are naught but a dream dreamed by sinners.

Messer Lanfredino's invective against old blood made me think of the Bardi family and took me back to my last year with them. Now at last I began to understand them. All their talk that year had been about marriage, about possible matches for Vanna first, then for Primavera. The elder brothers, who were about twenty, would not marry for another ten years. That was the custom for men. But each of the girls had to marry in the next two or three years, and conversation in the household named every honourable family in Florence a thousand times. It was a nuisance. I lived through a year of nothing but gossip about dowries, linens, dress, jewels, eligible men, rank, position, reputation, honour, physical traits, public office, rumours of scandals, the good and bad health of possible candidates, and so on. There was no end to it. The sisters listened in silence and were ignored or told to be quiet when they dared to speak up, unless they talked about their linens and the contents of their future wedding chests. They had never laid eyes on most of the men named as possible spouses. After listening to messer Lanfredino and thinking back to the Bardi household, I realised suddenly that I had become an encumbrance to them in the business of marriage. Already twelve at that time, who was I really, who was this boy living in their midst? A foreign cousin, an orphan, a servant, an adopted son, somebody's bastard, an odd sort of guest, a friend, who?

Since I was not a brother, I was beginning to present a threat to the virginity and honour of the two sisters. My mere presence in the household became ticklish. Therefore I had to be moved and so my guardians removed me. I also came to understand why I was unlikely ever to see the girls again, unless I located their new parish churches and went discreetly to a sequence of masses on a Sunday to spy them out. After all, what would they have said about me to their new families and husbands? Who was I? When one afternoon, in my cassock, I finally went to visit the family, after Primavera and Vanna had married, messer Andrea and monna Alessandra received me most kindly. They certainly talked about the girls, but there was no hint that I might be able to visit them. Had Jesus not distrusted the too-strong bonds of family?

I learned that the sisters now heard mass at Santo Spirito. Primavera was fat with child and Vanna had already given birth to a son. They had been placed beneath their station – Primavera with a rich vintner and Vanna with a linen merchant. But this had pleased their older brothers, who now waited to get their hands on all the family properties, because the girls, with their fine Bardi name, had gone to marriage with modest dowries.

Forgive me, father, for dwelling on what is sure to be dross, yet it all bears on my allegiance to the Third City. I am touching the roots of my sinning.

10. [LETTER, from a Florentine, a certain Zenobius, to a friend back in Florence]:

In Venice

. . . I tell you I could almost prepare a *relazione* on these bastard fishmongers. They live on the sea, don't they? Still, on this question [*mutilation and the sentence of death*] they are right. After all, is punishment not a remedy for sin? I heard a preacher here last week proclaim that punishment is nothing more than everyday justice done on the bodies of criminals, so it's best to perform the mutilations in public and with fanfare. It's the only way, he said, to hammer people into being civil and law-abiding.

At any rate, as I started to tell you, since the convicted man couldn't walk, they carted him out to one end of the upper city, to a point where the streets below, in the old city, jut out and go on for another . . . [half-mile]. Up above there, on a contrivance at the edge of a small square, the man was blindfolded and tightly held, as he committed his soul to God in a last prayer. To me he seemed out of his mind with terror. The hangmen – two giants from the other side of the Adriatic – then picked him up and threw him down to the lower city, on to a rectangle massed with pikes. This is the way they deal with traitors here. The pikes had been polished and the points glinted in the sun. How will I tell you the rest? The moment he was thrown, the man jerked into a curl to protect himself. He hit the pikes . . . I had to cross myself. Indescribable. The head erupted up through the legs and backside. Blood shot out in fine sprays. Look, Piero . . . never mind. There was a crowd at a little distance around the rectangle of those bloody pikes . . . 6 June 1509. *Vale*. Zenobius

11. [Vendramin, DIARY]:

iv March 1516. Florentines often boast about their city. The devil take them, the braggarts. Florence this and Florence that. We've all heard them as they carry on about their Duomo, their bankers and villas, their Dante and Boccaccio, their Lorenzo il Magnifico, their wit, and their other geniuses. Even the air above Florence is supposed to be the best on earth. No wonder they have a name for being big mouths.

But Venice? Now here is the difference. We were the ones,

we Venetians, to carve out a whole empire. From the shores of Constantinople to the Apulian ports [*in the far southeast of Italy*], that vast expanse was all ours. Silk and Eastern spices came into Europe through us. We took the armies of the crusaders overseas, out to fight the infidel. Ours is the richest state in Italy – a republic, freedom, no tyrants. We publish more books than any other place. And where in the whole world is there a city to compare with ours? With the upper one, a vast glowing carpet of towers and white palazzi? Let all Florence's merchants brag. We know what we were and are . . .

12. [Council of Ten, PROCEEDINGS]:
    26 September. Anno domini nostri 1529.
    Nicolo Baron. The Third City. Testimony.
    Ten: Nicolo Baron, citizen of the lower city, we are horrified by your deeds of darkness. The plan of your secret society was to slaughter the nobility. Therefore the results of our vote. You are condemned to be cast upon the bed of pikes. The sentence shall be carried out at dawn. We are informed that you want to say something.
    Baron: Yes . . . but I'm too weak to speak up.
    Ten: Secretary, take down the man's words just as they come. Then read them out to us.
    Statement: My lords, once I had been arrested, knowing that two of my confrères were already dead and that the other two had escaped, I planned to tell you everything I knew about the Third City, and I have. Why did you break my wrists and burn my eyes when you knew that you were going to have me impaled? We know the answer to this question in lower Venice. We know it too well. You were teaching me a lesson. You took the light from my eyes to

show that I am ignorant and in darkness. You broke my wrists to show that you can stop all action by anyone who wants to change what is evil in Venice. It is easy to read the lessons of your violence . . .

Ten: Secretary, omit the insolence.

Statement . . . my lords, it was not till the past three or four years that the Third City began to chart a course of action. Before that time, we favoured only the most spiritual means of renewal – prayer and meditation. We hungered to have an effect on others by changing ourselves. We wanted to set an example by talking calmly about a superior city, and we talked without anger or resentment. When in our best form, risen above all passion and at the crown of meditation, we saw the city we desired. We really saw it, a single third city, not the two cities of our day, one on top of the other, as in an act of obscene and unholy copulation. We saw our Third City in fact and in truth, hovering out there above this great lagoon. It was bathed in light. Despair was gone. The streets were wide. A gentle wind blew. Men were friendly. There was work for everyone. People moved freely through all parts of the city. The air was clean and fresh. And the horrors of execution were not flaunted in public like a happy pageant . . .

Ten: Guards, get this garrulous criminal out of here. He is not worthy.

[*Deletions* . . .]

Pietro Mocenigo: My lords, we are a thousand leagues from getting to the heart of this treacherous business, and I admit to you that I am afraid. I am particularly alarmed by the complicity of certain priests. We should all be afraid. Consequently, I am proposing a measure which requires us to do an exhaustive search through all the parish churches of the lower city, and let me single out, in particular, Saint Mary's in the Fens. I have a suspicion about things there. I promise you – I pledge it – we shall cut out this cancer.

Andrea Dandolo: My lords, I speak out at once in support of Mocenigo's proposal. There is no need to emphasise the dangers. We are confronting indeed a strange and pitiless sect. Once again, however, I urge that we bear in mind the roots of this conspiracy: the stinking and dark parts of the lower city. I simply say that in the course of our struggle against the conspirators, we also consider what to recommend to our Senate in all questions regarding space, light, water, air, pedestrian circulation and civil order in lower Venice. We must, in other words, begin to think about doing away for ever with the grounds and reasons for a conspiracy such as this one.

13. [Loredana, CONFESSION]:

Mother of God, come to my help. It's time to get to the point about Marco and Agostino, but father Clemence it's not what you think, not at first, though that certainly came afterwards. How will I set the cards of this story out for you? Straight is the best way I think.

It was about three months after the marriage, a warm September afternoon, we were in the country and I was still a virgin and Marco and Agostino had spent much of the day riding around, then sitting in the shade of a large chestnut tree reading through a pile of books, talking a lot and drinking little jars of cold white wine. I could see them from the upstairs windows. Our servants Giovanni and Daria had gone to Asolo with a mule and cart to fetch some barrels and horse-harnessing and were not due back until late the next morning, and our three local women had gone home for the day after cleaning and cooking and setting the table, so Marco and me and Agostino were all alone in the villa. An hour before sunset when everything is still and not a leaf moves Marco came into the house to invite me out for a walk in our woods and I was amazed because he had never done anything like that before, but I could see that he was almost a bit drunk, though Agostino was not, as I saw later on.

Well I got myself ready and of course Agostino came along with us too, and all the talk was between them, I was quiet, it was talk about a friend of theirs who had false hair, fur-lined sleeves, embroidered doublets, a hundred pairs of stockings, and different powders and waters for his face. We were out for maybe an hour and it was a lovely walk, and then Agostino wanted to have a short sleep before dinner so he went back to the villa before we did and of course I can't remember what Marco and I talked about, but when we got back I went straight up to my bedchamber and who was there stretched out on my bed but Agostino. I was stunned. I asked him what he was doing there, he said he wanted to have a talk with me and I told him that was no place for a talk, to please leave at once. When he refused I shouted for Marco but there was no answer and when I tried to leave the room to call Marco what does Agostino do but jump up in front of the door and bar the way. I began to be afraid and he began to talk to me and what he said was this, *that there I was a married woman and still a virgin.* I went all hot with shame and for a minute I couldn't come up with any words. Dear God what was happening, was I in a dream? It wasn't right for a wife to be a virgin he told me (who had ever heard the likes?), in fact it was shameful and even ugly, and he said he was going to do something about it now, that Marco had given him first-night rights, these were his words, rights of first night, and he started following me across the room.

As soon as I could talk I told him as I backed away around the bed that what he was saying was a foul and criminal thing, that Marco couldn't approve such an act and had no such rights anyway, and Agostino with a laugh on his face kept asking, *where's your husband, where is he?* Where indeed! I went on crying out for Marco till Big Hands caught me by each arm and threw me face-down on the bed, then keeping a knee on my back he tied my hands over my head with a stocking. He'd suddenly reached down with a violent swipe and snatched off one of my own stockings and brushed aside my kicking and hurt my back to stop my twisting, while all the while telling me to be quiet, that he was going to do me a big favour and would not truly hurt me. My voice by now was so hoarse that I'd stopped screaming and let my tears flow, while in a broken voice I did tell him that what he was doing was a crime, that my father and family would know about it and have his neck for it. I said other things too but nothing would stop him, and being on my back on top of me so that I couldn't see him he spread my legs apart and burst in, going in right through my pain and cries and curses.

But that still wasn't all because when he finished and there was blood all over my thighs and skirts and I was wailing like a child I thought I heard Marco's voice telling me to stop crying. I looked up from the bed and there he was, he was standing at the doorway, he'd been there the whole time and seen it all, he was grinning at Big Hands Agostino who kept saying *Stop it madonna Loredana, stop crying, you've now had your big wedding night, we've plucked your berry, you're now a proud married woman, truly married and maybe one day you'll be the mother of a noble family.*

Those were his exact words, they're carved in me, and the more he talked that way the more Marco grinned and even laughed. Can you believe it? And what about me, what do you think I was feeling? I'll tell you. Horrible shame at first, I was grinding my teeth, I wanted to crawl into the large chest and die there, but then, and then it came fast, I fell into a dead hate and fury. Marco had approved, he'd wanted the action, he had wanted it, and I wanted to see his face cut with a razor, his beauty slashed before my eyes, that beauty that Big Hands adored so much, and I wanted to see this man's proud member cut off.

God even as I write this down here nearly twenty years after it happened I begin to cry so that I can't go on writing.

My own husband, my companion of three months, I'd always obeyed his every wish and hung on his every word, not a harsh sound had ever passed between us in that time, Holy Mary mother of God, what do they say about what he did? Instigator. That's the word. My own husband was the instigator.

You don't have a tale like this confessed to you every day do you father Clemence? Then listen to more. Sometime afterwards (and how there could be an afterwards you're going to see), when fighting broke out between those two and Big Hands was cross with Marco, he told me that they'd made an agreement on the day he assaulted me. He would be able to sleep in the same bed with my husband if he deflowered me and he agreed to this, but he'd only do it if Marco helped to hold me down or if he stood nearby to watch it being done, which Marco was happy to do, and being the stupid butchered lamb I was, it took me months to see the whole thing clearly. My husband gave me to Big Hands to deflower and that business was now over and done with, no more worries and embarrassments for Marco, but Agostino's labours on me that day were also what he paid for getting to lie in the same bed with the beautiful Marco. I was the Venetian canal, the watery way to Marco. That was my husband, saintly Marco, named after the patron saint of our city. Well all that night, the terrible night of first-night rights, I was in a torment about what to do in the morning and it all came down to this – pack up a few things, get out of that house, get out of Asolo and rush back to Venice to tell my father. That's what virtue and shame and honour said I had to do, but it wasn't going to be easy. I locked myself in my bedchamber and didn't appear for supper, I was choked with disgust for myself and them and the next morning I didn't want to go down- stairs to breakfast to fight and screech or whatever else we were going to do, knowing that I'd be alone in the villa with them because Giovanni and Daria were not coming back until later. To fight was harsh and bitter talk, and what was there to talk about? I wanted to leave that house because just the sight of them made me want to tear at them with my hands, except when I was being a broken fool and wailing like a child. I'd been shamed, hurt and laughed at and had my woman's parts bared, all in front of my husband's pleased eyes, so I was writhing with hate, and where this fury suddenly came from I don't know but I also felt helpless and you're going to know why when you hear what those two said the next morning.

Here's what they said. *You tell your father and we'll say you should see priests and doctors, that something is wrong with your wits, that you're telling ugly lies, that after all, you've said nothing for three months, ha ha, and we'll get the servants to support us and Marco's two brothers and Agostino's family as well, and in a day or two your shame will be all over Venice and you can't afford such a scandal you fool, nobody can but you least of all after all the stories about your sister's lewd impediment, and we won't stop until you're disgraced and have to go end your sorry days in a convent, ha ha ha. We know your father has friends everywhere, in the Ten and Senate and all around the doge, bene, who doesn't know that, and do you think we are without friends, monkey brain? Have you ever heard of the Contarini and Barbarigo houses? Before you do any harm to us we'll make a jakes of your life.*

I need to rest again, my fingers are hurting from pressing down too hard on this quill.

Well this is what they said father Clemence and this time they weren't laughing or jolly with drink, they were nasty and cross and their faces dark and brutal. I spent days locked up in my room being sick, not knowing what to do and having Daria bring in water and a little food every day, and I'd rather have trusted the devil than said anything to her with her make-believe caring and fretting. She and her husband were Marco's prisoners because he knew something awful and evil about them, I don't know what it was, but I'd picked up many hints from Marco, so they were at his beck and call, and I've only reached the fourth month of this criminal marriage of mine. I don't know how I'm going to get it all in because you see that I don't know how to write out long things, I've never had to write much except for my favourite job of keeping my father's farm and rental accounts which of course are all in numbers and the same repeated words. Anyway back to that time after my husband's base contract with Big Hands, yes a contract, what else was it?

No matter how bitter and angry I was, Marco and Big Hands had me scared down to my heels with their talk of a scandal and the whole world knowing. I could already see my father's face and the faces of my aunts and all the Loredans, and I knew I wasn't a complete fool but I was trapped. Looking back now after nearly twenty years I see what would have happened if I'd told all to my father then. After many words and cross feelings, I mean words also about the sodomy of the two men, the three families would have found a way to save all our faces and then done a trick to say the marriage hadn't taken place, and next my father would have turned up another husband from an old but poor family of good standing in the Palace, and with my dowry that family would have been poor no more, though they'd have heard about what happened and known that I was already tupped and deflowered. Heavens. But at nineteen I didn't know about secret dealings of that sort.

Back to what they did to me. I swear by the virgin blood spilled by Agostino Barbarigo that I didn't know what to do because I was afraid and confused as if in a deep fog and I did nothing, and so as the weeks went by I seemed to float along with their crime and dark doings, I'm talking about their kissing and being together in the same bed. I saw this when we got back to Venice through a crack which I widened and then covered up again in the floor above Marco's bedchamber. But what I saw there, father Clemence, was about their strange sinning, not mine, so I have no business even pointing to it here though it does explain some things, doesn't it?

Anyway I say I didn't know what to do but then it came to me, I decided to tell my father, because there were many days when I didn't care if I was stuck into a convent for ever as long as I could hurt them, Marco and Big Hands, even if I was disgraced. Then in another mood I'd start to worry about the scandal and our family name and I'd fall into an

awful fright but even so, please remember this, I tried to tell
sier Antonio my father though it was nearly impossible because
I couldn't get to him alone, Marco was always close by and
watching us, till one day about two months after the violent
deflowering, when Marco was in bed with a very bad catarrh
and fever, just then my father came for one of his short visits
and as he was leaving the house I told him in a gush of
words, they just came out, that the marriage wasn't right, that
Marco wasn't doing the act of marriage, that he loved men,
that we'd have no family, no children, and I was just starting
to tell him about the assault on me when I think the look
in my face was too much for him and he pulled back, staring
at me as if not understanding and at first he didn't understand because he said something about his own marriage to
mother and something about that woman of his down in the
lower city, then he shut his eyes tightly, even in my fright I
saw all this so clearly, and he changed, his whole body went
stiff, and still holding himself away from me he said that
nothing is ever perfect in this life, no marriage either, and
we must bear our troubles as best we can. Prayer and a firm
heart were the only way, nothing ever came of fretting. *Please
Daana* he said (that's how he has always called me) *be a woman,
grow up, take hold of things, fathers aren't gods, we do what we can
and just now I am in the middle of hellish things at the Palace.*
His words rang through me like a warning bell, a scolding,
and before I knew it he was gone.

There you have it father Clemence and the next time I
saw sier Antonio maybe ten or twelve days later Marco was
up and around and still not quite well but sticking to us like
a leech. I had made my father shiver, he saw a queer look
in my eyes, he didn't want my woe, he didn't want the worry,
all at once he wanted me to be an older woman, not a girl

any more, and that's why his face said, Look by heaven, just stop it! No more shame and scandals! So how could I tell him? I thought of writing a letter to him though I'd never written one, and of slipping it into his hands sometime when Marco wasn't looking but that's the very thing he would have feared and hated, I saw this that time and in his manner too from then on, and he was always a little more friendly with Marco.

14. [Orso, CONFESSION]:

Father Clemence, I break into my confession here to say that I am fighting to keep this hand from shaking. By now you know the reason. In a minute or two I shall collect myself. Far from loitering, I am racing through a whole life, rushing it through a sieve.

Where was I? – I was nearly sixteen and my days at Santa Maria Novella were drawing to an end. Acting on messer Lanfredino's advice, my guardians decided that next year I should begin work on degrees in theology and philosophy, and so go up to Bologna, to that city of loggias, wonderful little shops, rounded spaces and colonnades. I was to love its huge blocks of well-cut stone, its graceful turnings and soaring towers. And though I lodged with other Dominicans in the friary of San Domenico, Bologna gave me my first heady taste of being on my own. I could wander through the streets, slip into out-of-the-way corners, have the occasional lunch in taverns, and get a closer look at workaday mortals. They had a different smell from clerics, us.

My last year in Florence brought a strange connection with Bologna and two-tiered Venice: this was Luca degli Albizzi, who turned up at the convent one day. He was seventeen and spent just a year there, before going on like me to Bologna, with the difference however that he was to read civil and canon law. Broad-faced, pink, carnally solid and visibly powerful, he was the very stamp of physicality. His fists were like hammers, his shoulders were a fortress, and his reddish hair often stuck to his head in sweat. Yet he was clever, quick and a better Latinist than I. He learned easily in an hour what I struggled to learn in two. At Bologna I discovered that he was also a glutton, a lover of wine, a friend of prostitutes, a genius at forging friendships; and that nothing, neither drink nor blows, could knock this tonsured creature to the ground. I liked him immediately, but we could not be friends in Florence because of convent rules. And now I turn to my Bologna years.

Luca degli Albizzi's energy made him a force of nature, a mountain, and at Bologna we were able to become friends because we saw each other around the student quarter. In the first year we were fond of rambling around the great cathedral piazza. His happy vitality drew staring eyes and I could have loved him. In fact, I did love him and could have loved him in a baser sense, but such love is an ugly sin, punishable, as you know, by castration or even a fiery death in some cities. What deterred me was not only the knowledge of sin but also a fleshy sense of what is right. Male bodies did not seem to me – *pace* Plato – to go well together. Therefore I prayed, I occasionally fasted, and I kept my distance. When separating, Luca and I embraced on occasion, but that was all the contact we ever had and we never spoke of our feelings. This, however, is not the point here. My sinning with him, if any, was in the heart, but it was confessed and purged long ago. The lesson and mystery in my friendship with him lay somewhere else.

Luca came from an old Florentine family, all but snuffed out by political enemies about a hundred years ago. Afterwards the family were foiled at every turn – in their desire for good marriages, in the hunt for office, in legal contests over property. Seeing Luca's brilliance, his father and uncles resolved that he should be the one to remake the fortunes of the Albizzi house by going into the Church, excelling, and rising at last to become a bishop. In their dreams they even saw him as a cardinal.

It was enough to look at Luca and to spend an hour with him to know that here was a man not cut out to be a priest. In tutorials, in logic, in argument, his tight reasoning could knock holes in mine or run circles around it, but he was not guided by reason. He was explosive, impatient, bold, ready to take leaps wherever his fancy took him. I marvelled at his ease and fearlessness. Yet by appealing to his generosity, his family cowed and tormented him. He had told them time and again that he did not want a priest's life, that he yearned for the everyday world, and each time they returned the same answer: he must stop being a selfish beast. He must serve his family and become a Dominican so as to help restore the Albizzis to their former glory in Florence.

Luca, like me, was already tonsured, but ordination was still some time away. For two years I tried to make him feel his religious vocation and he sometimes humoured me. Without thinking about it, I was simply conniving with the brute claims of authority. I wanted him to be obedient. But I also believed that I was siding with God and the Dominicans. Were Luca's gifts and powers not a divine grace? Then let him serve the pinnacle of all good action, God. Although hypocrisy and cynicism sliced through his family's ambitions, I argued that with a true commitment, he could rise above their pleas, make them see what was right, and get on with his divine mission.

May I be forgiven for my own hypocrisy. I was a willing captive to my work in the poor parishes and wanted Luca to take part in it. Within weeks of my arrival in Bologna, I had joined one of those companies of cowled men, the Confraternity of Saint Mary's Dead. I visited the sick in the poorer parts of the city and collected alms for the Foundling Hospital of Saint Joseph. Luca admired the things I did but had no desire to join me, and sometimes we went weeks when we scarcely caught sight of each other.

One morning, late in the second year, he invited me to breakfast to meet a dear friend of his. We went out to an inn near the city walls, just inside the Milan gate. He warned me on the way to prepare myself for a surprise. Well, his friend was Gismonda, alias Gismondo, who wore the tights and doublet of a young man, but when she removed her bulky cap and loosened a cascade of yellow hair, the woman blazed forth. She was the sun. Watching them touch and look at each other, I could see that they were lovers, and there I was at breakfast with them, a colluding witness. What was I to do, stay or go? Would I, by remaining, give approval to Luca's flagrant violation of our Dominican rule, though we were still only in minor orders? I looked at the man: this was Luca, a force of nature and more sharp-witted than I. How could I pretend to lay down the law to him? In every way but one – our divine mission – he was stronger, and he had never embraced that mission. As I sat gazing at the two over breakfast, I saw that they were being true to their natures, and I would have been a donkey to assail them just then with my devotion to the Cross. The tumult was all mine, not theirs. But worse was to come, much worse. Gismonda was a Florentine prostitute and they had been lovers for nearly two years. Unable to be apart for long, they invented an arrangement whereby, passing herself off as a man and his family's factotum, she moved back and forth between Florence and Bologna. But she had now arrived to spend the rest of the year near Luca, and she was going to lodge with one of his many contacts. He had friends everywhere.

It was impossible for me to stand up with a stern face against their friendship and good spirits. Gismonda was a warm and laughing presence. I was cut in two. They were knotted in sin, yes, but I was not Savonarola. I could not find it in my conscience to cry out at them in horror, and I knew that I could not prevail against Luca in argument. The winter passed, and the more I saw of them, the more devoutly I pursued my work with the sick in the poor parishes and with those on their way to die. I slept less and prayed more, though many of my days went into a special inquiry concerning the nature of sense experience in Saint Thomas and the notion of absolute singulars in the banned William of Ockham. Of all things, sense experience! What a laugh. For in due course Luca and Gismonda introduced me to Picchina, a Bolognese prostitute, and soon enough I got into a bed with her. Now in fact I was two men, living two separate lives, the one often frantically praying for the other and for his three companions.

Need I say that I received absolution years ago for my deeds with Picchina and breakfasts with the two lovers? Yet I am not just going over old ground. I have come to see the Bologna events in a new light. My religious life then was a discipline of routine and prayer, a thing of rote. My faith was deep but unexamined. I had tumbled into formula. Did I see – I think not – that Jesus had looked upon whores with a kinder face than we do? True evil has more horns and stench than anything to be found among the thieving poor, the women who sell their bodies, or the wretches who foul themselves with infanticide. Picchina was put into the streets by her mother, a widow who had her own mother and six other mouths to feed. At whom shall we point the accusing finger here – at the mother or at all of them, including the dead father, chance and fate, and carnal appetites (hence nature)? But the story of Luca and Gismonda is the paste that sticks in my heart and sinews.

Word of Luca's secret life in Bologna got back to Florence, though even the Dominicans – misled, I suspect, by the brilliance of his studies – knew nothing of his doings. Drawing on their Florentine connections, Luca's family had Gismonda seized in Bologna by order of a Church court. She was dragged back to Florence and repeatedly raped on the way. Her guards laughed themselves silly with the jovial question, how can a whore be raped? Luca was detained in Bologna for five days, but when released, he rushed to Florence to help his beloved – in vain. Neither was he allowed to see her nor to testify. Tried in a temporal court, Gismonda was convicted of having used sorcery and base carnal charms to enslave the affections and sick love of a student priest of good family. Her penalty? She was marched through the streets of Florence, backside exposed, whipped there until she was bloody, branded on the lips with a hot iron to stamp out her eighteen-year-old beauty, and cast into prison for two years. Luca himself, not yet twenty, was hauled back to Bologna to his studies. He had of course no trade, rents or income, apart from the monies provided by his family and a modest Dominican benefice. I saw him the day he returned. His colour had gone, his shoulders were sunken, I thought he limped, and his eyes sought the ground, but when he looked at you, the stare was fiercely unreal. He gave me the bare facts of the case, adding, with a terrible bitterness, that they would have branded her labia but refrained from doing so, the swine, only because they knew that her shame would not show there.

About five or six weeks later Luca vanished. Neither Church nor family could find him. Three years later, in my degree year at Bologna, a letter from him reached me through the old innkeeper by the Milan gate. Using local contacts, Luca had found a way to get into the imperial army as a foot soldier, passed over to a company of cavalry, and risen to the rank of battalion commander. No one had thought to look for him among the horde of hired soldiers recruited out of Germany and Spain. But he is now dead. God rest his soul. Word came to me through the [*Dominican*] Order that the sack of Rome two years ago began with his death. He was the second man killed in the imperial assault on the Holy City. The rumour is that he hated the Church and had become a heretic, a Lutheran. Even now, I want to rail against the stars. Lord, let me.

At eighteen, how could I contend with what I have just recounted, except by plunging into prayer and works of mercy? Luca and Gismonda were my dearest friends, my only friends. Never had I known such love and trust, a point the more borne in on me by the fact that I could not get myself – in private at any rate – to honour the head of the Dominican Order in Bologna, messer Guglielmo Pepoli. My feelings rioted there, and this obstinacy coloured all my relations with the local order, for Pepoli was known to be a soft, self-indulgent man and mere potter's clay in the hands of our real master, messer Gianfranco Savelli, adjunct bishop and distinguished professor of canon law.

Now here was a true jackal in the golden hide of a lion. This Savelli – but you must have heard of him – groaned with pleasure under a cascade of moneys from benefices scattered throughout the Patrimony of Peter [*the papal states*], yet he was always hungry. You had nearly to pay for just laying eyes on him, a Roman aristocrat who in Bologna was only comfortable in the houses and banquets of the city's nobility. He was a small, brown, good-looking man with graceful movements, the eye of a hawk, and a keen taste for furs, silk, young priests and fine foods – he only ever dined in state. In the legal science of this eminent canonist, the Church could do no wrong; but he defined the Church as the clergy arrayed in all their incomes and privileges. He argued that all religious services deserved a recompense, that office in the Church could be treated as an investment and was therefore justly bought and sold, and that canonists, in their heroic office as defenders of the Church, should be among its highest-paid officials.

Savelli tried on a number of occasions to be charming and friendly with me. I can still hear his words and seductive tones: *Young man, don't be sulky. Let your limbs rest easily. You may discover one day that you have need of me, and your handsome face will not be, I can assure you, a hindrance. Besides, I am told that you're not a bad scholar.*

Savelli also said: *Look to your soul of course, but look to your present life too. Paradise does not come as a reward for ugly discomfort. What a delusion that idea is. The world cannot be without princes, without riches, without pain, without commands and obedience. This is all in the natural order of things. Otherwise, with our exceeding stress on charity, all the rich and powerful, every one of them, would lie under a sentence of eternal damnation. But the Church has never taught that, how could it? It is realistic. How do you think it survives?*

He added: *Come and see me, come and have a happy lunch when you want. We could help you . . . you must know that. We won't sully your proud heart. All we want is to civilise you. Don't you see? We want to teach you the ways of people who know how to live in the world — the ways of courts, fine houses and graceful conduct.* Nearly laughing, he said all these things in a gentle, bantering, honeyed, fluctuating voice. But I could not respond to the man, and I did not take up his invitation.

I remember a final encounter. Summoned one day to a meeting with my religious superior, I found Savelli there too, seated beside Pepoli. They wanted me to spend less time in the poor parishes; and my Roman lord in particular insisted on our canonical right to be paid, whenever possible, for every religious service rendered. He demanded that I observe custom and not cheapen our labours by excessive zeal, for my example would take daily bread away from other men in holy orders. As the recipient of a generous annuity, I of all people should be thrifty about my doling out of services in the city's poor parishes. This instruction, Father Clemence, may seem astonishing to you, but so it was. I agreed to be ruled by their warning, but I took no notice of it and thereafter was simply more secretive about my doings.

Savelli knew everything. His memory was an account book of infinite entries, and he had a hand in every stew, so it is likely that he was the one who, getting wind of Luca's secret life, then got all the details to the Albizzis in Florence. At any rate, Luca and I despised this perfumed miracle in priestly garb, and you can see why. I could not forget my old mentor's lines:

Riches, place and worldly honours
Are naught but a dream dreamed by sinners.

* * *

Yet Savelli was the man whom my fellow-Dominicans most talked about, admired, courted, emulated. And not just they but others as well – Augustinians, the top men of the secular clergy, and most Franciscans, they all looked up to him. He rode, hunted, kept a train of servitors, and was never so much at home as at wedding parties and grand luncheons for ambassadors and visiting dignitaries.

I have said too much about this gentleman, but only to throw light on my isolation in Bologna, which also explains my surpassing affection for the honest Luca and Gismonda. Yet I was hounded by guilt over my ties with them. It was horrible, and my speech developed a stammer. Words would catch in my mouth as if in a cage. So after Gismonda's arrest and Luca's disappearance, though I was cast back and forth between rage and despair, I also verged shamefully on relief, because I no longer had to go through a daily labour of cutting myself in two. After a few months I began to be whole again, but the stammer lasted for a long time.

I regret the sinful blot in my relations with Luca, Gismonda and Picchina. Another obligation also defeated me. I could not rescue Picchina from her infamy because she would not abandon the six hungry mouths. *Yes*, she shouted at me one afternoon, *I'll give up this trade, this public shame, I'll give it up! And will you promise to bring in daily provisions and the yearly rent? Charity, you'll tell me, rely on charity! The devil take charity. There isn't enough to go around and you know it. We would starve. So damn it, Father Orso, stop talking that way till you're ready to bring us our daily bread. Let me go on earning it for now.*

What could I say, Father Clemence, that I would bring prayers?

For any obscure anger that still remains in me over the fate of the two lovers, for this I beg forgiveness. It is easier to purge bodies than souls. Yet those who worked their will on Gismonda and Luca, I am bound to say, will also need forgiveness, for they strangled two joyful lives in full bloom, however sinful these may have seemed. Their beauty threw a happy light on the face of the earth.

In the second year of Gismonda's prison sentence, I was finally able to get away to Florence to see her, and though I tried brazen bribery on top of my honest claim that I was there to bring her spiritual comfort, I was refused permission to see her and told the prison had a monk to look after the needs of her soul. Perhaps it was just as well: I did not have to look upon her scorched lips. I wrote a letter to her, bearing my prayers and blessings, and to help with her meals I also deposited whatever I had – some four or five florins – with the Hospital of Santa Maria Nuova.

In 1522, my twenty-first year, I completed my work on sense experience and took a degree. That year too I was ordained, but when messer Lorenzo Campeggio, the bishop of Bologna, touched my head, I was not moved. I might as well have been chewing stale bread. An inner freeze protected me. In my perennial black and white garb, I was so much a Dominican already that I did not see how my life could change. Teaching and work among the poor were to be my primary tasks, not celebrating of the mass. The truth is – I must confess it – that I was ill at ease with the mysteries of the bread and wine. Although my heart was there, my intelligence was not. I was too ready to push raw reason into places where it had no business, and sometimes I asked treacherously: Outside the slippery words and constructs of philosophy, O Christ, how *do* you enter into the bread and wine?

Was nothing in the miracle in the least accessible to sense experience? Of course not, but here was a simple-minded notion of the senses perfidiously nagging at me. Such lapses inevitably brought confession and absolution.

One day a Dominican from Venice paused in Bologna on his way to Rome. Spending several days in our convent, he sought me out and wanted to hear about what I did in the Confraternity of Saint Mary's Dead and about my charitable work in the outer (near-the-walls) parishes. Some of my stories aroused his wonder. I told him that if you stay with old women and poor folk, if you hold their hands and help them with kind words and prayers, they can often bear intolerable pain. Later I was to realise that in my dealings with this Dominican I had my first encounter with the Third City.

In a second visit, he talked to me about a group of devout men, most of them living in and around Venice. To my astonishment, he said that I had come to their attention. Inquiries had been made. They even knew that I was born in Venice, despite my Florentine speech, and he offered evidence of this, such as the fact that I had spent my infancy in the country near Venice, but he refrained from giving any family names. He indicated that if I elected to join them − though in this case our conversation had to be held in confidence, as if under the seal of confession − they could have me transferred to Venice. Their interest, he emphasised, was in the common people of the cities of Italy; but Venice, the two-tiered city, was at the head of their list. They saw it as the main ground of study and zeal, simply because the two tiers of this raised city boldly separated rich and poor, noble and commoner, and high public affairs from the lowly world of petty trade and manual labour.

He went on. All cities, to be sure, have these divisions among men. Florence came to mind. Bologna too with its depressing peripheral precincts. He pointed out that hilltop cities such as Bergamo and Perugia were crowned by fine old centres but that grim habitations lined the streets of their low-lying parts. In Genoa, to move away from the grand, sea-fronted enclaves was to walk up into alleys of shame, past clusters of shacks and crooked houses. Milan? There too was a place of melancholy in the outer parishes, far from the palazzi, squares and wide streets that circumvent the cathedral and citadel. Could we not change our ways and the faces of Christian cities?

His words were a shower of light. Suddenly a new mission loomed up, and without more ado I assured him of my interest. All my life I had been hearing about Venice. In daydreaming, when I wondered about who exactly I was, I had often seen myself as a Venetian. The lagoon and its two-piled city, that ancient republic, the Most Serene, rising wondrously out of the sea – I yearned to see it. Entire forests had been felled along the Adriatic to be turned into piles, the underwater foundations of Venice's tiers of dressed stone, and into its sea-roving fleets, which four centuries ago had transported thousands of crusaders to the Holy Land. An instant traitor to Bologna and Florence, I was ready to go to Venice now. Did I respond too readily to earthly glory?

As I write these lines my stomach does a turn. It is fear, a feeling which I have come to know again during the past two weeks. But it will pass, it will pass or I learned nothing in the desert. I may lose Lady X, and the Ten may get their horned hands on me – these threats keep merging and separating: the loss of someone who is life for me, and that council of masked men. Did you know, Father Clemence,

that the Ten wear masks when holding their sternest interrogations? It all began as a joke at Carnival time a few years
ago, when some of them had taken to arriving at their afternoon proceedings in costume, before going on to their rois-
terings. The joke turned out to be so fearful for those whom
they ply with questions, that answers flowed, and the wearing
of masks quickly became procedure. Imagine the scene. Each
of the Ten hides behind a ghastly vizard. They gaze down
on the accused from raised benches. In the background the
pale faces of other councillors look on, and the speakers for
the Ten, gathered around the prisoner, assail him with questions. Do you think they ever fail to get what they want?
Their masks and tools of torture seem to be joined; and
accused men have been known to end in madness.

I confess that I am afraid. This is why I conjure up the
scene, to fix it and move around in it. I want to recite and
memorise the details now, in case I am ever thrust up before
them, face to face, face to mask. The details be my litany. I
will see behind their masks, imagine them as they strut around
in the upper city, and I shall remember that they are
Contarini, Mocenigo, Loredan, Trevisan, Barbarigo, Venier,
Vendramin, Grimani. I will know that they are flesh, bone
and sinew, that their bodies too can feel the cold tongue of
fear, that they fret over family, money, tenants, servants and
trivial passions, and that each of them – for the powerful
ones are for the most part old – worries about death. Yes,
they worry about death. Some are afraid to die because they
carry a fearsome load of sin; others cannot see the face of
God and meander through their days, lost, plagued by a vision
of desolation on the other side of life; and a few, already
ailing in their feeble bodies, are afraid because they associate
dying with unspeakable fear or even pain. As if they had

never considered Him, the crucified Christ, who at that point was only a man!

All this I will remember if I am ever put in front of the Ten and they rise up before me in their gory masks. God forgive them, but still, may they be more afraid than I.

15. [Bernardo Loredan to Pandolfo, in code, LETTER. The outside of this missive, in a different hand, reads, *To Pandolfo, at the sign of the apothecary's dragon, in Vicenza*]:

In nomine dei.

Worthy Pandolfo. What of the lambs? Wolves streak across the high ground. This is my third letter in two days, tripling the perils, and still no reply. What in heaven's name has become of you? Have you lost your tongue, like our poor Maffei? He cannot speak a syllable; his lips do not move, nor his arms; and I cannot read his wide troubled eyes. It seems he is trying to tell me something. Yesterday he broke into a sweat. Did you send anything to him last winter?

It is check here. A thousand eyes are out on tenterhooks, in search of the kiss-of-death seekers. You take my meaning. When I withdrew from the shop [*the Third City*], we agreed that I would no longer have any knowledge of details or proceedings. But this . . . I plead with you. I simply must know now whether or not the friar is in these parts. A voice spoke the name, reported that he was in Venice, lives here, works here, runs the shop. Runs it? Is this possible? If so, who took the decision – how, when and where? But don't in God's name write anything openly. Use the numbers. My servant Beringaccio will bring this letter to you in bales of Naples linen and will attend your reply.

Again, I must hear from you at once, to decide on ways to govern myself here. There are a few things I can still do (the chief secretary is all mine), but everything is now moving so fast that every hour cuts my choices, and I will soon be a shorn Samson. I pray God you will tell me the report is false, that the friar is not here. Say it is false! If in two days I have not your answer, you are on your own.

Christ shield you from evil.

Yours in Venice. xxi Septembris. MDXXIX. Bernardo

16. [Vendramin, DIARY]:

xxiv September [1529]. Piera says that I'm too gloomy. That it's bad for the children. Well they're bad for me sometimes. I have yet to be elected to the Ten. And until you've done a term there, you're no part of the top group. But Antonio [*Loredan*] assures me that my day will come.

Last night I had a picture of the Ten. Alberto [*Giustiniani*] was in a talkative humour. Hands restless and voices on edge, they seemed uneasy, he said. But there was also laughter. Two of them clowned with their masks. The Ten sat around the prisoner. Behind them, up higher, were the ducal councillors, then the outside group [*zonta*] of lesser councillors. Alberto sat among these.

The prisoner either stood or kneeled. There were four guardsmen nearby, their dress a reminder of the instruments of torture. These are in the next chamber. The prisoner speaks only when questions are put to him. The light comes from behind the Ten, falling full on his face. Two clerks sit nearby, recording everything said. Other members of the Ten may inject comments or questions. When they disagree, a vote is taken. Six of the Ten decide. Ties are broken by the ducal councillors.

Alberto was struck by the mixture of fear and humour in the proceedings. Odd but effective he said. You need moments of laughter. Otherwise matters lurch out of control. Prisoners go to pieces. The Ten snap at each other. Or the terror reduces men to near-idiocy. The masks are bizarre. Alberto himself was put on edge.

[*Deletions: private matters, a baptism and a violent quarrel between two noblemen. Next:*]

Here are the rumours racing through the city.

That the conspirators are a round hundred, some of them living on the mainland.

That they are made up of small groups, with many priests among them, all secret heads [*capi*]. Priests who hate the Church.

That they want to raze upper Venice.

That they are occult Lutherans.

That they are Mohametan mystics, not Lutherans.

That they were founded by the Jews out of Spain.

That they hold women in common.

That they only pray on water, in boats, and pray only for bizarre visions.

I conclude that these rumours are mostly rubbish and Alberto agrees.

[*Deletions . . .*]

i October. The Franciscan, Fra Dolfin Falier, was executed. We woke up this morning to find his body on the pikes. One spearhead came out through a cheekbone. He lay beautifully twisted, as if spread out to please. Shortly before his execution, he broke down and wept uncontrollably. He claimed to know a certain Fra Orso, claimed he is a posturing, fraudulent, would-be saint, seeking a grand name for himself.

In this autumn of galloping rumour and poison, our sky has held nothing but a magnificent sun. Not I hope too late for our vineyards.

The following source has not been previously cited. As a genre, family chronicles were more often produced in Florence than in Venice. Such narratives were usually based on family papers, family oral traditions, or even on material culled from official archives. They are much used by historians.

17. [Alvise Falier, A SECRET FAMILY CHRONICLE]:

I present a brief account of the Loredan lineage, of their hidden and disgraceful history. Their good deeds, if any, I leave to them and their adulators: they know how to trumpet their own virtues. Thus, I shall say nothing about their holy Saint Bernardo Loredan, who was as much like them as Saint Francis like Tamberlane.

Why a Falier should write a chronicle of the Loredans ought to be made clear at the outset. I desire the reader to know why I have composed this account.

The Loredans worked the destruction and moral murder of my house in the fourteenth century, and ever since then we, one of the oldest and most noble of all Venetian houses, have lived at the margins of civil life in Venice: poor, despised, banished from high office, and stymied in all our efforts to forge marriages with other eminent families. The only thing they could not despoil us of was our nobility and ancient standing; these leap out of the public record; and of course we still have a place in the Grand Council, admittance to minor offices for patricians, and even some properties in the lower city.

I make no bones about it then, my chronicle is an indictment, but justly so, as my evidence will establish. Even as I sit reading and correcting this narrative in my study, I am afraid. Will I be discovered? Such is the long arm of the Loredans. Together with other prepotent houses, such as bearers of the Dandolo, Mocenigo, Venier, Contarini,

Vendramin and Barbarigo names, they hold in their hands the power of the Venetian state and could easily end my career, indeed my life. For as I am the official archivist and historian of our Most Serene Republic, I depend entirely on the favour of the ruling families. This is why I am forced to write in secret, to keep my chronicle under lock and key, and to conceal its existence from even the nearest members of my family – my wife and sons.

An apostrophe just here will help to place me and to explain the origins of this chronicle. *The Secret History* of Procopius is my model, and we know what horrors he exposed.

I descend directly from the doge Marin Falier who was barbarously decapitated in 1355. He was the grandfather of my great grandfather, Paolo. As chief archivist, I work behind the scenes of Venice's world stage, and I have my father to thank for this. Although having two daughters to dower, however modestly, he scraped enough money together to give me an honourable education, and I was able to take a degree in humanistic studies at the University of Padua. After teaching for several years, I returned to Venice, and there my literary talents proved to be remarkable enough to enable me to win the post of archivist. This gives me access to state papers going back in time for hundreds of years, and among these are the official duplicates of wills, deeds and contracts, as well as trust and other property transactions. I have gone through these papers on the pretext of putting together a genealogy and profile of my own house, the Faliers, but my unique purpose has been to chronicle the misdeeds of the Loredans. With this end in mind, I have also searched through baptismal registers and old family logbooks. In other words, in keeping with the practice of the most respected Roman historians, my account is based strictly upon evidence taken from the public record; and wherever I depart from the facts, such as to conjecture or to report gossip, I make an honest admission of this. I need no inventions; the crimes of the Loredans convict them.

Unless he be a Venetian from upper Venice, no man can know the pain and infamy of descending from one of the great lineages of this city, while yet having to live bent over, near the knees of unscrupulous families like the Loredans and Mocenigos. Since the judicial murder of Marin Falier, all my male ancestors have had to live in shame and obscurity; all, I am sure, have longed for vengeance, the most sweet of cordials; and I am here to provide it. My forebears will weep for joy in their graves when this true chronicle is published after my death, issued through booksellers in Rome, Florence and Milan.

18. [Orso, CONFESSION]:

In my time at Bologna there was a preacher, one of my Dominican confrères and much favoured by Savelli, who gave fiery sermons on the beautiful justice of public floggings, brandings and amputations. To lop off a man's thieving right hand and to tie it around his neck, before a baying crowd, seemed to him a ceremony of truth, the will of God, the king of lessons, and government in its finest hour, performing a sacred right. You know the sort. He was an older man. And when I sought in private to approach him, to challenge his school of argument and engage him in debate, he lashed out at me. He was preaching sound doctrine, he shouted, whereas I, an enemy to punishment, a snivelling intruder, could only belong to the devil. My claims were not a plea for mercy but an invitation to crime and rebellion. I deserved to be cast into the papal dungeons. There could be no discussion with the likes of me.

Forgive me, I have veered off course here.

The Third City – though I did not yet know them by this name – were a quiet group, eager to remain in the shadows. I understood this from the start. Their views required secrecy if ever they were going to be realised.

Several weeks after my second talk with the Dominican emissary, I received a sealed letter from him. It was handed to me as I came out of San Petronio, where I had just spent part of the morning lecturing on Albertus Magnus and tyrannicide. That whole day remains with me. The letter made a proposal: if I was seriously to take up the work which awaited me in Venice, I needed new armour. I had to harden myself against evil and reach the highest plateau of concentration, which would also be a new leap of faith in the Cross. This required a pilgrimage to the Holy Land, to be followed by a period of solitary existence and exercise in the desert. The model was given by the early Church fathers. Was I ready to go?

The invitation brought a rush of excitement. Are we not moulded to see that life is a pilgrimage, a journey through trial and error? My feelings had already detached themselves from the University, where my noble lord, Gianfranco Savelli, held forth in state, and from the city itself, where doctors of law swaggered around in furs and every fashionable attorney read Petrarch or scribbled lofty love sonnets. I was ready to set forth tomorrow. My reply was sent off at once, and fourteen weeks later the papers came through. My Dominican brothers gave me a hearty farewell, but knew nothing of my planned movements, apart from the fact that I had been suddenly called to the two-tiered city. There was nothing extraordinary in this. The Venetian with a Florentine tongue – my epithet – was on his way home. I was to go to Venice for five days to make my acquaintance with its two souls, the upper and lower cities, and to meet members of the Third City, after which I would board a galley for Alexandria and go overland from there to Jerusalem.

No first impressions of my birthplace can I give here, because they have since been fused with later ones, and anyway Venice will too soon have a place in this confession. I want only to note here that for all the descriptions which I had heard and read, nothing had prepared me for what I saw as I approached the two cities over the waters from Chioggia. Venice seemed to float on, and partly to be suspended over, a vast dish of water. Towers and stacks, spires and statuary fretted the sky above. Cornices, colonnades and great symmetrical windows ran their course. The two tiers were clearly visible: gigantic suspensions of pale stone. I wanted this first illusion to endure. I savoured the sense of being a Venetian born, of coming from salt water, sand, sailing vessels, great beams driven into the sea bed, misty skies, huge blocks of stone, and the smells of the sea. As if place, earthly place, can touch the soul! But what else does? We force the temporal and the eternal to intersect, unless we cut ourselves away from what is earthly. Yet if we do this, how can we test and know the self? Earth is the place for the soul's trial.

I lodged in the friary of San Domenico di Castello, where a long leave of absence awaited me, issued by my Dominican superiors. But I met only two of my Dominican mentor's special associates, a Venetian nobleman and a physician from the lower city. For three days we talked zealously about the Third City and my coming mission to Jerusalem and the desert. Each of them having been to the Holy Land, we also discussed the dangers and what awaited me – burning sand, burning rock, the sun, flat bread and bean pastes, the murderous attacks of disease and bandits, and the sharpening of piety down to the bone. They took me in hand and guided me through the lower city. I was appalled by the dim light of the streets and by the fact that the sun on the tier above seldom breaks roundly and fully through to the underlying tier. They also took me to the silent *piazzetta*, to see the impalement pikes arrayed on a low platform: the bed of justice for high treason. But time was short and I had to hurry away. For since I was travelling to Jerusalem incognito, not as a priest – and God forgive me for this – my head was shaved clean, and I had to spend the better part of the next two days buying clothes, linen, headwear, shoes, medicaments, eating utensils and a sleeping mattress. I was to cross the sea on the two-decked *Contarina*. The Third City saw to all expenses and provided me with a purse of Venetian ducats, together with letters of credit to be presented in Jerusalem and Damascus.

Came my day of departure. About 170 pilgrims got on to the galley, including thirty women and two thin-faced hermits. Most of the voyagers came from Germany, France and Italy. The women were so clad that they were covered from head to foot, much of the face as well, like our own unmarried girls from upper Venice. The Italians were mostly usurers and merchants, some of whom in a panic about their souls. The moment we set sail – it was early August – a peace descended upon me such as I had never known, and the feeling remained so for weeks, even when the vessel tossed violently and all about me fellow-travellers prayed and wept, persuaded that their last day had come. I led them in prayers on occasion, though as a layman. The voyage to Alexandria took twenty-four days, broken only by a single stop at one of the Greek islands.

I pass over Alexandria and Cairo, the second of which, like Damascus, is larger by far than the biggest cities in Italy. And like these they also squeeze their poor folk into honeycombs of stinking squalor. But I must not deflect the arrow of this confession.

At the meetings in Venice I was told that the purpose of my journey was to prepare myself for work with the Third City, a secret society whose aim is to see Venice's upper tier removed, so that rich and poor, weak and powerful, can be drawn together, as is more nearly the case, however imperfectly, in other cities. But I was warned that the Council of Ten thereupon became our capital enemy, for how could the Third City, with its levelling purposes, not be seen as a threat to the Venetian nobility? And how could the Ten fail to strike with all their might, at the first whiff of our intentions? Each of us had to be ready to die. This demanded a focus pointed enough to lift us out of the body, above pain. To alter the two-tiered city, moreover, would require impeccable planning. Here again was the necessity of discipline in the deepest recesses of our being. My pilgrimage was to be all about this.

We hired mules, donkeys and cameleers in Cairo, then headed east into the desert, making for Mount Sinai. Our tents, water and food – the heaviest things – were borne on the backs of camels, strong beasts, but we rode either mules or donkeys. The horse is forbidden to foreigners and is, in any case, a poor animal for distances in the desert. We lived on biscuits, pastes, salty cheese, almonds, dried grapes and dried plums. Although fresh at first, our water, borne in goatskins, took on the rancid taste of the fatty leather and came out with many goat hairs. Imagine the pleasure. And the pilgrims who had not already passed over to a rhythm of occasional fasting now did so.

Since I was to be away two years and alone for most of that time, I began to turn away from the other voyagers, whose ordinary expression for the Saracens was *those dogs*.

Before leaving Venice, I had decided that I would not look to the relics of saints – bones, hair, teeth, bits of cloth, wood and the like – to focus my meditations. Not all men hear the summons to the Cross in this manner. Instead, I searched for moments of intensity. So as we traversed the Sinai, I found other things to contemplate in the limpid light of the dawn. The splayed soft feet of the camel. The flowing white calico of the cameleers. The stark blue of the skies – *there* was the blue robe of the Madonna or of Christ – bluer than anything we get in Italy. Endless stretches of luminescent sand. Even the long centuries and genius which had gone into finding the right foods for the desert.

More than by the many points of interest in Jerusalem and Bethlehem, tiny desert towns, I was swayed into silence by simply being under the same skies which had covered Jesus, by looking at the same baked earth, taking in the same smells of spices and being brushed by the same hot winds. The world is a miracle. I came to feel pushed so far into myself that my ears blocked, and I entered into a daze, letting definitions slip away, as I lost touch with the other pilgrims and barely responded to them. At night, as we sat eating a light meal, their voices broke through and reached me, especially when in a fury with those dogs, as they called our Saracen interpreter and the cameleers. They claimed that these men had betrayed us to bandits in the desert or that they were forever conniving with petty officials to make us pay more taxes, more service fees, more tolls, more gratuities.

After a week or so in Jerusalem, I wanted to rush back into the desert. There was too much casual holiness about. It was too easy to think that I was truly there, in the hot streets which He had walked, in the same sun, on the same slopes, in the same shadows. All Christians have this flaring conviction in Jerusalem, in the here and now of ochre earth and stone. Responding to brute matter, our faith for the first time comes to feel glowingly alive, because an assault on the senses is our truest reality. Suddenly I rebelled. I got the odour of paganism: I was being seduced by surfaces, by mere things and stuff. Jerusalem had turned into the earthly city, a corrupt Venice. And for five days, too, I was violently ill, feverish, almost certainly from the sting or bite of an insect, for I had convulsions and nearly died. So, feeling no regrets, I left Jerusalem and the Holy Sepulchre for Damascus.

On the way out and for many weeks, this was my litany: I am here to make myself unafraid. I have come for the Cross and the lower city. My business is to gather strength for the work that lies ahead, and I shall be as knives and stone for the Council of Ten.

Therefore I was eager to journey into the desert, to go through my trial. On my return to Italy, I had to be able to summon up and see – truly see – the Third City, a new Jerusalem floating whitely out there, beyond the great lagoon, along the sandbars that face the open sea.

Damascus is a vast beehive of buying and selling, three times the size of Florence and enclosed by two rings of great walls. It has many Christians and a scatter of churches where we are allowed to worship. Damascenes are a handsome people. They flow as they walk through the streets in their long gowns and wide sleeves. I saw sugar there as white as snow and solid as a rock, and in an attack of gluttony, I ate a pomegranate with juice that was all sugar and the colour of goats' blood.

In Damascus I was swiftly in touch with Ibrahim Hurayra, an old Christian and Damascene who had lived in Konya, where he studied the ways of a Mohametan heresy. I had a letter for him in Arabic from my Third-City Dominican, the Venetian. We conversed through a clever and quick interpreter, a retired pepper merchant, as Ibrahim's wrinkled fingers flicked beads; and for the next three months he taught me the rudiments of thinking about God. I would take an object, such as an orange or a jar, and stare intently at it. The aim? To wear it away by an act of sustained concentration. Either it dissolved into everything around me and I was locked into an intense cognitive exercise, or it diminished to a point so charged with shimmering delicacy that all creation seemed to be there. Here too was an act of pristine perception and mind. The object contemplated is absorbed into the One through the contemplator, and God is thus understood to be as near to us always as our own eyes.

I could go on with these ideas for hours, Father Clemence, but I have put the matter into a few lines, to keep to the spine of this confession – the risen chain of actions that have put my salvation in danger.

In Damascus I rented a room beside the church of Saint Ananias, in a house belonging to a Christian family. I did some begging but only, of course, outside our Christian churches; and at the end of the day I would turn my takings over to one of these and occasionally hand a few coins out to the beggars who stood outside mosques. I also fasted, the better to attain an astringency of thought. The less the body works on food, the more force there is in the faculty for focused thinking, as in the thinner part of the lenses of spectacles.

For days after my arrival in Damascus I found that the worst trial for me was to stay away from the company of people, particularly in the vaulted bazaars with their massive siege on the senses. Solitude and the crowd are the two extremes for the trial of the spirit. We should at some point enter into these, and this was my time – or it was coming – for a plunge into seclusion and silence. I picked up bits of Arabic, but all the while, on top of my talks with Ibrahim, I was making plans to spend fifteen months in the desert. I had to be back in Venice by Christmas, 1525.

Two memories eddy back to me from those days – the inexpressible depth of Ibrahim's green eyes and the eyes of a beggar who sat outside the entrance to the Umayyad Mosque. This man's eyes were a sermon, and whenever I saw him, I could not rid myself of their look for the remainder of the day. I began looking to him as my human point for a departure in thinking. I would go to that mendicant, nod and smile, and then stare into his eyes. It seemed to me that I was staring into a pattern of pain – the pain in all of us. He would then hold out his hand, I would put a coin into it and go on staring, and he would stare sternly back at me, until at some point, released from myself, I would move away from him – I do not know how or when – having lost all touch with everything around me, and find that I was sitting in shade, each time in a different place, leaning against a wall and coming out of a stupor.

Just after sunset one day, emerging from one of those contemplative dazes, I was hearing a conversation in a dream. The speech was Italian, Venetian to be exact, and one voice was saying to the other: *Tomorrow morning will be the perfect time. A great caravan arrived this afternoon.* I strained to catch every word and, doing so, realised that the voices were coming from outside myself, for I had turned to one side and, looking up, saw two men engaged in the gestures of that conversation. One was in black silk, Venetian dress, the other in a white gown, a Saracen, but he was speaking, I thought, a flawless Venetian. Paying no attention to the beggar sitting nearby, myself, they went on talking about a shipment of slaves, mostly women, all taken in raids near the coasts of the Black and Caspian seas, in the Caucasus. The figure in white was saying that such a wonderful gathering of slaves had not been seen in two years and that the field of buyers would include Genoese, Neapolitan, Florentine, Greek and North African merchants. The prize lot, he declared, would certainly be bought by a great merchant or desert chieftain. They were a mother, aged thirty-one, and her three daughters, sixteen, fifteen and fourteen years old. He had seen them when the caravan arrived. Who knew what had happened to the father. All four were beauties and would fetch the highest price by being sold together to a single bidder. The Venetian, however, had more modest intentions. He wanted only three healthy girls of passing good looks, and the man in white – another Venetian, I was now sure – was going to do the bidding for him.

Early the next morning I put on a clean white robe, along with good headdress, and went out to the slave market, which was held just to the north of the Umayyad Mosque, in a small square, where I placed myself close to the two Venetians. I observed the sale of eighty-five to ninety slaves, about seventy of whom were young women and girls, mostly fair-skinned but with a sprinkling of sandy and olive-pale maids. All had obviously been bathed. There was no wailing or gnashing of teeth. The vendors had bullied them into silence and resignation. A few held hands. Others, standing alone, quietly cried. Others still clutched lostly at their garments. The suffering of captivity and rape was in their eyes. To guard their value they had been well fed and, I assume, forced to eat all along the way of their long journey over water and desert. For a minute or two before each transaction, the slave who went up for bidding was led, naked, across the sale proscenium and turned slowly around with her arms raised. Every time this happened, there was a hush among the crowd of merchants and then, when her gown was put on again, an outburst of comments on the different parts of her body. Some of the boys were shown so as to suggest that they were meant for sodomy. Most of them, the girls too, as far as I could tell, were to be slaves for carnal, as well as for domestic work.

I saw the mother and her three daughters. They were brought forward and proudly displayed. The slaver guaranteed that the three girls were virgins. A wise woman had examined them. The fourteen-year-old was the tallest. Her fair hair fell to her elbows. She stood straightly, but the tears in her eyes flashed, as did her handsome limbs, when she was turned around; and though her jaw went hard, she could not control her crying. The mother, on being sharply turned, fell at one point but was at once got up and made to pace gracefully back and forth across the platform, to show that she was healthy. She too was indeed very fine-looking, with auburn hair. In fact all four were too distressingly handsome, and the particulars stick in my memory not only because it was so woeful to look upon their enslaved grace, but also because the beauty of their flesh outlined the lechery, violence, paganism, villainy and murderous barbarity of the slave trade. Yet all the buyers were Christians, Jews or Mohametans, who laughed and chatted, as they sat and ate comfortably, looking very pleased with themselves and quite at peace with their souls. They accepted the world just as they had found it. They were perfectly, happily accepting, Father Clemence, and that is where hell is.

What was I to do, turn myself into a strange knight of Christ? Rush into their midst, a protesting madman, to be hacked to pieces? I wanted to attack them all with blades and jagged stones. Every last one of them deserved a vile death. Could I at least walk up to the two Venetians and spit in their faces? I thought my veins would burst with rage. If I did nothing, I also deserved to die. And I was filled with disgust for my spiritual exercises and my retreat from the world. While children and their mothers were being sold to be used as sheathes for the male member, I was taken up with the schooling of my spirit and a higher order of contemplation. Wasn't there a supernal self-indulgence in this, one anchored in hell? Where in heaven's name was the self-denial?

It took days for me to pull myself out of that spasm of doubt and self-hatred. The mission of the Third City *has* something to do with the freeing of slaves.

19. [Loredana, CONFESSION]:

After being back in Venice for about three or four months, I mean after our first summer in Asolo, Marco and Agostino began to quarrel and from then on had bitter fights and I didn't know at the time how their quarrelling was tied in with the next thing but it was. One Sunday morning when I got back home from mass with our two servants I let them go for the day as by arrangement and they went off. Marco and Agostino were hiding in my bedchamber and as soon

as I walked into it Marco grabbed me violently from behind
the door and tied a stocking around my mouth while Big
Hands held my legs to keep me from kicking out but I
fought them anyway, I tore my nails scratching at them and
I bruised my lips doing all I could to get my mouth free
from the stocking so that I could bite Marco and I tell you
that if my teeth had found any part of his body I'd have
bitten off a piece, I was so blind with rage but they were
too strong for me, they broke up my rosary beads, scattered
my pearls, ripped my headdress and tore my bodice and
underskirts, even my hose, and then Marco held me as
Agostino entered me for the second time. There was but
little blood from between my legs this time and not too
much pain either even though Agostino was as brutal as the
first time. All the pain instead was inside, down deep, a lump
of shame and rage, what honour had I any more? Only my
family could have that if I held my tongue, and how could
I blurt things out now? How, after all the time already gone
by since my wedding day and also considering that our
servants must know something, they saw my bruises, they
had to know about Big Hands and Marco, and I knew they
were ready to say things against me and tell lies and do
anything to please my husband. I can still see myself then,
wife to the noble Marco Contarini but whore to his lover
the noble Agostino Barbarigo. Yes but it wasn't quite like
that, something bizarre was happening because a few weeks
later Big Hands had the face to come and tell me that he
was losing Marco. In those days I barely spoke to them and
had most of my meals alone, I hated them but I hated Marco
a hundred times more because he was my husband and the
shaming attacks on me were all his doing and his idea because
Big Hands doted on him and was ready to do anything just

to hold on to him, even violence and anything lewd. So slyly I began to let Big Hands talk to me because I had to know what was going on, I mean their secrets, but he couldn't talk to me except when Marco wasn't there and that was only a few rushed minutes at a time when for instance we were in the middle of a room and could see that there was no one else near by, not the servants either.

By shutting up that whole dirty business inside myself where it kept getting bigger and more twisted I was letting my feelings against Marco turn into an animal thirst for vengeance and it came to rule my life, I gave myself to it, it made me look at him more closely and start to talk to him and be watchful so that one day I could strike. I guess I had this in my Loredan blood, I wanted to revenge myself on him in a terrible way, I didn't care how as long as it was terrible, and I wasn't thinking of poison either or any kind of death because then I would have to die too and why should I? No no, I wanted him to taste and go on tasting my clawed vengeance, I wanted him to suffer as he was making me suffer, I wanted him beaten and humiliated. He deserved it because he was so clever with people and secretive and knew how to get the lowest things out of them while always seeming courtly and kind and so handsome and as if honey wasn't sweet enough for his beautiful mouth. Toads and poison were too good for it. He was truly strange that Marco. Listen father Clemence I'll go right to the next thing. He got an evil pleasure from seeing Big Hands put his member into me, that's why they got at me that second time and Big Hands did it because it thrilled Marco and made Marco desire Big Hands who told me all this. Well now the light entered my thick head, I began to see how to get my revenge on Marco, though even as I write this, in case you think I forget, I know

I am standing as a sinner before God, I know that but I never stopped praying to the Madonna. In my own eyes yes I was a sinner and I went through each day being afraid, sometimes my whole body would sweat from fear, but with prayers and tightened fists and kneeling before the big panel of the Madonna in my bedchamber I'd come to feel that I was wrapping myself in her merciful folds.

Here I have to break off this confession because I need a rest, I'm writing it down as fast as it comes and it comes fast. There's no time to waste because I may have to go out and look for Orso.

Now I'll give you my thoughts of revenge against Marco nearly twenty years ago, here they are, I never confessed them. He takes pleasure from watching Big Hands enter his wife, enter her like an animal, though knowing I would be ready to stab or batter him from the disgust of it all and maybe this thrills him too, I don't know. Well I'll change, I WILL CHANGE, I'll stop feeling what he expects, I'll make myself take the violence, I'll get myself to like it and he'll hate it, but if I show I like it he'll stop and my revenge stops so I won't show it, I'll hide my pleasure, I want to like it and I'll have to like it if I'm to make him a dirt-low cuckold (that's what he is anyway) and bring his name and face and all that's in him down to the filth where he belongs. When he thinks he's hurting me I'll enjoy it and hurt him instead, and when he dishonours me I'll dishonour him by liking what he thinks is a disgust to me. This was my thinking, it was evil and frightening but I went on with it, I seethed with the snakes of cold rage, I was turned into a demon, I sewed these shameful thoughts into the skin of my head and I worked on myself to make me change and be the way I had to be for vengeance's sake.

So one day maybe seeing some sign in me, when that beast Big Hands was shameless enough to hint (I can't remember how) that they might assault me a third time, I was ready for them, I just waved him off and said I looked on them both with such *schifo* [*disgust*] that I didn't care what they did and I would always rise above them, base animals that they were, that their souls would end in hell, and that I didn't even care if Marco's gossiping servants knew and told the whole world about it because then their dirty sodomy would come out too and be known to all the world and how right *that* would be. I said the last thing about the servants really as a hint to Big Hands so they'd get them out of the house if there was a third assault, and that's the way it was because one morning a week or two later Marco sent them off for the day to the lower city and the house was empty except for us and I knew at once that it might be going to happen. But everything was going to be different this time, I was ready, I saw details, I'd see everything, I'd not give in to blind rage, I would be sensible and know exactly what to do. Big Hands Agostino arrived just as Marco and I were sitting down to lunch, he joined us, I ate next to nothing and at the end as we got up from the table they fell on me. I pretended to fight hard and heaped insults on them since they didn't even bother to bind up my mouth and I bit Marco, but not too hard as they half-dragged and carried me to my bedchamber where the deed was done. Big Hands was worked up because he thought that would excite Marco more and it did, I heard it in Marco's voice, and the more aroused they got the more Marco himself held me and the more things Big Hands did. I kept shutting and opening my eyes, I cried more than enough to keep Marco pleased but I saw everything, I saw the branch with a fat head (Agostino's member), I saw his enormous veined hands, I saw the fingers of one hand spread the hair and me down there by rudely parting the lips, I saw the other hand push the branch forward oiled and glistening, I saw the head and neck enter slowly because happy Marco had pressed my head down so I could see, and after Big Hands was in me all the way I shut my eyes and grabbed Marco's wrists and squeezed them with all my might, I also bit his arm through the sleeve so he'd think I was feeling pain and hating it, yet all the while I was thinking of nothing but Agostino's member, I was seeing it through my closed eyes, I was letting all of that thick thing come in and fill me up and I was holding my place or maybe pushing, not pulling back, while still insulting Marco but always taking and taking Big Agostino's brushing branch until I heard the far sound of bees and I began to feel as if the top of my head was going to burst off and I screamed and screamed and then Agostino's weight wasn't on me any more.

I was on my side sobbing and Marco was delighting in my shame but this time he was wrong if he had eyes to see because I'd just got the strongest pleasure of my whole life, a great wide blow of pleasure but so sharp I couldn't bear it, that's why I squeezed and screamed and insulted him with farmyard words because I had the feeling of losing my senses but also of standing over him in strong animal pleasure. There was something else, Marco should have seen through my acting and biting, he should have seen what was happening, the violent pleasure, only he didn't because he was too stirred up himself and too crazy with watching Big Agostino, but Agostino knew what happened because after he was in me I held on to him down there deeply, it was like a grabbing at him with a secret mouth. That was my vengeance, I need to say it again, that was my vengeance, and I needed no help from my family for that, my father could have his honour and yet I'd get back at Marco by stamping on his pride with my own pleasure. It was deep sinning, I knew that but I thanked heaven for it (that was blasphemy) and I was so satisfied I was ready to die. I felt I'd urinated on Marco's face, that's the best way to say it.

20. [Orso, CONFESSION]:

In June of 1524 I left Damascus with a caravan bound for Persia, on my way to a place that would change me. My route had been charted by a Damascene merchant, a Christian. We crossed the Syrian desert with stops at Qasr al-Hair ash-Sharqi and Halebiye where, abandoning the caravan, I was taken north along the Euphrates River to Raqqa and then into the desert again to a shrunken oasis, R'safah. Here is the tiniest of Christian enclaves, an assortment of seven monks. Each spends his days alone. Having been given three large camelloads of almonds and dried grapes in my name, and informed that I was a Dominican friar, they had offered me a place. Five of the monks are complete and perfect eremites. The other two, while living a hermitical existence, must occasionally be in touch with bedouins and the few local families for the replenishment of their small stocks of food – olives, nuts, chickpeas, beans, dates and rare oddments of salt fish. An ancient well provides just enough water. But the seven men rely mainly on a trickle of provisions from Christian traders in Aleppo, Deir al-Zor, al-Ladhiqiye and Safita.

The place names spring forth easily, as if the sun had baked them into my awareness. They conjure up the desert, which armed me against the towering pride of the upper city. But if this armour also increased my own pride and distance from God, I repent the effects and see the more reason to recite the words by which I am able to call up the desert. Let those words too figure among my confessed sins. Father Clemence, please pray for me. How I long for the sun, the sand, the baked rocks, the scorpions, and madonna X. We shall come to the scorpions.

R'safah [*Resáfe*]. The desert, the ineffable desert. I fumble for a beginning, the *non*-desert, and therefore I name Picchina of the loose hair, the Bologna prostitute in whose body I rooted. I hold that image for a moment. Then I make it pass. In Damascus, the gliding movement of Saracen women in their long robes reminded me of her, and I sought to make that picture point the way for me. On my arrival in the desert, I laboured to convert all carnal memory of that sort into the very ends that I was seeking in Syria: self-composure and tautness in thinking. The image of Picchina and the long-robed women soon came up no more, and soon too I blended into the land like a Saracen. I wore a headdress and a loose white gown to shield me from the sun.

Although it is now a desert heap, R'safah was ancient Sergiopolis, a flourishing early Christian city, named after Sergius, an officer in the Roman army. He was brutally martyred for refusing to offer a sacrifice to Jupiter. In his life and nailed feet, the seven hermits have their champion. Rather than pretend belief in a pagan god, Sergius insisted on professing Christ and so was forced to run over eighteen miles of burning desert in shoes with exposed nails. At the end of the race his head was cut off. In my first weeks at R'safah, I concentrated on imagining the pain, the blood, the blows, the blazing sun, the burst feet, the bruised face, the cracked lips, the scaled skin, the being spat upon, the infamy. Why

was Christ so dear to him, so terribly dear? Because He was
the pulsating heart of meaning, investing every single day with
a purpose – love, decent action and salvation; and Sergius
could not bear to live without these. He could not for a
moment bear to live without meaning. If that is the case, is
it so much to put belief above all bodily pain? To rise above
our tormented clay?

Curiously, I remembered among Boccaccio's tales the
profane story of an embittered lover who traps his naked ex-
beloved in a raging sun until she nearly dies, as her skin
reddens, swells and then splits. I considered getting into the
sun that way, but I was not in R'safah to die. The Syrian sun
is not a Tuscan summer sun, with shadows and water all about.
In God's name, how could they do that to Sergius? But it
was in God's name, Jupiter against Christ. Would Christ –
does Christ – condone killing in his name?

R'safah either kills or revives. A curt discussion [*in Latin*]
with the two caretaking hermits, one of them a German, gave
me all the advice I was to have. Unless concealed in a safe
shelter, I was to be alert at all times. The dangers were both
obvious and hidden – to lose my way in the desert, a sudden
illness, the surprise assault of wolves, a marauding panther, or
a murderous band of desert thieves, though what could these
take? Next, poisons from snakes and golden-backed insects.
It was almost better to be bitten. I had already been all but
mortally ill, most likely from a poisonous sting just outside
Jerusalem. If I wanted, I could make brief forays into the
open desert, but it was best not to, though if I must, then
better to do so in the high heat of the sun, because dawn
was the time for dangerous animals. But first I must find a
secluded spot, a point for prayer and meditation, inside the
great perimeters of the ruins of R'safah, and build a shelter

there for protection against the sun and beasts of prey – not, however, too comfortable a shelter. My commission was clear: to make the act of thinking triumph over physical discomfort. This is the proof of hard, pointed meditation.

For some weeks I slept in the shade of an ancient wall and closely examined the whole of R'safah. In ever-widening circles and in the hot sun, I also walked in the adjacent desert, striving to prepare myself. Back in Sergiopolis [*R'safah*], I found the surface rubble of what must once have been the church of Saint Sergius – great hardened mounds of yellowed stone, most of it buried deep in sand. I made a shelter out of fragments of stone, putting these up against a corner of the old city wall. From where I sat I could see the half-sunken head of a buried column. I dug out the surrounding earth and scraped it, exposing a delightful row of acanthus leaves. Who had carved and moulded it ten centuries ago? Some lowly stone cutter? Slaves?

In the beginning I was always thirsty and there was no way to avoid goatskins. I drank water from one and ate small amounts of nuts and pulverised beans mixed with herbs and water. Eventually I learned to work dried dates into this mixture.

When I got down to prayer, I used Ibrahim's way of seeing and thinking. He had prescribed measured breathing to go with the exercise of sustained perception, the exercise by which the thing gazed at then fades and vanishes, or becomes the point of everything. You know what it is, Father Clemence, to hold a thought for a few minutes, or a reasoned prayer for an hour. But imagine clinging to an idea for three or four hours at a time, and then again the next day, and so on for weeks and months. Men can often pray for an hour or two, while scheming for office or quarrelling in their heads with a neighbour. And many women can intone a hundred Hail Marys, while lingering over a hundred household details. The two activities are neither thought nor prayer; they are habits.

Bedouins love and couple in the desert, but hermits may as well couple with the hot sand, for apart from possessing the most spiritual of the senses [*our eyes*], the desert is miserly. It is as well to seek God. After gazing down and scrutinising the countless shades of yellowish-brown or greying sand, the eyes look up – sky, dunes, horizons. The hours pass. The eyes look and peer and stare, until they lapse into wonderment, dissolving the contours of the dunes and the blue intensity above, in the summons – we are summoned – to something vast, to the apex of possibility in ourselves, which is also out there in the void. That something can only pertain to God, of all ideas the most noble, because it gathers up all other ideas.

When the short winter came and there was the rare burst of rainfall, I had to scurry around to warm myself. I came down (or moved up) from thought and returned to reconsider the visages of the desert. There was a new look out there, grey-gold and wind-tossed. I could describe the many animals seen, racing across the sands, including, several times, a large beast, black and catlike, but I dare not let myself be deflected; my hours of confession may be numbered.

I realised how attached I had become to that mournful rubble, the quondam City of Saint Sergius, though I often awoke, turning on my bedroll, with ears and nostrils full of fine sand. The wind blew up the powdery stuff. And sandstorms, like a cold blaze of pure thinking, blotted everything out into a white night; they brought total loss. There was no need to pursue thought in a sandstorm. Nature did it for me: a white night resolves contradiction.

When the spring came, I saw that I had climbed to a new knowing plateau, that a change was necessary.

One afternoon, in the self-appointed task of going over every mound, stone, nook and cranny of R'safah, I came on slitlike long openings in the ground, allowing slivers of light into three vast caverns – subterranean cisterns. Stupefied, I was peering into the underground space of three Florence cathedrals, entirely covered over by brick, sand and rubble. Three cathedrals! All at once I saw Sergiopolis, a teeming city in the heart of the desert, and its heart was in these mysterious caverns. The desert here had once been darkly graced with water, the rain and wells a gift of abundance. Where had the water gone, and where the grace?

When the sun was at the right angle, I could make out tiny patches of the gigantic base of two of the cisterns. Were they the traces of a brick flooring? I spent weeks trying to find a way into them. The broken vaulting in the ground above made it too dangerous to attempt an entry through those openings. So I scoured every bit of land that seemed to be above and around the cisterns. I could find nothing. Then late one evening, close to the ancient southern rampart, at the base of a mound of buried masonry, I discovered a large hole loosely but carefully sealed by rubble. Removing it all, I looked in and saw a ribbon of brick stairs leading down into the pitch black, but the hour was too late for me to do anything more. What was down there? I replaced the fragments of broken stone. To go down I needed shafts of strong sunlight or I would certainly lose my way. Others, I realised, must also know about the entry. Was it a hiding place, that black void? That night I slept badly, or only half-slept, as I rose through a vapour and toppled buildings in a dream of anxiety about what I would do and find the next day.

Apart from the New Testament and a sheaf of writing paper, my only luxury was a three-pound bundle of candles, which I had lugged along with me in my trek over the desert.

In the light of the early morning I returned to the spot and again removed the concealment rubble. Stepping inside, I sat and waited for several hours, until the sun hung closer. I then went down the worn, undamaged steps as far as I could go in that black hole, often looking back up, but also searching the black nothingness below for other rays of light. As my eyes got used to the void, I detected other lines of light, and at quite some distance off I saw more brightness still – slanted shafts of light. These I judged to be coming from the dangerous apertures that I had first found weeks before. But the base of the cistern was still far below me. Needing more light, I climbed back up to the entrance to find that there was not a breath of wind. My heart alone beat against the absolute stillness of that day. A candle was unlikely to go out suddenly in that immense cavern. With flints and a handful of stubble I started a fire and lit two candles. Bearing one in each hand, I went into that night again, back down the steps and slowly, cautiously, edged my way to the bottom. There I stood. My innards seemed to slither. After a few minutes I put out one candle. I breathed deeply and prayed. After another while – but I could see the light, barely, at the distant top of the brick stairway – I blew out the other. There was an intolerable silence. My ears strained to invent screams. I felt fear in the form of slow-moving vast wings. I fixed my eyes on the spot of light far, far above, through which I had entered into this infernal cavern. My fear passed. What if someone suddenly sealed the entrance? On hands and knees I would grope my way up to the top of the stairs and throw myself against the rubble to knock it out.

A strange desire had taken possession of me. I wanted to spend three months down there, in an exercise of prayer and perfection, but I faced inexpressible dangers. Would I stick to the base of the ancient stairway, which must once have been used for construction and repairs, or would I venture out into the void? I studied the black sky of the cistern. There was a meagre scatter of points of light, some a little brighter than others, yet all making the expanse look remotely like our night sky. By fixing a map of those lights in my visual memory, I judged that I might be able to move around in that night and find my way back to the staircase. But there were other dangers, such as from possible spiders, snakes or large pits in the cistern floor. How would I crawl out of a deep hole? And was this the secret hiding place of outcasts or escaped convicts? One of the hermits – I suspected that one or more of them knew the way in – might block the entry at the top of the stairs and cut off the light. What then? Or was there an understanding that when the rubble had been removed from that point, only the man who had descended could put it back, and might no one else then go down? Perhaps I could feel my way around those vast perimeters by cleaving to the walls, but this would not help me to find the right place, *my* place, for reflecting and for prayer. I wanted to be somewhere near the middle of the cistern. Particular places give us a feeling, and some are right for us, some wrong.

In the end, by using both candles and the fine rays of light that came in through the cavern's vaulted roofing at high noon, I found a raised point not too far from where a sliver of sunlight struck the base. There, with bricks prised lose from the flooring hidden under the sand, I built up a brick surface just large enough for me to sit and sleep on.

There were few beetles or other insects around, it seemed to me, and I saw no snakes, but who could tell? And there was not a drop of water anywhere. The brick flooring, lying under a coat of sand, felt as dry as any bone bleached by the sun.

To find a route to the other two cisterns was out of the question. In time, with the help of a candle, I felt my fearful way to a tunnel which I believed led into the next cistern. I concluded that there had to be tunnels connecting the three hellish cathedrals, but I sensed that the dangers of finding and groping my way through them were insuperable. As I said, I was not in R'safah to look for my death.

21. [Falier, SECRET CHRONICLE]:

The Loredan name was first heard in the 1200s, when our name, Falier, already betokened celebrity. We were doges in the eleventh century . . .

Like many Venetian patricians, the Loredans came up on the silk and spice trades, so let there be no prattle about a line of descent from the ancient Romans. Great emporia – Antioch and Beirut, Aleppo and Alexandria – figure large in their early history. But the Loredans added a new twist: they were also pirates who preyed on Christian vessels. Hence their history has its beginnings in theft and violence. I append writs of litigation, dating from the 1290s, where we find that two Loredans, Zaneto and Zorzi, were being sued by Christian merchants from Amalfi. They had seized a vessel off the coast of Malta, and the documents also show that they were already slave traders . . .

Their first houses were in the parish of San Vitale, but after 1300 they decamped to the northern arm of the Grand Canal, above the Rialto Bridge.

[*Falier next provides a genealogy of the Loredans and does a sketch of their activity in commerce and high office. The highlights follow:*]

The role of the Loredans in the bloody Tiepoline Conspiracy of 1310 is shady indeed. Many scraps of evidence (Appendix iv) indicate that first they supported it, having recently married into the great Tiepolo clan. But from the moment two defectors, on the night before the uprising, began to unfold the particulars of the plot to the doge and his advisors, the Loredans passed cravenly over to the other side. Afterwards, to display their loyalty, they were the most implacable accusers in the hounding of the conspirators.

[*Deletions* . . .]

Thus I conclude that this Leonardo Loredan (+1349) was one of the most notorious usurers of his day. He was far worse than the Jews, who only bilk little folk. Leonardo stole from rich and poor alike. He had a heart of granite. He took interest at rates of from 65 per cent to 100 per cent; his agents did not hesitate to put widows and orphans out of their houses; he drove borrowers to suicide; he battened on war loans; and he was arraigned by ecclesiastical courts to answer charges of aggravated usury, but always managed to confute the charges by means of gifts, bribery and occult levers (Appendix vii). Later, much of his wealth went to build two of the Loredan palaces in the upper city.

[*Deletions* . . .]

Having reviewed the whole body of evidence (Appendices xii–xiv), we cannot but conclude that the leading parts in the martyrdom of the doge Marin Falier were taken by none other than Andrea and Daniele Loredan. To speak plainly, they were lickspittles to the Dandolo and Gradenigo families; they were seeking distinguished marriages; and they had been snubbed by doge Falier, who sought to keep the dishonest members of that lineage out of high office. Consequently, Andrea and Daniele managed to put him in touch with discontented commoners; they produced false testimony against him, regarding his secret machinations against the ruling caste; they manipulated the Council of Ten; they led the call for his brutal torture; and they even circulated indecent jingles about his young wife.

> Marin Falier has a wife too fair,
> He is the payer but other men lay 'er.

In short, no deed was too vile for them in their rabid determination to destroy the doge; and over the space of a few hours on the night of 17 April 1355, Marin Falier was questioned, framed, tortured, and beheaded – a woeful event that makes for the blackest page in all the annals of Venetian history.

[*Deletions: pages on the deposition of Doge Francesco Foscari, 1457*]

The pestiferous crime of sodomy illustrates an aspect of the violence and double-dealing of the Loredans. In early May 1408, when the Council of Ten unearthed a secret company of sodomites, involving men from both the lower and upper cities, the Loredans, sensing an upsurge of public fear and disgust, led the column of those who demanded the most savage penalties against the accused, namely death by fire, a sentence then imposed on a number of minor noblemen. Twenty-eight years later, when Andrea di Leonardo Loredan was seized *in flagrante* and at night with an eleven-year-old boy from the lower city, the Loredans rushed in to keep a lid on the case, and Andrea was condemned to pay the boy's family of menials the derisory sum of seven ducats.

As in sodomy, so in cases of corruption, assault and the scandal of brothel-like convents: when members of their own clan are involved, the Loredans always pursue a policy of lenience or outright toleration; but wherever they can wring name and advantage from a terrible severity, they lead the chorus of the terrible. I grant, however, that they are no different in this regard from the Morosini, Contarini, Dandolo and other families of the ruling caste.

22. [Loredana, CONFESSION]:

A low filthy evil confession, that's what you'll think father Clemence, how can you think anything else? So I have to warn you here, it's going to be lower, God help me, if I write things down the way they happened, and I've described the third base doing just as it was so you can know how far down I had gone in my sinning revenge against Marco. You could say I wanted that violence from Big Hands or even (once it started) that I was the one who attacked him with the blows of my pleasure, and I didn't stop committing that sin, I couldn't, how could I, Marco wasn't going to stop, and anyway the story wasn't going to get out to all the wagging tongues of upper Venice, no one knew, the sin was always held in, always there, a toad squatting inside me, so I went on dishonouring Marco in my imaginings too because he did the same to me, I hadn't any honour left except on the outside in the lady who pranced to mass on Sunday mornings, also, remember that he was the one who had started that downward pull, the violence and lewd pleasure, and only he my husband had the power to stop it, I couldn't. I'll say this too, never once did he show any regret or sorrow or shame and the only time he ever touched me was to give my woman's parts to Agostino who knew I'd stolen pleasure that third

time, after all I held on to him, and now I think of it this is
why I didn't go to my father again or write a telling letter
to him, I was caught in vice and wouldn't give it up though
I gave myself other reasons for not telling him. This is the
first time I've ever admitted this so you see my depths and
you see why Agostino began to think he was giving me a
big treat every time Marco forced him on me. It was Marco's
way of getting his snaky pleasure and Agostino's only way of
holding on to Marco.

There we were the three of us each wanting something
else and all wallowing in a strange sin, but I was the worst
because I saw the evil of it and I think they didn't, I could
see all three of us in the furnace of lust when they had eyes
only for each other. Also my God I was the prize vessel of
honour, the finest flower of Venice, daughter to maybe a
future doge, holder of the two proudest names in the city,
Loredan-Contarini, yet up to my mouth in the swills of sin
together with my husband and his lover. So I say it again, no
matter what I just admitted, that with the ugliness of Quirina's
impediment fluttering over my father and me like a banner
we couldn't stand up to another scandal. What then? Time
passed and the sinning went deeper because it took new and
more things to excite Marco, till those two reached the point
where after tying me up with my legs apart Marco himself
with his own criminal fingers spread me open down there
for Big Agostino's member, then weeks later in the next
change he forced the knobbed branch into my mouth. And
what did I do? I ran a lewd race against them and won.
They'd blindfolded me but when the thing was pressed into
my mouth the herby taste and feel of it made everything
flow and suddenly I didn't care a fig any more if Marco saw
how much I liked it, here was the crown of all revenge, my

noble husband of the mighty house of Contarini was now fetching my pleasures for me like a lackey, and I sucked hard till it gave up all its sap into my mouth and I imagined my warm urine down below trickling over Marco's face and gorgeous locks.

I have to stop here, I don't know if I can go on, I can't face that preacher's word, my depravity.

Two hours have passed father Clemence and I must start writing this again, you see I'm going to have to go out to look for my dear Orso, so now back into the confessing because the evil goes on and there's a lot even just sticking to the facts. From here on I'll tell only about the main sins and deeds.

In June my monthly flow didn't come, we'd been married a year and I remember its not coming because we were about to go out to the villa for the summer and there was no flow in July either so I told Marco and he called in the physician Pietri and Pietri said I was with child. Can you imagine our feelings with Agostino as the father? I was horrified and happy too, it was a tug of war, Marco was horrified and in a rage the cretin (what did he expect?) and he didn't know what to do but we said nothing to Agostino who anyway wasn't at the villa then. Marco stormed around like a wild man insulting me and said he'd kill me and I gave him back as good, I called him a cuckold of his own making and he knocked me down but I reminded him that he was the animal who had started it all and what could he say, that I had no business being with Big Agostino's child? After a few days he calmed down and the next week when Agostino came out to Asolo he told him. Well in a day or two they were drunkenly happy and dancing around the villa because you see Agostino said right away that he would leave their child all his estate and their child was what they kept saying, I didn't come into it, it was their child. Listen maybe this was a new sin on my part, you tell me father Clemence, but I was soon happy for two reasons, first to be a mother is why women marry and second it would pull all three of us up out of our sin because the two of them would have to stop using me for their strange lusts, I'd stop hungering for the evil pleasure of what they did to me and I'd also turn all my thoughts to the child who would have Marco's name but be Big Agostino's and nobody would ever know the difference. That way if the two of them wanted they could go on in their dark ways but now I'd not be one of them, I'd stop being the animal that they had made of me, especially that tart Marco who was always looking for new pleasures and wanting to be admired for his beauty and wooed by big men like Agostino. Two times that year he'd gone off with other men for a few days and made Agostino suffer. Anyway now I'd be free of them, they could play their own low games but not with me and I would be truly Loredana Loredan Contarini, so day after day I prayed to the Madonna. I used to touch my stomach when I was alone and I could feel it growing so I started to eat for two, Agostino saw this. But it was not to be alas, it was not to be, I had only two months of peace and near-happiness out at Asolo because in the fourth month, September, the seed all came out in pain and a bloody mess of a tiny baby in the middle of the night, and Marco had to go out and fetch the local midwife, a good woman. Well picture our feelings now. Agostino was very sad, Marco couldn't decide how he felt about it and I was more miserable than the lowest beggar, every day was black night but I saw the hand of God there. I understand accounts, we had to pay for our sins and me especially for mine, and the debts were huge, they'd mounted up horribly. I also saw that it could happen again and again, the clotted mass of bloody seed coming out, not the curse of the devil but bloody payment for the evil we had done. There was no easy way out of our sin and I shouted this to the two of them one morning in a wild crazy rage, I screamed it into their faces and would have written it with fire on their vile bodies. Again I have to stop.

Well there was no return, the world knew I'd lost a baby and whose could it be but Marco's, so we were now in everybody's eyes a good wife and husband trying to have a family. We squeezed through that second year somehow, I wanted a child and I got Big Hands to enter me a few times but I miscarried again. Heavens if only I'd been able to carry it without the sin. Agostino was almost sweet but mostly in pain over his own suffering because Marco was really turning against him no matter what he did to me under Marco's nose, and my attachment to Agostino's member was Marco's dishonour but revenge wasn't all, remember that I yearned to have a child, I would have given an eye for it. In the meantime everything was changing, a great naval captain was just starting to come to the house and of course he had (has) one of those grand old names from the upper city so I won't write it because you'd know it. He's still in this city and anyway first I'd better tell the whole story of Big Hands or you won't understand the part coming about the captain.

What I haven't told you yet is that I began to think of Big Hands as my true husband, after all he was the one in the act of marriage with me, not Marco, he even started being tender and three times I carried his seed for months so how could I feel any other way about him? Also the more he lost Marco the closer he got to me and I tried to comfort him, I confess I did, so that whenever he was staying in the villa or overnight in Venice he sometimes slipped out of Marco's bed in the dead middle of the night and in great secrecy stole into my bedchamber where we embraced and he entered me because as I said I desperately wanted a child, but I did help him too with all my sympathy. That big man couldn't stop talking about his troubles and I got to know him better, he was not evil, he could even be kind and he was dog loyal, he had a big heart but he was pulled around and bent by Marco because he wanted Marco so crazily that he'd do anything for him. It was a fever, and Marco ended by treating him like a dog. Yet even so Big Hands defended him, he told me a strange story, I had trouble believing it, about how much Marco suffered from being a man and being in his beautiful man's body, something I wouldn't even have dreamed of. Marco hated his body and many times had wanted to die, though to me he seemed to show it off in all that fine dress of his but Agostino said it was all fanfare and acting like on a stage, every morning Marco got up and got through the day by performing, too proud to show his misery, but look at his eyes sometime, Agostino told me, look inside them, look at his nose, it flickers, look at the tight lines around the mouth, something awful is happening there, the agony of not being a woman. Think of that, the agony of not being a woman. This is what Big Hands said. Also Marco hadn't wanted to be married to me or to any woman but he couldn't get out of it because of strong family ties and talk, his uncles and family business at the Palace, yes especially the Palace. Marco didn't hate me, not at all Agostino said but he could never be my true husband in marriage and I must be careful with him because he could get into very nasty and evil humours. I was confused, I couldn't make head or tail of Marco, but I think I've said enough about all this and anyway everything came to a head in the third summer.

Marco caught us one night, he caught us, he woke up and saw that Big Hands wasn't in bed or in their great room so he went all through the house quietly looking for him and heard us in my locked bedchamber (I always locked it) though we were more quiet than two ants, but he held his tongue even after Big Hands got back to their bed, he said nothing till morning when he sent the servants off on a long commission and then threw himself into a violent jealous quarrel with us, his eyes went crazy. Agostino was ordered out of the house for ever and I was called a base whore and every other filthy name and told I'd now be his low slave under his strict commands because I was a dirty willing adulteress (he loved that word), so he was going to make me do things he said that my slow wits couldn't even begin to imagine. One of the last things Agostino ever said to me was this, *Marco is dangerous.* Well but I knew that, by heavens I knew it. Still, hearing it from an older man who knew Marco so well put me on guard, but being on guard, always watching and weighing things, wasn't good enough, far from it because like Agostino and much more than Agostino I could be ordered about (remember the blind obedience of wives) and forced to kiss evil through my own lust, and tell me how was I going to put a stop to that if Marco put pleasure up against my lips? I lived in fear for months after poor Agostino was barred from the house and there were those frightening last words, *goodbye, goodbye.* I didn't want to live any more. Look, Agostino's end was this and I weep to report it, he went to sea on a boat belonging to his family and a few years later was taken by Saracen pirates off the coast of Candia, he was enslaved for eleven months and killed when he tried to escape while the pirates were still waiting for the ransom money. God help him, may his soul rest in peace, I have often prayed for him, it was a bitter end and I think Marco was partly to blame. I have to say it father Clemence, my father and uncles had married me to a kind of woman, if only they'd married me to one of the better sort, Venice teems with loyal women but dangerous Marco, I don't know how to make this fit with Agostino's picture of him, dangerous Marco looked to me as if he adored his own good looks, he dressed too well (silken robes, puffy sleeves, furs, fretted linens), he craved flattery, his interests flitted around from thing to thing, he was always putting on a show of grace, he was disloyal from hat to heel and he always had an itch for new pleasures. This made me wonder and now suddenly here I see it, he must have been too tormented in that body of his (or why all that lewd craving and panting too?) even if it was so handsome and graceful. Anyway by comparison Big Agostino was good, I'd grown to like him very much and he liked me, I needed him terribly and that was all.

Let me pause here. No I won't.

Then came the captain, the man of the sea, another big man, little did he know what he was getting into, or did he? Yes he did. You should know father Clemence that Marco had plenty of time to read his Plato and make himself clever with words because he didn't do anything else, nothing, from his high nose he looked down on trade and affairs at the Palace where his brothers, not Marco, took care of family things like lawsuits and getting our men into the right office. I've lost my thread here.

I think I'm trying to say that after what he did to Big Agostino, robbed him of his dignity I'd say, I couldn't bear to look at Marco's face any more, to me it looked like a mask, and after the captain started coming to the house I used to think of Agostino's last words to me about the danger, that made me more afraid but at the same time I was also pulled down to the danger of sin (you see the depravity) and there was sin all over that captain, most of all in his eyes when he looked at Marco and even at me, but he looked at Marco most of the time as Agostino had, only the difference was that Big Hands loved Marco if that's possible between two men.

23. [Orso, CONFESSION]:

Christ, only his wounds and mercy can save me.

There, I break the surface of this confession. A calm flow, you thought, Father Clemence; but no, my stream of words is nothing calm, for I hear feet and calls, shouted orders and passing voices outside my window. When will they be those of the guardsmen or spies of the Ten? When will they break down these false walls?

I take hold of myself again. R'safah again.

In the first two weeks, keeping a skin of water beside me, I came out of my black cathedral, the cistern, once a day to get my bearings and have a bite of food. My courage grew. Using a candle, I had found dangerous holes in the flooring between my place and the distant stairway, but I was learning to feel my way around them in that black night. In the third week, having taken food into the dark with me, I emerged only twice. In the fourth week I remained inside. My way of breathing and fixedly staring at the distant points of light on the cavern floor turned into the final stage of my journey towards God. I gave up all sense of an immediate self. At the end of the fourth week, making several trips, I fetched in a provision of water, nuts, pulverised beans and dried fruits – enough to last me a month. In pitch black I lived, but for a few hours a day, when points of light appeared far above and also, at some distance from me, on three narrow strips of brick flooring where I had cleared off the sand. Looking back, I see that I was drifting insensibly far from ordinary sense experience. For at the start of the second month in my cavernous night, a terrifying occurence enveloped me.

One day – it was day, as I could tell by the remote points of light – the cavern exploded with screams and howling. My shock, coming out of meditation, took me so that I passed into a swoon, because when I regained awareness, I was crouched down beside my bed of bricks, stunned, shaking. The screams and howls began to come through to me again. Having just died, it seemed to me, I was on my way to the place of every horror and black secret. Slowly then, on that horrific edge, as if verging on becoming a creeping spirit, I returned to myself. I listened. The sounds now and then turned into shouts and moans, and while their brutish source seemed to move, I could not tell where they were coming from in that eternal night. I remained crouched and terrified. Then too slowly, whatever it was, a tormented creature moved near to the base of the oblique shaft, the hair-thin line of light, shooting down from the main aperture above; and after a long time I thought that I was almost able to make out (or was I?) the contorted outlines of a man. Was it possibly one of the hermits? The creature was sunken, I imagined, in a furor of madness, reminding me of two crazed men in a Florentine hospital and of a sick woman whom I had known in Bologna. It came to me that I must not go to him, that I could offer no help in that infernal cathedral. And when, long after, the creature finally crawled or reeled away, until I could hear him no more, I wondered about how he had entered that hole of night, where he had gone, and how he found his way around in it carefully enough to avoid the pits in the treacherous floor? Was his madness light in that darkness? Some unnatural, God-given vision?

Breathing hard, as I now remember it, yet determined to seek an explanation, I felt my way to the stairway and returned to the surface to look for the German hermit, but was unable to find him. I spent the night in my old shelter and the next morning again set out on my search. True eremites avoid all meetings and conversation with others. The whole point of their lives is in the flight from people, from chatter, from human articles, from vanity, from lies. Generally, I saw one or two of the hermits, though always at a distance, about every ten or twelve days and I had a vague idea of their preferred haunts. They spent a good deal of time in covered holes in the desert. I finally came on my German in the late afternoon and said I had to talk to him for a moment. I told him about the mad creature in the cistern. His gaze moved over me and then he asked accusingly, *What, you too?* The question, ambiguous, wanted no reply. He told me that Robert of Paris had lost his reason in the cisterns two years ago but was otherwise harmless. Four years before that another hermit had perished there, simply disappeared. One thing, however, he warned me about, something which he had pieced together from Robert's incoherent testimony. Unless I was courting death or madness, it was unwise to penetrate into the second and third cisterns, as each went down more deeply, finally reaching an absolute blackness, despite apparent slits in the earth above. The third and deepest cistern had snakes and traces of water, and Robert had lost himself there, yet somehow managed to grope his way out. But he had left his reason down there.

Our brief exchange ended. A man in his forties I surmised, he had gone on searching my face and concluded by saying, *I myself would not go down there. Insanity is not a gateway to God.* Whereupon he blessed me. We then stepped forward, embraced each other and he went off.

My fear of those ghostly caverns flooded back. I had to sit down. My knees had turned to dough. One man mad and the other dead. What was I going to do, go back down? Certainly I was going back. But that was not the true question. No, the true horror was connected with cisterns two and three. Snakes. Could I resist the temptation to grope my way into them? The question prostrated me. It gnawed at me for hours. That night I returned to my old shelter, and the next day I roamed under the sun in the open desert. I knew the contours of those gentle dunes, the scatter of rocks, the horizon, and the subtle shifts in the colour of the sand as the sun traversed the sky. The answer came. I was a catamite to pride and the devil. I was being tempted to go into the second and third cisterns not to perfect my faith in the Cross but to put something of myself – vain and mortal stuff – on trial. This stuff remained to be burned out. It had nothing to do with God and self-discipline.

Although anxious about the ill-fated Robert of Paris, who might still be crawling around down there and whom I knew not how to help, I went back into my cathedral. I made six trips, taking in provisions enough for two months, and I resolved not to emerge until that time had expired. Every day the total night of the cistern lasted for seventeen or eighteen hours. I could see absolutely nothing. Then the fraudulent stars above began imperceptibly to brighten, and I saw that a new day had come, even if my hands and everything else in front of me remained a tomb of blackness. I began to count the days, and since I had already spent a first month there, I needed to count another sixty-one days.

There I remained, then, in that inky void, in a stupor of contemplation. Whenever I felt a small object move finely over some part of me, I remained either perfectly still and let it pass or brushed it instantaneously away. In time, I learned to remain as still as an owl, and I am sure that when I was intent on the deep fixing of a thought, if an insect crawled over my skin, I felt nothing. I was bitten or stung several times but the swelling passed. Having encountered something poisonous outside Jerusalem, I became more and more fit, like people who live through an epidemic of murderous plague. Scorpions at any rate do not relish human flesh. They prefer their own kind. I saw this in the desert and again in the cistern. I made a little study of them. They are natural beasts of prey, in colour like the hair of angels in old altar paintings, yellowish or very pale brown, with eight legs extending from a trunk, a pair of little claws in front and in the back a slender tail, thinning out to a sting.

During my months in the darkness, I used to examine one point of sunlight as it moved across a strip of exposed flooring. There I observed a scorpion, nearly half the length of my hand, as it disabled, dismembered and slowly ate a fellow scorpion, until the victim vanished altogether. Something about this sixteen-legged event seemed fitting, even if the scorpion was eating its own kind: brute was eating brute, or better, something in nature was eating itself. In the world as divine creation, how does absolute ugliness fit in? If divinity has any part there – and it must – that part is mysterious, a prodigious contradiction. Divinity's part in us, however, is not mysterious: it is not fitting for one man to eat another, nor even to hurt a hair of his head. For each of us *is* made in the image of God, and so we naturally cast Him in our own image. Each of us has the power of reason and a view of – an opening out towards – grace.

Robert returned to the cavern one other time during my weeks there. He must have had occasional flurries of insanity, yet his darkness was strangely in keeping with the night of the cistern, for he found his way safely across that pitch blackness. This time again his howling possessed the whole of that hellish place. He exploded into my being and held my spirit for hours. Could he see, sense or even smell me by some gift of madness? I feared so. What would I do if he came so near as to touch me? Take hold of him, shake him, or pull away? Might the shock of being grabbed and talked to in that dire night knock him back into his senses? But he did not approach. Judging by his sounds, I sensed that he was on the far side, crawling along the great wall, and once again he did not go suddenly silent. His cries and howling faded gradually as he moved farther away. This meant that he had gone into the tunnel leading to the second cistern and then even, perhaps, farther down into the third one. But when he did not come back to use my own point of exit, I realised that there had to be at least one other way in and out of that measureless night. I could not conceive where.

The wretched Robert was tracking some parallel to the darkness in his head. When he had pressed into the final cistern for the first time, was he already more than half-mad? Had he been looking to complete his madness in a higher perfection? But then he and I were not so very different. For although I was seeking light, there was also a delirium in me. I went on being tempted by the other cisterns. I was haunted by the feeling that they were waiting for me. Against all my supplicating, the temptation reached the intensity of a fever. I started out for the second cistern twenty, thirty times, even getting as far as the tunnel, and each time I drew back, more than once in a jelly of terror. On one occasion – the memory stops my soul – I went into that tunnel with a candle and edged my way to the very end, where at last I faced the vast trembling night of the second cistern. With my back to the wall, I moved left and sidled into it the distance of six or eight feet. Then I retreated. If a gust of air had blown out the flame in my hand, I think I would have ended my days like Robert.

As long as that struggle against temptation went on, my rhythms of prayer and reflection were an anarchy, and in a fury I tore at myself with a shattered brick – I still bear scars – wanting desperately to know whether I was being held back and saved by fear or by Christ. In this very question, with its demonic common sense, there sparkled the cruel allure of the devil: pride and then the plunge into the abyss. I knew this, I saw it, I kept rejecting the question, but there was no help for me: the question would not go away. Was I being saved by fear or Christ? Reason could not rescue me. And then mysteriously, after some weeks, but now easily and brightly, all at once a new vision came to me. I was called upon to bury myself in Christ's suffering, in His compassion for us. I prayed for the power to make His loving wounds real, tender, flowing and large. I would immerse myself in their sacred blood, as in the darkness of that awesome cistern, and those wounds would be my light, my cleansing, my new day. Grace was given me – grace and then serenity. The stars of the cistern came and went. I took command of myself and held to the true way for the last forty days. On the sixty-first day I emerged fully into the light. I went back to my old shelter.

My emergence from the cistern appears to have been an act of simple necessity. I was abandoning a horror. But this was not so at all. After grace came, I settled down. I came to love the darkness, the isolation, the silence, the peace. Looking back now, I am certain that I had drifted over into a form of madness. During my months in the desert and cistern, I had rejected the world for God, but I did it in such a way, unknown to myself, that the renunciation could be everlasting. I wanted to remain a hermit; I had found God; here was finality. Peace.

The splinters of another perception came through to me. To be one with God in this world is a perfect irrationality, a kind of insanity. I might never bay and scream like Robert of Paris, but I would live literally inside a vision and be as turned away from people and from the world as he was. The mystic from Damascus, Ibrahim Hurayra, had warned me of this danger. The Florence and the Bologna which had made me were no more. Luca and Gismonda, and all those others who had been whipped until they were bloody, belonged to a different universe. The months of isolated meditation had removed me from humanity and hollowed me out. I had taken in a new infusion and was so stamped with remoteness that I had to wrestle to enter the world again; but I omit the particulars of this struggle. The Third City brought me back, summoned me.

Some days after I emerged from the darkness, the German hermit sought me out and looking me over asked, *Are you well? Yes*, I said, *thanks be to God, but I shall be leaving next month*. Then I urged him to tell me what Robert of Paris looked like and where I might find him, claiming that I had to see him to offer my blessings before I left. I also said that there must be a second entrance to the cisterns.

Robert, he said pointing, *lives in that part of the desert. He has crazed blue eyes and a dark beard. You must have seen him, he's bent over but very strong. He gets into the cisterns by climbing down the long, pitted shaft of an ancient, concealed well.*

There it was, the other secret entry. But I was not even tempted to ask for its location. My horrible temptation had passed, though I no longer saw it, then at least, as horrible.

Keeping an eye out for Robert, I saw him come into R'safah late one morning to fetch provisions. Though he was skinny as a reed, he shambled like a bear [*orso*]. I wanted to thank him, I knew not why. I wanted to embrace him, touch him. I wanted to pray with him, and so, rudely violating his distance, I went up to him and said, *God be with you. I also have been in the cisterns.* His eyes, remote and uncomprehending, looked at me queerly, then full of hurt, and when I raised my hand to bless him, he turned quickly away and hurried off. His body spoke of a shattered soul and I kneeled down in prayer for him, longing to know what his youthful life had been in Paris, what losses, terrors or humiliations he had suffered, and what agony or ambition had carried him out to these pitiless dunes, where the light of so much sun may turn into a darkness blacker than night. I loved this land and I also feared it.

Early September had come. In the past fifteen months I had exiled Venice from my mind. That was the future. The desert is for the present hour and for eternity. Lying between these, the foreseeable future is an irrelevance. It is too far; eternity is closer. Since leaving Jerusalem, I had tried to make each present hour a preparation for a final reckoning. The profit-minded Florentines never tire of saying that we are all entered in the account books of Sir God, Who may at any moment call in His debts.

Sometime in the first two weeks of October I was to be picked up by bedouins on their way to Aleppo, and so I was. They were a blue-eyed clan with sixteen camels. The cameleers sang certain songs to quicken the pace of the camels; with other songs they slowed them down. The bond between man and animal here was a grace to behold. In Aleppo I joined a caravan bound for Beirut, and there a two-decked galley again, laden with returning pilgrims, started out for Venice on 10 November. We sailed into the Venetian lagoon on 23 of December 1525. Many of the pilgrims cried with joy.

All along the way of the journey back to Venice, I fixed my thinking on the Third City and the work ahead. I saw that we could not go on dragging our feet in a mire of talk. That was philosophy. We had to get on with a course of action. Our dream was to make one city out of two. Then let it come to pass, bring it about. Where, in any Christian or pagan writing, even in Plato, was there an argument in justice for cutting the society of men into two different physical communities, separated by a tier or by huge walls? One for the rich and powerful, the other for those who work with their bodies, one up above facing the sun and the other underneath, turned away from the glorious chariot? Even Sparta had not put its helots in a dark city.

My return to Venice was a charge into activity. I plunged. Dominican friars are in the world to lead the laity in spirit, not to live buried in the desert. In that first year after my return, I seldom slept more than four hours in twenty-four, what between sacred offices, my tasks in the wretched parishes, the Third City, and reading through the chronicles of the Most Serene Republic.

What shall I say about the lower city? You have been there many times, Father Clemence, but have you ever looked around in it with an eye to change? Go for some walks there, notice that there are few open ways in the under streets, so that stench and noises get boxed in, as are poor old people, beggars, cripples, rambling mad folk and the sick. Have you ever had them lurch at you? As if they could harm anyone! Should they not be in the sun when there is sun, where they can warm their bodies or expose their needs and wretchedness? Instead, they are hidden away in darkness. Venice hides its shames. In other cities, when convicted evildoers are flogged and mutilated, they are marched out before the noses of rich and poor alike; in Venice, this spectacle is confined to the lower tier even when the offender is a nobleman. Burned and torn flesh are not allowed to violate the upper streets, as if crime and swindling belong solely to the dark city.

What about the squadrons of prostitutes in the lower city? Are they flesh only for sailors and lowly merchants? Or the expensive ones, the courtesans in the more open, peripheral quarters? Are these not for the carnal pleasure of foreign dignitaries and gentlemen from the upper city? Our noblemen do not keep their paramours in the sun above, because they want such women far from the bodies of their daughters, wives, mothers and aunts. Knowing every crack and cranny of the dark city, I say that the horrid squalor of its inner neighbourhoods so darkens the eyes and soul that the promise of God there is dimmed or vanishes. Yet what can God be in this life if not a promise, and who more than the wretched need it?

The nobility could not live for a moment without the lower tier. How could they be without food, labour and the arts and trades? Naturally, therefore, servants, tradesmen and other commoners go daily through the upper streets, but they must be attached to noble families or have legitimate, brief commissions there, and may at any point be arrested by an alert constabulary. The penalty for fraudulent dressing like a noble is a public flogging in the under city.

24. [Falier, SECRET CHRONICLE, cut to the generation of Loredana's father, Antonio]:

Francesco di Francesco Loredan (+1497), whose father was one of the key figures in the disgraceful deposing of Doge Foscari [1457], had three sons and four daughters by his wife, Orsola Venier. Surviving one and all, they were married thus between the years 1488 and 1499:

Francesca to Nicolo Gradenigo
Leonarda to Nicolo Mocenigo
Corona to Bortolo Steno
Graziosa to Andrea Morosini
Antonio to Laura Vendramin [Loredana's parents]
Bernardo to Apollonia Dandolo
Tommaso to Paola Dolfin

These marriages were all ducal, for in each case the other family had doges in the direct line.

The Loredans usually put their daughters out in marriage with magnificent dowries of 6,000 to 8,000 ducats of gold, but they do not insist on equivalent returns from the families of spouses for their sons. This is to say that while the daughters are easily married into ducal families, the sons may take wives with lesser dowries, provided only that the girls come with a natural endowment of health and beauty. The male lineage, in other words, has long insisted upon *bellezza*: the striking and healthy good looks of their brides, with the result that they have spawned a line of good-looking men and women, reaching up to the present generation. Just as two of our noble families have a remarkable reputation for ugliness – and we all know who they are – so the Loredans are known for their good looks; and they keep a proud sense of this in nicknames, as well as in family anecdotes. Yet such pride does not escape the ever-watchful eyes of *fortuna* and the higher powers. The Loredans have paid dearly for their handsome flesh – one of the springs of their arrogance. For all their grace and enviable beauty, they too have produced their lot of idiots and monsters, whether from incest, bastardy, *fortuna*, or the reaping of their just deserts. Luca di Leonardo Loredan (b. 1398), a humpbacked dwarf, spent his life with a peasant family in a hamlet near Asolo, shielded from the eyes of the world. Agnese di Andrea (b. 1419) was an idiot who made strange noises and could never speak; she shrieked. Her father deposited her in Santa Lucia, a convent for grotesque nuns, located just outside the western gate of Padua. Then came Pasquale di Lorenzo (b. 1431), who never stopped laughing: he was kept under lock and key in an attic in Chioggia. Daniele di Jacopo (b. 1488) was born with two heads, and no one ever established whether he was one or two. He lived four years, having been turned over, with a sum of money, to a foundling hospital in the lower city, from whose records I have extracted this item (Appendix xviii). Do my examples suffice? I see no point in adding to this catalogue of horrors.

I had reached the present generation and am up to the 1520s. In our day, Antonio, now nearly seventy, the eldest son in the main line, was luckless in having no legitimate male heirs. He had only four children by the lady Laura Vendramin; but the two boys died in childhood; then Lady Laura died, leaving only his two daughters at home, Quirina and Loredana. In 1504 the elder of the two, Quirina, was in the eye of a shaming scandal, which in this case the Loredans were powerless to suppress. Married with great fanfare to Marcantonio di Giacomo Mocenigo, she was examined four days later by two physicians and a midwife. They found an impediment in her vagina. Quirina could not be penetrated, and the marriage was immediately dissolved. Although pretending sympathy, many people saw the event as hilarious, and a rash of scabrous couplets did the rounds in those days. I still remember one:

> No art can cleave Quirina's cleft,
> Too tough e'en for a Landesknecht.

In fact, she was a very good-looking girl at the time, but thereafter became a most pious lady, a tertiary to be exact, and took up serious fasting. To this regimen she later added the mortifying of the flesh. I have seen her in their local church and attest that she is nothing but a sack of bones. Fortune saw to it that the lushness of the Loredans was punished in Quirina's stark bones. It is not often in life that we get such poetic justice.

[*Deletions* . . .]

The building of the upper city cannot be separated from the pride of the Loredans and other mighty families, such as the Mocenigo and Contarinis. Leading the field in the will to construct a new city, they built it to affirm and celebrate the establishment of the Venetian ruling houses as an hereditary aristocracy. Here are a few particulars for those who may not know the story. Venetian courts and government had ended in the hands of a select circle of families by the year 1300. Birth alone put men into that class of powerful citizens. It seemed right, therefore, to separate the nobility from the people by erecting a new city, particularly since the riches for such a stupendous undertaking already filled the coffers of the ruling families. I refer to the wealth from their traffic in spices, sugar, silk, dyes, slaves, shipping and piracy. The new city represented their triumph as a dazzling physical reality. But however legitimate, it sprang from an act of moral violence, for it was built directly on top of the old city, thereby eliminating most of the sun and light below. The upper tier was given many more squares and wider streets to take up the space which is occupied by denser settlement in the tier below. Nevertheless, the under city spreads out beyond the perimeters of the upper one, with the result that those peripheral parts have the sun. This ample fringe is reserved for the richer class of citizens, government clerks and great merchants. The lower city itself thus has two zones for the differing conditions of men, the well-off margins and the unhappy inner heart. Here, in the covered parts, under the uneven stacking of the grand buildings in the city above, there are thin shafts of sunlight at many points, enough for the work of craftsmen and shopkeepers, for carting and vending, and for the movement of animals through the streets. But winters are long; clouded skies cut off the dim light; rain-waters hiss or leak down; and the denizens of the shadows rely heavily on lanterns and candles. As if to make up for their stealing of the sun, the ruling families – I mean the Loredans and their ilk – provide all the wax and lighting materials for illuminating the dark parts of the lower city.

25. [Orso, CONFESSION]:

Beware, Father Clemence, I have been fighting back the particulars of a plot to kill me. Here are the facts.

On a day in late March, 1527, after sunset, a stranger fell upon me in the lower city as I came out of the church of San Barnaba. Carrying a small hidden sword, he brought it out suddenly and made a violent lunge at me. I was all but wearing armour, since, unknown to him, he struck a large book under my cloak (I had just fetched it from the church), cutting my left arm. I broke away by swinging the book hard into the man's face, turning instantly and plunging back into the darkened church. Knowing it well, I lost him in the shadows and darkness of a side aisle – he had run in after me. A priest and two parishioners, hearing a shout and the racing feet, rushed into the street to call for help. My assailant fled and I, meanwhile, had edged my way down into the crypt. The din, fortunately, failed to reach the ears of the night-watch; I was able to silence the three or four witnesses; and soon afterwards I reached the house of a friend, a neighbouring barber–surgeon, who dressed the wound so wisely that five weeks later the healing was complete. Remember? You have noticed the scar.

I had been marked out somewhere for a sudden death. But how could I alter my movements, with all the offices I had? Go and hide, give up my spiritual functions and the Third City? Hire secret guardsmen to protect me, as is the way of certain priests and cardinals in Rome? Of course not, none of these was possible. Yet I was never going to be careful enough. So I lived every day under a sentence of death. Something had to be done.

The Third City is, I confess, split. A tiny group sheared away from us three years ago. I knew my would-be assassins;

there were three. A ravening anger had taken charge of them. But the third one, as I shall call him, was in truth a Franciscan and would be governed – I had reason to know – by the fate of the other two, the two laymen. Accordingly, I held discussions with members of my circle from outside Venice. And this is what happened: they had the two men slain.

Father Clemence, the executions were carried out with my consent: I am responsible for the murder of those men. I killed in self-defence; but I do not for a minute think that the action was right.

It had to be done for the sake of the Third City, and I would do it again. But I am tormented by it; I wake in the night with its hand on me; for killing another, whatever the cause, is always a foul deed – the violent thieving of a divine right. I repent; I feel a deep and true sorrow; and yet what good is this, what good *is* it, if, as I say, I would again commit the same crime against Christ?

I see in logic here a leering death's head. To kill is wrong, and yet to have to kill? Does necessity not justify us? Can we do wrong in order to do what is right? May there be the imposition of evil by a higher moral necessity? No no, that kind of thinking is a cave of evil intention. Then let us put the matter differently: to punish evil is not evil. But who tells us what is evil, who defines it? Governments, assemblies, churches, neighbours, communities, men simply? How so, if they are fallible, sinful, self-interested, self-righteous, fickle, proud? Yet they cry out, *Let's kill this one. He's bad!*

Yes, let's kill this one, since we live in a world of foolish animals and utter illogic . . .

I turn and turn in a vicious circle and make no headway. So I can but cast myself on your mercy, Father Clemence. Your prayers alone and blessings will have to save me from this sin, because my repentence sinks at once into a mire of incoherence. I see nothing clear or straight. God help me . . .

Now for the story of a conspiracy.

In the early days, the Third City was all about meditation. Members toiled to imagine a superior city, extending dream-like, over the far-vanishing sandbars of the Venetian lagoon. In time, their own logic drove them into recruiting more followers in lower and upper Venice, in Padua, Vicenza and other cities under Venetian rule. They moved with a fine circumspection – the way they enticed me into the group. I was in before I knew it.

When I came back from Syria, I took up the plea for action. I argued fiercely, but I am not a hothead. To the objection that the kingdom of God was not of this earth, I replied that we were seeking no such thing – heaven on earth, a foolish notion. On the contrary, we desired something only too practical – the sun and the equity already found in other cities.

The call to action made me an obvious emissary, and I was picked to travel, in my Dominican habit, to Vicenza and other neighbouring cities, to carry a new plan to our men there. Those encounters, always wrapped in a religious air, were a very trial, and in some cases the task required passionate argument, especially when the obstacle was none but the fear of our members. In other cases, if the reports of our observers and my sense of the group bespoke danger, I served up a bland mixture of religious ideas – bread and milk, rather than our new agenda. For a single defector could destroy his quintet of men.

Though it surprise you, Father Clemence, I happen to know that you and your family in Padua once came close to being crushed by the Council of Ten, and that in your youth, despite your innocence, the Ten held you in prison for six years. So, to keep from compromising you, I shall give no names . . . [*Water damaged the confession here*] resistance.

If in seeking to demolish parts of the lower and upper cities, to make them one city, we should seize a handful of patricians and hold them in custody until the work of reconstruction is done, would this imperil my soul? And if, worse still, some of them should die because of their choosing armed resistance, would I then run a graver risk? Of course I would, even if their deaths were to be seen as inevitable sacrifices in the clash between good and evil. And there it is again, that clash. Therefore, you may well ask, but who am I, a friar and priest, to decide where the good is in *worldly* matters? I answer that the operations of good and evil do not sort themselves out into two different orders of being, the spiritual and the temporal. That distinction is sophistic. Render unto Caesar? But what *is* Caesar's, the right to maim the whole human race as long as he keeps his hands off the Church? That's a strange licence. The leaders of the Venetian nobility have no doubt about where their good is: it lies in denying the sun to the lower city, while they themselves bask in it. How can I doubt that theirs is an evil view?

These questions, I pray, will have a resolution by the time I get to the end of my testament.

26. [Falier, SECRET CHRONICLE]:

The scandal caused by Quirina's vaginal impediment cast a shadow over her younger sister, the fourteen-year-old Loredana, a ravishing beauty who in those days was rumoured to be the loveliest creature in all Italy; and I own that to see her gracing her way down a street in a blur of silk and ribbons was enough to stop any man. The light around her seemed a trembling clarity. She had deep grey eyes, a splash of pale brown hair, radiant skin, an enchanting smile, flawless long-fingered hands, a well-turned body, an erect and light carriage, and lips as fresh as the morning dew. Yet it took her father, Sier Antonio, four years and a princely dowry to arrange a marriage for her. This, some people claimed, was the result of the Quirina scandal; but many others alleged, and certainly many believed, that her father had delayed things because he so loved and cosseted the girl that he could not bear to give her to another. Surprisingly, although having no male heirs legitimate or natural, he refused to remarry, and this again gave rise to endless whispering about his unnatural attachment to Loredana. To be truthful, however, I should add that he also kept a pretty mistress in the lower city and seems to have been much enamoured of her. Thus mistress and daughter, the great delights of his life – apart from intrigues at the Palace – kept him from an inevitable second marriage and legitimate male heirs.

What had he in mind? What is the good of great estates if they cannot be passed on to the male offspring of one's loins?

27. [Loredana, CONFESSION]:

I've now come to the part I'm most afraid of, the captain, and I'm not going to say too much, it's too shameful I confess it. You're bound to think *first she's ashamed, then she tells her stories and they're nothing but filth and sin.* Yes and again yes but it's also true that by telling, by writing down these words, I change things, I mean in me. If I tell my stories this one time I'll rake them out of myself because they are the toad still squatting there, and even if you think I arouse myself by describing things my answer is I have to, I have to do this to pull out all the buried feeling and leave it truly behind me, not only the sticky deeds but the words and the rest too, the sin that goes with the words because words and sin are stuck together in me when I tell what happened. I don't know any other way to get the sin out.

Well now for the captain, the most frightening man I've ever known. Marco never forgave me and Agostino, he wanted to think I was a base adulteress and a whore, he also wanted to punish me for it, that's why he got together with the captain I think and why the two of them waited around and planned and plotted. I didn't know what they were getting up to but they weren't lovers yet, I knew this because Marco wouldn't give himself to the captain without somehow first putting me his wife in the middle. Anyhow I waited and by now we were in the third summer of the marriage, but I forgot to say that the captain was often away at sea that year, he went back and forth, so we didn't see much of him, then in the summer and autumn he came to the house much more, I mean out to Asolo where we spent the summer. Well the day came at last, they had their plans. Now I'll confess to my last mortal sins, the doings of two days and I'll number them like this <1> and <2>, the way I enter items in my account books where only the essentials count, and even so I won't get things right by not going down deep enough because I'm too ashamed of the details. You see I want to tell you all but then I frighten myself and back away and next again I tell too much, something depraved, so it'll be crooked instead of straight.

<1> Early one afternoon Marco ordered me to prepare for a trip and cover up well, especially my face so I wouldn't be known, he said we were riding out to an inn just over an hour away to spend the night there and I wasn't to take my

mount, I was to ride behind the captain on his horse, not to worry because the inn was on one of the captain's properties. Well I locked myself in my bedchamber and said I wasn't going, that I wanted no part any more in his evil doings. Then we had a low insulting argument, I shouted through my door and he said he'd smash it down and I called him a sodomite. He just laughed and said he'd bare my buttocks to the captain if I didn't come out and that he'd get our two servants to help tie me to a horse and force me to go, seeing as I was anyway a tricksy adulteress. I knew he'd do all that, he was twisted enough for it, so in the end I had to give in, he would have smashed the door down.

Then, listen to this, he made me wear a pair of his riding breeches under my skirts and as I mounted the horse behind the captain I was trembling with fear and even more so when we started out and I had to grip him tightly. Well it was ice and fire all the way to the inn as we cantered along and I slipped back and forth between fear and a sinful pleasure tugging at my innards. Remember I was holding the captain around the waist and he was a fine firm riding figure, though he scared me and that was part of the sin. That ride to the inn undid me and by the time we arrived there Marco's breeches had a wet place in the middle. After we got into our rooms and I'd had time to wash and change they came to my chamber, came right in talking and friendly and you won't believe it but the captain picked up the breeches from the bed and ran his fingers over the gusset and laughing showed the wet patch to Marco. I was struck dumb, my face burned, I turned away from them, I wanted to flee, and then the captain said, *My heavens, what a good start, well done madonna Loredana.* The two of them laughed like fools and right away I knew their game, it was going to be to pull me down and right there and then I told myself I wouldn't let them do it without my helping hands, I'd join them, I'd be as good as their tricks, as good as they were, I'd do the dance with them and get whatever I could out of their secret plans, and I also thought, very well Marco I'll make you pay for your fun with interest right into my purse.

I'd come into the inn swathed in a veil and anyone who saw us maybe thought I was their courtesan or who knows what. Many candles were lit and dinner was served in my chamber and they gabbled on about their horses and sailing the high seas and the ride to the inn, but I said nothing the whole time, to be a mute animal I decided was the best way to keep my distance and watch them and know what to do. The captain was a big man like Agostino, with a massive nose, greying moustache, funny teeth, hard brown eyes, boots to the knees, lots of talk, clever too and with a high lordly way just like sier Antonio my father. When we came to the fruit course at the end of dinner the captain got up and locked the door and next he made me a little speech and this is what he said. *Lady Loredana you're going to have a lesson in obedience tonight, dear Marco here is always complaining about you, he says you're proud and stubborn and disobedient and always want things your own way. Can this be so? I invite you with all due respect to remember that you are a woman and barely ten months beyond your twentieth year. Have you forgotten that your husband sier Marco is your legal lord and master, am I right about this? Of course I am, well now come over here like an obedient young lady and kneel down at the table, yes you're to kneel down right here between me and Marco and don't look at him, no don't look at him, in this lesson I'm the lord and master.* My heart was heaving but my mouth was sealed, I was quiet and I did what the captain commanded, I got down between them, then he made me put my head and shoulders under the tablecloth till I was down on my hands and knees and only the lower half of me remained out between them, that's the way it was and all I could think to do was to fight off shame, to choke it down, so I ground my teeth and I must have gripped a chair or something down there as my husband Marco sat there looking on. Monster, let him swallow the shame, it's all his shame, women are in the lesser image of their husbands, and as I was thinking this Marco or the captain, I don't know which of them, began to lift my skirts up so gently that I barely felt the hems rising to the tops of my legs till a slight chill passed over my buttocks and I knew they were bared. Well there we were, that's what my honoured husband wanted, to show me off to the eyes of his dear friend so I could learn obedience. Then I heard the captain's husky voice say, *Ah my dear Marco, you lucky lucky man, oh beautiful Loredana, we're gazing at fine art here, your lady has the most divine rounded parts in the whole world, a glory worthy to be worshipped, look at the delicious line of the upper leg, look at the blush here and the dimple there, and look at the way everything comes together in this handsome patch of dark bush. Well, we shall certainly know how to part it won't we Marco? Let's enjoy what heaven has provided.* The captain reached down then and began to touch and feel my secret garden (his words) but his hand was too caressing, too good, I liked his fingers too much and I was me no more, no father Clemence I was me no more, I was melting, I was only that part, nothing else mattered.

Follow my thinking father at the very point where I am now, it is the sin, the toad to be got out. The captain's fingers felt and probed and went on feeling and soon he said, *How wet we are there madonna Loredana. Wait, don't move, steady there, that's good, now I've just warmed the handle of my fancy poniard here, I'm going to put it delicately between the lips and press it around, yes, like that. Ah you like it, I can see you like it, that's right, push back more and rise to meet the handle.* This is all just as it was father Clemence and I'm going to go on writing it, I must get it out. Well the captain worked the handle round and round me there and knew where to press and rub and hold the knob and go more deeply and my garden rose each time to meet his pushing till I had to pull away and clench my teeth and clench all my sinful parts and stifle every sound and not show that I loved it. Then I heard him tell me, *I wish you could see your husband's face, he's been watching the handle in your garden and he's in a swoon of pleasure.* After a little he said, *Now lady Loredana let's get on with the rest of the lesson, you've got more to learn. While your handsome lord sier Marco and I are having our fruit up here you're going to be having your after-dinner sweet down there under the table. You have to show us what a truly humble and devoted servant you are.* He reached down and took me by the hair of my head and pulled me round under the table until my face was between his booted knees. He had powerful hands like Agostino and in the dim light I saw them unbutton his gaudy codpiece, out came his hard member (his hawk he called it) to brush and press up against my face, then he moved it around to find my mouth while he and Marco went on talking and laughing, but by now I needed no prodding, I sat up on the floor between his legs, I was bold, I pulled him out to me at the edge of his bench, I pressed his knees apart, I grabbed his hawk with both hands, I took the head into my mouth like a dog gnawing at a bone (that was obedience) and as my lips pressed hard on the neck and eye I was deep in vice, deep enough to find myself comparing it with Big Agostino's. I couldn't tell which of the two was thicker or more spicy but I knew I was liking the captain's more because of the danger, something heaved in me. The sweet bird began to shudder and spit hard, a groan came from the table and I got a burst of seed into my mouth, I swallowed it and went on pulling at the beak for more till I drained it and I could feel my swollen labia (another one of the captain's words), I needed to touch them but when I started to let go of the hawk the captain took my hair again and pulled to hold my mouth in place. He said, *Now little Loredana, bite the hawk gently because if you bite it hard it'll hurt you. I once killed a boy in Alexandria that way, he bit it too hard and it was rammed down his throat. Ask Marco about it, he knows the story.* So I was all gentle teeth and tongue with that wild hawk and you see what I meant about the danger.

I want to give more details here but I won't and even so I'll tell the truth. When the captain after a while drew me up to join them at table again and I stood exactly between him and Marco, that pleased me, they were still sitting, so then I arranged my sleeves and bodice and pearls as they watched, slow movements, I didn't rush, I got those things just right, also my hair, and next I hiked up my skirts to pull my hose up tightly, and they could look on at what they didn't see every day, then I gave the captain a smile and tapped his chest and laughed but I said nothing, not a word because I didn't trust myself, I could only say something low and there'd be tomorrow and I'd regret it. Anyway they had a gift for me, that's how pleased they were with my obedience. Marco and the captain said that I'd been truly humble and obedient and a brave falconer, so they decided they said to give me a reward, and the reward was one of the captain's servants, a young Greek who'd been ordered to come out from Venice to meet us and he was already at the inn. When Marco went out to fetch him the captain took out a linen mask and slipped it over my head to hide my face and made me sit across the table from him, then Marco came back with the youth who at once got under the table, he had his orders. Next the captain reached over the table to me and took hold of my hands firmly and told me to let Giorgio do what he was trained to do, I was to let him be my happy slave. Then the captain said some words in Greek. I felt myself pulled out to the edge of the bench, my skirts were gently pushed up, my knees were pressed apart, my thighs were kissed all over, hands moved over those parts, fingers probed around the garden, playing about till more nectars came, something else began to touch me, an eager mouth was there. The captain let go of my hands and as he did so told me, *Giorgio is your slavie, a thing to order about, use him right, be a lord, make him obey, reach down, grab his head, pull his face into the garden, he's expecting it.* Well then Marco who was sitting there seemed to sink under the table too and I saw the captain reach down I think to grab his head but I shut my eyes so I'd see nothing and anyway I was behind a mask which was a good thing because bursting labia were up against Giorgio's face as he licked and licked, and the more he did that the more I pulled and pressed him to me, oh how I pressed till I let myself go as he was pushing mouth and nose and cheeks and his whole face into my cloven part and we were pushing with the same desire, and when I wanted to cry out with pleasure I pulled poor Giorgio's hair as hard as I could to make him stop and I shut my legs together tight against his ears and held his face there. After a little the captain made me go over to the bed and lie down and turn away from the three of them, I did and I covered my ears so that I would hear nothing just as I was seeing nothing.

The next morning the captain had to go to Venice but first he went back to Asolo with us and I rode behind him again and he had another surprise for me. On the way back he took my left hand from his waist and slipped it down under his riding robe to put it firmly on his codpiece and he commanded me to keep it there so I could feel his roundy things. He also taught me a word I'd never heard before not even from Big Agostino and I wished I'd known it the night before. Cunt, that was the word and he said that mine was most definitely for kings and warriors, and all the way home I could feel it half-hitting and half-brushing against the saddle, so I pressed up harder against the captain pushing myself into him as we rode and I handled his hawk too but he pretended nothing was happening and said nothing and I don't know what he was thinking because he went on talking about other things, who knows what, I can't remember. When we got back to the villa he had to rush away at once on a summons from Venice and I rushed up to my bedchamber and locked the door and touched and touched my new word until all was well.

28. [Orso, CONFESSION]:

Father Clemence, minutes ago the liveried agents of the Ten were here, at the point where the waters of a canal nearly lap a window of this ancient church. Crouching behind a false wall, I became a model of stillness, as in my desert cistern.

I come to the second part of this confession: madonna X. Heaven be my witness.

The story briefly is this. Last April I was called to tend a lady from the upper city; she had been ill for months, and having an obligation in her parish, or so I understood, I was urged to bring religious comfort to her in her final days. I went to a poor creature, wasting away in bed but hard and ardent in her devotion to Jesus and Mary. She used to wait anxiously for me, and on my arrival would grasp my hands and stare at me, as I sat beside her for a few minutes nearly every day. I prayed with her, for her, and while I did so, she was all tenacity. Astonished by her hidden strength, I found it vivifying to be with her. Body and soul in her seemed to be rivals. As the one got weaker the other got stronger, and I am prepared to believe that the soul wished her body dead, so that it could be off, trouble-free, to find eternal peace. I have more often found this virtue – moral strength in the face of death – in women than in men. At the core of being, curiously, men are more frail.

During the last ten or twelve days of her life, she often slept or remained steeped in a faint, and when I arrived to be with her, I sometimes had to wait or go away and come back again at an unusual hour. The door of the house was always opened to me not by servants but by a tallish woman clad in black and partly veiled, a widow. She was madonna X, the dying lady's sister.

Since I am in hiding because my life is in danger, I will not allow shame to hold back any events that properly belong to this part of my confession.

Whenever I arrived at the house to see her sister, madonna X greeted me with eyes averted. She would look at my shoulders, chest or arms, or at the floor beside us, but never at me, my face. After some days, since the dying lady was not always fit to see me on my arrival, and we had to talk about what I was to do, madonna X began to raise her eyes. Perhaps my devotion to her sister helped to ease things. She looked increasingly into my face as we spoke, and I returned her gaze. One afternoon she had removed her veil. I found her visage a place of light – fresh, pensive, troubling. Her words, as she enunciated, were neatly shaped, as if not allowed to leave her lips unless they went forth with clear outlines. The whites of her eyes had a tinge of blue. She wore no rings on her fingers, not even the dutiful ring of the widow, nor a spot of artificial colour anywhere, unlike most Venetian women of her condition, who go about ablaze with powders and jewels. Her only gem was a small ruby worn at the throat, where the pale flesh made it stand out. I was arrested by the simplicity of the person, the strong eyes, the serene oval of the face, the wide forehead, the rounded lip and chin. I offer a picture in words, because that candid presence, all tranquillity and grace, came forward to change my life.

Her widow's veil had been removed because in the vast distance between her face and mine – how to invent the right words? – the world had moved; the gigantic gate to a city had opened; we were tilted closer together. She held my eyes and I would not let go of hers, and the longer we held on, the more her lips produced words and the more I also spoke, so that in a day or two I did not know whether I went to that house to see the dying woman or to listen to X's words and see her eyes. I was surrounded and held: I could not loosen the enclosing force, nor step out of it. Her eyes came forth as light from her widow's black cladding. Eyes large and almost rueful, eyes with a whole life illumined in them, the profuse grey eyes that I had seen in the faces of certain Saracens, the eyes, somehow, of the desert. You will think this perverse and conclude that I had lost my reason to a love sickness. No, I had found reason of the sort that leaps over syllogisms, and I had to go back to her to talk, to gaze, to be utterly there, or find myself unwell. I could not be without that presence and daring spirit. Daring? I only sensed it. Though daughter to one of the most unprincipled men in Venetian politics, she yet reminded me so very much – and mysteriously – of that other luminous being, my dear Luca degli Albizzi.

Sometimes I saw two or three servants in the house and three times I was briefly with her father, who spent most of his days in the Palace. All my dealings were with her.

Early one afternoon, when greeting me at the door, X said that the doctor had just been and gone, convinced that her sister had not more than a day or two to live. As it happened, she lived another four days. I encouraged X to be happy for her sister on the grounds that she was marked for heaven in the passionate fixity of her faith, and since I had anointed the lady the day before, I invited X to come into the bedchamber, where we could both add our prayers to the masses that were already being said for her. After kneeling and praying beside me, she left the room and waited for me outside the door. The dying lady gave life to her sister and to me. When I came out, X had removed her headdress and for the first time I saw the entire face. It was as lucid as her grey eyes, framed in dark hair with reddish hues. I stood in front of her, not knowing what to say: I had entered a new world. One of her hands was rising. It came up to my face. There were tears in her eyes. I did not stir. She said, *I have to touch your face.* Her fingers lightly pressed my left cheek. I took the hand, without taking my eyes from hers, and kissed its palm and fingers and felt a tear trail down my own cheek. What is a most particular tear, do you know? May it be, once in a life, a fallen star, a poor spark fallen from heaven? Her eyes flooded into me and washed through memories of the small boy in Florence, the student in Bologna, the late hermit. My solitude lifted and passed away. There was no difference between us, between X and me, no space and no distinction.

Every one of these details is a fresh incision, and it all might have happened this morning.

Unlikely as it may seem, Father Clemence, apart from her hand on my face and my lips on her hand, there was no other physical contact. We had already glided over into each other, and anything more, anything fleshy, would have been less. Tears, hands, fingers, my cheek and lips – these are all watered clay, and through these we had got rid of our difference.

We agreed that I should come back to see her sister the next afternoon, unless a message reached me announcing her death, and then I was to come at once. The next day, having rushed to the house after racing up a great flight of stairs from the lower city, I was still breathing heavily when X opened the door to me. As soon as I stepped inside and she made fast the door, our bodies touched. Hearing me breathe, she reached out to me, to the place where my heart was beating, and placed a hand there. As her arms started to reach around me, I clasped her to myself and our lips met, for how long so I do not know. I was too far lost and wanted never to return. Nothing in the great scatter and geography of my life had prepared me for this. My learning and memories turned spectral, and I was led by lip and mouth to far and undiscovered places. We go through the sense of touch and our liquescences to the frontiers of earthly being and then strain to see beyond, to something nebulous, still nebulous, to something we crave, something grand and beyond the seas and elevating. Words? Yes, but is there another way to tell you of this mystery?

What did I think I was doing? I have no answer. I was being borne away, beyond self-knowledge, and being reborn. Yet what did I know of her? Of women? I had known Gismonda and Picchina, little more than girls, rough-spoken and coarse I suppose, but generous to a fault and prostitutes who inhabited the dark fringes of life. I had known Primavera and Vanna, girls again and near-sisters to me — practical and even hard-headed, but sensual and without a drop of worldly experience. The other women I knew or had known were mainly poor old things or young girls, victims often and often in tatters, frightened, hounded by hunger and cold, wasted by work, wretches, poor penitents, sick prostitutes. Seldom in Venice had I ever been called upon to help or to confess a woman from the upper city. With madonna X, therefore, I could only follow my nature; I could only be as I was or longed to be — helpful, loyal, courteous, compassionate and oh far more. But all these feelings had now melted down to their primal substance. I wanted to hold that kiss inside the door throughout all the centuries to come. And I did not know that I had raised X up from the ground, as though she were not of the earth, until there was a sudden loud knocking on the door behind me and I had to put her down. In an instant I was upstairs in her sister's bedchamber, listening to the dying, ghostly breathing, with the odd wish to follow it out (that almost non-movement of the air) as far as it might go. Soon X and her father stepped into the room. He asked about his daughter and I replied that she showed no signs of awareness, that I would stop in again later. He thanked me and saw me to the door, where he handed me a gold ducat.

On my return that afternoon, X came to the door with a tradesman and servants. Still telling them about their commissions in that sonorous Venetian of hers (they were on the way out), she invited me to go upstairs. I give these drab particulars because the animating reason of my actions was here, in the parts, or how could it pervade the whole?

Let me remind myself that the penitentials warn us of the dangers of morbid delectation: the treachery of sinning a second time in any pleasure gleaned from recounting the history of a sin in its details. Yet the particulars of this testament hold the secret of what I have done, of how and why I proceeded from one step to the next.

When X came upstairs, I was trying to see if her poor sister might be awakened by a recitation of gentle prayer, but she lay stick-straight and still, apart from her faint and impossible breathing. We again kneeled down and prayed for her. The dying sister, that patron saint of love, once again touched life directly. We went into the first adjoining room and X invited me to sit in my usual place, a straight-backed chair set against the wall. I used to sit there and wait, as X prepared her sister for me. On this occasion, having asked if I would drink something, she came back with a small glass of wine, sweet and red. When I got up to take it from her hand, she made me go on sitting and handed it to me. Our eyes were strung together, never breaking that single gaze. I sipped slowly at the wine, until she touched my face with both hands, with the backs of both hands she touched my face, and again her eyes had tears. I put the glass down on the floor, into a tiny patch of light just there in the darkened room, and then no distance was between us, nor anywhere a sound. Nothing around us moved. We moved. I had drawn her over to me. I sat and X was sitting on me, her silk and linens rising, as I rose to find her, found her, and went on finding. To close our eyes was still to be one, but we kept them open so as to see, if possible, to the far ends of our being. I yearned to become her. I desired no self of my own, only her self; and as we rose and declined, this came to be. I felt the weight of her wide tenderness engulf me, and I fell out of myself so far that I felt I was becoming her. Loss is the utmost possession.

Afterwards, I again visited the never-waking sister. Everything about her had collapsed, except the bones of her face; and her hands were ashen spades. Never did I pray so well for her, nor ever with a finer sense of my office. A knocking at a distant door barely reached my ears. Later X told me that her father had come home for a change of robes and gone straight out again to the Palace.

The next day I went back in the late morning. The dying sister endured in her profound faint. Groups of relatives had been to see her and others were due in the afternoon. But once the great outside door was shut, the main part of the house, perched up very high and turned well away from the cries of the Grand Canal, was nearly as silent as the first cistern and gave me the feeling that I could hear the sunlight streaking through the slits in the shutters of the big windows. I associated madonna X with an order of silence, with the secrecy of a whole past life which I had no need to know. Let it be, I thought. We jabber endlessly about paradise, but which of us has ever heard its sounds? Has it sounds? In any perfect silence is our paradise. X was sitting. Spots of sunlight fell next to her chair. I was before her on the floor and when she moved, I could see points of light flickering over the edges of her face and hair – glints of gold and reddish brown. She leaned forward, with her hands against my knees, looking down at my face and eyes as if to hold them in memory everlastingly. We changed places, and then my eyes sought to fix that face of hers in my very bones.

What did we talk about? What kinds of words did we use? Words and talk were the last of things. Sight was primary; and touch was second, the sense that most tells us we are here, on this earthy earth. She gave me knowledge of herself through her way of touching me, and so gave me knowledge of myself through what I came to see I had to have. I buried my face in her and was surrounded, enfolded, undone, until all loneliness was scattered.

Was I so feeble in my faith, or so wrong in the way I keep it, that I could not cling to the Cross fiercely enough to free me from madonna X? Was there a sneaking heresy in my way of clinging to her, of seeking that route to paradise? To be with God alone can be a thing of loneliness. How can Christ be an intimate friend? Infinite mercy does not dissolve omnipotence, and He is God the Father too. Ever since my return from the desert, I had found no annihilation of myself in God. Being lonely was my daily lot. In giving to the sick and poor, I received and was content, but some covered part of me lurked unfulfilled. And the work of the Third City was too secretive, too dangerous and charged with worry, to dispel my solitude. I needed another, someone as mortal as myself. From the Cross all the way to madonna X: I lived joyfully on this bridge.

29. [Vendramin, DIARY]:

xxvii September [1529]. New tidings. The execution of Nicolo Baron, impaled. He was hurled down in the middle of the night. At daybreak, there for all to see, he was a gory sight. Three pikes poked through his gullet and jaws. The

Ten otherwise are silent but for a new decree. There is to be no loose talk in public about the conspiracy. The penalties: 100 ducats for the first offence, three years' exile to an island for the second.

This morning I went out beyond the Lido to say farewell to Paolo Giustiniani. His galley was departing for Alexandria. The winds were strong, so the vessel shot forth. More than 150 pilgrims on board. Their destination, the Holy Sepulchre. I never feel the pull to go. Prayer is surely enough. Besides, the dangers are appalling.

One rumour concerning our troublemakers is that their ideas come from that republican rabble in Florence. Reports claim that thousands of Florentines are ready to die defending their city walls. They hate the Medici family and will not have them back in the city. Florentine aristocrats have always taken baseborn people into high office. This is their idiocy.

xxviii [September]. The Ten gave out the first solid piece of news this morning. Astonishing. One of our own, a Falier, has been in their custody for eight days. Frightening echoes of the arch-traitor doge, Marin Falier. The man, Dolfin Falier, is a Franciscan. He claims to be the secret head of the whole conspiracy. But few people believe him. Some say he is a decoy, sent to draw eyes away from the capital criminals. He springs from the poorest branch of that ruined clan. They live in the parish of San Biagio. Occupy a few rooms on the top floor of one of those palazzi built for the poor nobility. It needs saying. Many of these noblemen are such a rabble that they would be better off in the lower city. But how, listed, as they are, in the golden books of the nobility? Well bless us! They cling to a respectable robe or two. And they cling to their rights in the upper city. Some of them boast a glorious past. Others even pretend to be more patrician than we are. What? When the truth is that they live mostly on handouts or paltry sinecures. We invent little offices for them with high-sounding names. This because they sit in the Grand Council and we need their votes to get into high office. So, we buy them. It makes me sick. They try to put on fine, honest and honourable airs. In fact most of them are half-famished and in rags. You can see it in their shifty eyes and greasy garments. All their honour is in a name. They would sell the backsides of their sons and daughters for place and money. Yes, of their beloved daughters too. Why so? Why would you think? To save the maidenhead in front of course! The girls can then be put out to marriage as undamaged virgins. I shall name some names [*afterwards deleted*].

The case of the treacherous Franciscan wants a few more words. Fra Dolfin Falier is nearly sixty years old. Before he took holy orders he was a scribbling secretary to a cardinal, a military engineer, a merchant, even a soldier. We see from all these pursuits how truly called he was to his religious vocation, the villain. Suddenly he presented himself to the Ten with the story of a secret confraternity. This was more than a week ago. Had a part in it he said for six years. How could their plotting go on for so long? Something here smacks of lies. They call themselves by a droll name, the Third City. The conspiracy includes priests and laymen. But a hundred questions remain unanswered.

The Ten do not admit to what I have heard from a friend. This Falier has been made to hawk up no more than five or six other names of conspirators. Why, if the braggart is the head of the sect or confraternity or whatever they call it? Is he shielding the true captains? The disturbing thing is that two or three of the names belong to recent suicides. The other men, when arrested, provided the same names. We are going around in circles.

The Ten have ordered a sharp reduction in the pealing of church bells. A most unusual measure. And the two cities are strangely quiet. It is thought the silence will frighten the hidden conspirators, or put their teeth on edge. No outsiders are being let into Venice. Prostitutes are stopped and questioned by the night-watch. The colonies of foreign merchants are under scrutiny. So are all inns, taverns, churches. I was amazed to hear this. Churches too. Amazed and pleased. Our saintly Franciscans writhe with embarrassment. It serves them right. They deserve worse. They have long had criminals in their ranks. Yet being ass-stubborn they say that they alone are competent to try their own villains. The Ten will ignore this insolent claim. We will not be pushed around by priests.

xxix [*September*]. At sunrise today the body of a young prostitute was fished out of the Grand Canal. She had a strange mark in one armpit. Her hands and feet were tied. And she had vicious teethmarks all over her backside. Bites on the breast I can understand. But on the backside? That was no fish. I would look for a foreign pervert.

xxx September. Alberto tells me that Fra Dolfin Falier has made a disgraceful claim. So disgraceful it cannot appear in the Ten's proceedings. They ordered it struck from the record. Falier says the Third City was born eleven or twelve years ago, the work of two Venetians. Noblemen both but from ruined families. A Dominican, Lorenzo Tiepolo. And a Franciscan, Pietro Ziani. The first was killed by Mohametan dogs in the Holy Land. The second, an old man, died of chest pains two or three years ago. He had also travelled to the Holy Sepulchre. Fra Dolfin has offered many details. Those two got him into the sect, he claims, and put him in touch with four men from lower Venice. Of these, one says he knows nothing about Tiepolo and Ziani. But he acknowledges Fra Dolfin and insists that the aims of the Third City were religious and peaceful. Not even torture has made him renounce this plea.

This blamed diary. I get distracted. I have neglected to say – Bernardo [*Loredan*] is on the Ten. We were together for a little early this morning. He said nothing. They take an oath of silence. So he is not allowed to talk about the scandal, or do I mean the plot. Still it is strange. Not a word about things escapes his lips. Gloom is his mood and he has been so for days.

i October [1529]. Something has gone terribly wrong, the unheard of. Cousin Loredana Contarini disappeared yesterday. No one knows exactly when it happened. Our jaws fell in amazement. Women from the upper city do not vanish. Not our sort. Antonio [*Loredan*] got a sudden report of the matter last night. He had been in the Palace all day. Knew nothing, suspected nothing, until a discreet servant turned up there to hand him a notice. Naturally he is hellishly worried. He says that everything at home is in order. Nothing was taken. The servants however say some dresses and linens are gone. We are spending the day looking for her. Where are we to search? Would she take refuge in a convent? But then why keep things from Antonio?

30. [Falier, SECRET CHRONICLE]:

I turn next to one of their more secret and curious histories, the story of Lady Loredana.

She was finally married in 1509. Her spouse was Marco Contarini, a man whose own good looks were nearly a match for hers. Although I could treat this marriage at length, such treatment would make me seem a mere gossip and call into question the veracity of my chronicle. Consequently, I restrict myself to the main points.

During Loredana's marriage, but above all afterwards, the couple became the subject of many rumours, of which the following were the most persistent.

(a) That Marco Contarini was devoted to the art of silk [*sodomy*].

(b) That Sier Antonio wanted no man to enjoy his daughter because of his unnatural predilection for her, and that therefore he had given Loredana in marriage to a man who was not a man.

(c) That she was not a maiden at the time of her marriage, hence who deflowered her?

(d) That being debauched by nature, she seduced all of Marco's male lovers.

(e) That she had four pregnancies during the marriage, none of which by Marco Contarini, and four miscarriages.

(f) That Marco's mysterious drowning of 1512 had in it the hidden hand of Loredana, who was in the throes of losing a lover to him.

(g) That after Marco's death, instead of remarrying or withdrawing to a convent – the customary alternatives for a Venetian lady of her age, beauty and wealth [*dowry*] – Loredana chose to live with her sister under her father's roof, where, hidden from the eyes of the world, she could carry on with him or even others, contrary to all her feigned piety and severity.

I need no lessons on the iniquity of the Loredans, but it must be averred that most of the preceding allegations lie outside the possibility of any binding proof. Such is the nature of clandestine, private activity. Yet I shall try to get as close to the truth as the facts of the case will allow.

By the time he drowned, it was well known that Marco Contarini loved men. You cannot keep such turpitude eternally hooded, at all events in a watchful and gossip-mongering city like upper Venice. For all his discretion and secrecy, Marco's vice had come to be known, and were it not for the scandal to the families involved, I would list the names here of three of his lovers, one of whom, now a powerful senator, is always surrounded by bowing and scraping office-seekers. Next, I myself looked into the story of the miscarriages, out at Asolo too, and have found evidence of only one such occurrence. Thirdly, Marco's brothers, Domenico and Giacomo, were greatly upset by the alarming manner of his death and, summoning the help of other eminent families, they pressed the Council of Ten to get to the bottom of the mystery of Marco's drowning. After many weeks of investigation, which included three cloaked visits to Loredana, carried out to question her in private, the Ten found no suspects and nothing to warrant anyone's arrest. Not a scrap of evidence was ever turned up against the enigmatic lady, though some people still entertain suspicions against her. From all of which we may conclude nothing but the obvious: namely, that Marco's death was an accident – he had been drinking – a suicide, or a cleverly executed murder. However this may be, women are unlikely perpetrators of well-reasoned crimes. They are too unstable for focused action. We have only to look about us.

It is impossible to challenge or verify the rumours concerning the beautiful Loredana's maidenhead, her natural bent for the brutish sting [lust], or her father's incestuous love. The only true witness to her virginity, or want of it, on the night of her marriage has been dead since 1512; and it is not at all certain, in any case, given his taste for men, that Marco

Contarini had carnal knowledge of her on that night or any night. In short, how could he have known anything about her virginity? Yet in view of his accursed proclivities and the fact that he was known to receive his lovers at home, the likelihood is that Loredana also was carnally known by one or more of those visitors. This would account for her pregnancy and miscarriage. Denied, it is thought, all physical congress with Marco, why in her lush beauty would she have denied herself others? Nature has its needs; strong natures have stronger needs; and Loredana was known to be both ardent and demanding. Lastly, on the question of her alleged incest, the circumstantial evidence favours the presumption that there was and perhaps still is an unspeakable bond between father and daughter. I refer to the evidence of her delectable beauty, her late marriage – she was nearly nineteen – her refusal to marry a second time, her father's refusal to remarry, and their cohabitation. Why did she not retreat to a convent, where carnal licence is, at any rate, often rampant?

I have heard men say in private that Sier Antonio Loredan has so disgraced the nobility by his incestuous tie with Loredana that he deserves to be tried for treason and hurled on to the piked enclosure. No harsher accusation is possible. As one of the capital men in state, he may be brought to trial; he most certainly cannot be served with a mere reprimand. The Council of Ten have the authority and instruments to bring him down; but could they try him for such an unholy crime, however secret the proceedings, without soiling the reputation of all the ruling families and thus staining the republic itself? Too much ignominy would be laid bare and noised about, and we would be the scurrilous talk of all Italy. To extract confessions from Lady Loredana and Sier Antonio could only be done by means of torture, the torture of their servants as well; and not many of his enemies would go so far as to consent to this. Let us not, after all, forget his formidable circle of powerful friends and relations in the top tier of the state. I say, therefore, that his fall is inconceivable.

The Venetian nobility produce two kinds of women. There are first of all the women of the poorer gentlefolk, including those once great but now fallen, owing to the twists of fortune. These ladies are brought up to be thrifty, modest, chaste, practical and sober. Then there are the ladies of the ruling families and rich nobility: they go into marriage with immoderate dowries and are likely to be vain, extravagant, impractical and sensual. Although brought up chastely, they are flanked by so much luxury, and the servile attention of slaves and servants, that the abundance and flattery go to their heads, and they fall prey to every temptation of the flesh and spirit. With notable exceptions, this has been the lot of the Loredan women.

[*Deletions . . . Jump to October* 1529:]

The Loredan connection with Fra Orso and the Third City provides my chronicle with its natural conclusion: a portrait of this arrogant house in a pageantry of disgrace, for all its money, honours, violence, web of clients and lack of scruple. I am, accordingly, all the more obliged to make a comment about my distant cousin, that Judas, Fra Dolfin Falier.

He was born into the poorest of the Falier households, but being graced by nature with a quick wit, he was always a compulsory overreacher, as if in revolt against the shame of his poverty. His love of Latin encouraged a local priest, a follower of the Ciceronian style, to educate him, and Dolfin pursued Latin letters up to the age of sixteen. Thereafter, he began to discard order and discipline; he ran away from home; he travelled with a merchant, possibly as his lover; he became a soldier; and being of a rich fancy and rapid intellect, he tried his hand at a variety of artful pursuits, architecture among them. Then late in life, at about the age of forty-eight, he was infected by religious enthusiasm and became a Franciscan. I knew him. He was an unquiet presence; he showed no loyalty for his clan or family; and he attached himself to people and to unusual causes, never to Venice or to blood relations. Well aware of his own talents, he could not bear to see dull and dimwitted men climb above him in the ladder of dignities, even in the Franciscan Order, just because they were born rich and well-connected. Whereupon he was seized by a desire for drastic change. If, in his black labours for the Third City, he had been animated by a notion of the common good or by hatred for the iniquity of our corrupt ruling clans, I could almost have sympathised with his dark intentions. The core of the lower city is an odious place. But he was driven by envy, pride, fantasies and a liking for mere novelty: that is to say, by nothing worthy. Hence he ended rightly on the piked stage. We have no choice, we the Faliers, but to bear him as a blot on our family history.

31. [Council of Ten, PROCEEDINGS]:
    27 September. Anno domini nostri 1529.
    Session restricted. The Ten and seven advisors. No other.
    [*Text of an anonymous denunciation*]:

    To My Lords, the Mighty Ten, Cowardy Custards.

        One you want is all around,
        High upon your lady's mound [*Venice?*],

Yet in churches to be found.
Go and catch him by the tits
Lest he fry your fickle wits.
He's the making of a Jesus,
Pulling noses where he pleases.
I have paced him through his days,
Here he prays, above he slays.
All the poor get Heaven's keys
And the rest the pikes of trees.
All in fives as five they go,
Praying you to the gallows go.
Tonsured, tall, an angel's choice,
Find a winsome Florentine voice.
All decked out in black and white,
Bombard of your peaceful night.
Last of all I tell you this,
All in fives as five they piss,
On the Zen and Mocenigo,
Vendramin, Loredan and Gradenigo,
Contarin, Trevisan and Barbarigo.

Ten: Gentlemen, three of our members have pored over these insolent jingles. They are clearly the work of someone who is seeking to betray the Third City or to foil us. At one point we suspected that the author of the vile rhymes was none other than Fra Dolfin Falier, but he has denied authorship under torture. Moreover, the squib was affixed to the main doors of San Marco four days after Fra Dolfin delivered himself to us, and at about the same time, as some of you know, a copy was thrown boldly through an open window in the Palace. This also indicates his innocence, at least in the contrivance of the scurrility. One of our numbers, Loredan, still believes that Fra Dolfin composed the lines and then, by previous commission, had them put into our hands by an impudent third party.

If the jingles can be trusted, we are meant to look for a man in holy orders, possibly a Dominican with a Florentine connection. The suggestion is that he spends much time in the lower city, while also displaying himself in our midst. His mission is to destroy the nobility. He is reportedly tall and with pleasant features, but this may well be false and calculated to throw us off our scent. Finally, the rhymes make him out a would-be saint. We take this to be irony, for the man we want is set to be a pitiless murderer.

But can we lend any faith at all to the lines? They may be little more than another Third City trick.

Meanwhile, one of our many inquiries has fixed on the name of a certain Fra Orso, a Dominican and Florentine, and this of course would give us a link with that lower class of republicans in Florence. The same inquiry also sees a line there running back to Savonarola. In that case, we would be confronting an emotive and mystic rabble; but we do not believe this to be so. Our Third-City conspirators have been alarmingly judicious. A rabble they may be, but they move with care and cunning.

Every known suspect has been seized and questioned. More are being arrested. Our soldiers and constabulary scour the two cities for the named Fra Orso and we expect to have our hands on him before the day is done. We know his haunts and daily movements. All exits to the sea and mainland are being closely watched.

My lords, let us get on with the interrogations. Secretary, summon our other external councillors.

32. [Loredana, CONFESSION]:

I'm going to write in here a *storia* that all Venice knows about, a double murder. We even know who did it but nobody tells and you'll see why, so I can't give names, but it has to go here because it saved me from many base and low acts, and maybe it saved my life.

A little before the time I've been talking about, maybe three or four years before Marco and the captain, there was a lady, we knew her of course, who used to spend five months in the country with her husband summer and autumn. Some people say she was a brazen tart but others say she was too unhappy because her husband liked to be only with courtesans. He kept one and very dear she was to him. Anyway the lady his wife was young and very pretty to look at and she was often alone in the country, I mean together with her maids while her sier was off in Venice at the Palace or with his courtesan and their friends. Well the lady, no one knows how, took a fancy to a young peasant who was the miller out there near their villa. I guess it was a mad fancy, and the way it started was that she was bold, she walked a straight line into his mill one day when he was alone and right there boldly reached out for his member, she just took hold of it. This is what everyone says father Clemence, though I'm not sure how they came to know. Many people report that one of her maids knew the beginnings of the story and told all afterwards. Anyhow the lady just went into the mill and took hold of the peasant and things went on from there, there was no stopping them. Well, that miller became a slave to her, she being so pretty and a noblewoman, and besides she also gave him clothes and money, one time a whole handful of ducats, enough to cover his member they say. But don't think she was careless, certainly not, she took great care not to be seen because she was afraid of her husband and losing good name and honour. You know all the reasons. She used to post one of her maids nearby, near the mill to look around carefully and see that no one was coming.

Well to get to the point, no one can throw light on how her husband got the scent of it but he became suspicious until he was nearly certain, and one day he invited a burly lancer, a soldier from Saxony, out to the villa to help him train two horses. It was a trap. Two days later they pretended to go back to Venice, off they went, but after three hours very quietly and secretly they crept straight back to the mill, they saw the maid keeping watch but went around her making no sounds and not being seen by anyone. Then in they crept to the mill so quietly (they were hearing the moans of pleasure) that they found the miller on top of the lady. Listen, I'm sorry for her and I think she deserved prayers and masses, so did the peasant miller because a horror came next. The lancer now was carrying a pike and he thrust it down so hard into the miller's back that he pinned them both together, him to her. Killing them on the spot. They couldn't even move. Then the two men crept off as secretly as they'd come, not even the maid saw them (and she'd heard nothing) and somewhere they collected their horses again and hurried off to Venice. Does it surprise you that no one was ever arrested or punished for the crime? Nobody knew who did it but as I told you all Venice knew and knows, still nothing was done to the husband and soldier because no one, not even her family and no servant either would speak up against them. Everyone said that the peasant miller and vile lady truly deserved to die. I don't think so, and of course her family were too shamed to speak out, most of them even thinking the deed was right.

Why have I put this *storia* here in my confession? I told
you, it saved me and here's the reason. After my lewd deeds
at the inn and the morning after too, remember that the
captain rushed off to Venice and so there was I feeling too
much, just pushed aside like that but all stirred up, nearly
panting and desperately ready for more evil, though I certainly
couldn't tell Marco my husband that, could I? This is a truthful
confession to a priest and I must say it, I wanted to go out
secretly and find a man to enter me, I thought of it all the
time for days and I thought of all the peasants out there, it
was like having the hand of lust inside me grabbing at my
parts, I thought of their faces and hands and bodies, really
seeing them, and I wanted to undo myself on a man's member,
but how could I ride out through all our lands and look for
someone? I wasn't brave enough, not me. Remember the
story I just told you, the two people pinned together. O Lord
I would have done it, my cunt was all alive, I would have
gone into ditches, I would have been with a thousand peasants not just one, forget kings and warriors, that's what Marco
and the captain had done to me but I couldn't think of a
way and I was too cowardly and afraid to die. You see the
way it was, it was being a base coward that stopped me, not
that word chastity.

So now I must confess it, I began to touch myself every
day, I'd lock myself in my bedchamber and do it and this
went on for days, for more than a week maybe until just
before we went back to Venice. I would touch myself hard
until that sinful part was so open and wet I could almost
put a hand in and die, and I did worse than that in those
days, I also used my mount every day, I used to ride all
around inside our lands, it helped, and I ground my wet part
into the horse, I punished that part on the leather there, I

punished it everywhere, and I wanted to punish it on the horse's snout too, that's how lewd I'd become. Marco never discovered what I was doing, no one did. Then I forced it to pass away, I mean the lust, my darkest shame, and I confess all these crimes as a true honest and evil penitent. The word is contrite. Forgive me father Clemence, I regret it, Dire Regret, I was dirt low and I had no shame, I repent, I turn against that evil sin of lechery, I abominate it, let it all go away from me and be cursed, forgive me, forgive me, lift me from it, Lord forgive me.

Now stop, I went away from this paper to try to take hold of myself and then I came back.

I said I'd call those two times of lowest sin <1> and <2>. Touching and riding and punishing it were part of <1> and now that's the end of <1>, a full examination of conscience and of memory too. It was all depravity. No, wait, no more apologies, and don't think I wrote down all the details of <1>, far from it. But I did use most of the words because they trouble me and sometimes worry me even more, much more. Tell me, why are all the words for shameful deeds men's words or words for preachers, like depravity cunt hawk lechery fornication vice adultery and debauchery? The good words too are mostly used by men, like chastity modesty abstention and immaculate. I'm afraid of all these words but especially the ones for being pulled down to the lower parts, they're a danger just as words, the sounds are, and they're strong because they applied to me, that's why I often think my soul can't be saved no matter how much I pray to Mary and Christ. When I think of those days with Marco only men's words come to me, I was a sack of carnality, I took to sin like an animal sucking at things and I can't be saved because just in telling, in the words, there's a base filthy feeling, a being gripped again and the feeling goes on and on like that murdering captain, monster and dog who still lives and laughs with all the honours of the upper city, and you think he doesn't know I'm alive? God in heaven he knows my father! He knew my mother!

Stop, I've lost my way here, I don't even know what this hand is writing because I can't see what needs seeing, I need better words or even book-reading to help me and I don't mean poetry, I mean books with sermons about low matters. I have a question and I need an answer to save myself. My question is, how can I confess my sins of lechery and wash them all out when by just writing things down after seventeen years I get a feeling of new sin and lewdness? Remember I've lived unconfessed for all these years, *unconfessed*, and now the old vile deeds are words, they turned into words and they're limed in my memory, set words like a witch's prayer, that's why they have to be said and written and pulled. Are words evil, are the pictures in words evil, is talk about sin evil, so is confession evil, and would not confessing, not telling, not writing things down, be better? But then the old sins would stay in the muck like ugly anchors at the bottom of memory, toads I've called them. If you decide to confess deep-down sin don't you have to dig it up by using words, by digging out the words too, and not put limits on what you say, or if you do put limits how do you know where to put them?

Dear Mary mother of God please help me, I want to do what is right, I reject the devil, I want to tell and stop telling, I want to save my soul from hell, I'm going to have to tell you about fra Orso but I don't know how to write without first saying the words out loud so that I can hear them, that's the way I learned to write, and how can this mouth that did what it did and talks about the captain then talk about Orso too? Next to Orso I am the jakes. As the wife of Marco di Domenico Contarini I turned into labia, I wanted what my shameless openings wanted, there was the utmost of feeling and being alive, there was the highest tower, pleasure, lust in my hidden parts, in what the captain called my vulva and cunt, that was me and that's what the two years of Big Agostino were all about, my lord and master Marco had seen to that. Christ help me. But those parts have no soul, they're dead and when they live for themselves they're of the devil, so how can they deserve to see God seventeen or a hundred years after the crimes, also because I feel as I tell my tale that I'm still vulva. I thought I'd revenge myself on Marco by cuckolding him even in my soul, I mean far inside myself in the me that is always there and doesn't move, not just in the me of my shameless parts, and I did it by sinking down as far as it was possible to sink to hurt him as much as possible, but it all turned around on me, I became a slave to the pleasure and I can say that I found this most in the devil's member, that's what Loredana Loredan Contarini was kissing. Father Clemence can you save me, can you do anything to help save me? I have never in all my life tried to hurt anyone but Marco but I wanted to hurt him with my whole soul and so deeply that it all got twisted into horrible sin. I repent, I repent, I feel burning shame, I am unworthy I know, even if I could have God's grace.

I have to stop.

I'll now confess and write down the last of my dark acts <2>, I want to face the whole truth of what I am. Even so may I be saved.

<2> It was the third October of our marriage [1512], we came back from the country early in the month, the captain

was soon to go away to sea for five months and Marco
fretted about it, he kept telling me he'd miss his dear
company. Family affairs and the Palace had kept the captain
in Venice, he couldn't get away, so I'm glad to say that no
other wicked things happened after we returned to Asolo
from the inn (I mean apart from the lewd touching) but
still every day once we were back in Venice I was afraid of
the captain, though I only saw him maybe every week or
so because Marco used to be at his house much of the time,
and seeing that captain wasn't easy for me because I knew
the evil in him. He was that inn for me, though none of
us, not Marco either, ever mentioned the vile deeds of that
place, never once, I couldn't have borne that because I
couldn't allow such talk to be a part of every day and a part
of me all the time. On the way back from the inn (Marco
didn't hear this and it's one of the things I do remember)
the captain told me that my husband was just like me, a
pretty woman but by mistake in the body of a man and so
he'd always be unhappy, still the captain would do his best
to keep the woman's part happy. How strange that was, but
later what scared me even more than this talk was the turn-
around, it was now Marco who started to dote on the
captain. Almost every day I tried to find good ways of telling
Marco that I wanted nothing to do with the captain, that
I didn't want him around the house now we were back in
town, that if he came to lunch I could say I was ill and
have the meal in my own bedchamber, I even said I was
afraid of the captain and threatened to go to my father sier
Antonio. But Marco had lost his head, he'd fly into tantrums,
he'd call me vile names, he accused me of being a disobedient painted jade, a few times he slapped my face and he
often barked that he was master and lord of our house, *that*

was Venetian law he said. But one thing I swore to him and to myself and it was this. That they might be able as cowards to make an attack on me in my own house though I'd fight it tooth and claw, but I'd never leave the house together with the two of them, Marco and the captain, they'd have to kill me and carry me out.

Marco held me like a prisoner by keeping me away from my family, that was the start of the disease, so now being more afraid I tried to see them as much as I could, my father, Quirina, my aunts, sister Polissena and two uncles, but it wasn't easy because Marco was nearly always around during the day and he wouldn't let me go out or would always come along with me, he was afraid of what I might say, and naturally I couldn't leave the house at night when he was out to supper with the captain. There were times when I even thought that to save myself I might have to kill Marco with poison or his own knife when he was asleep, that's how much afraid I was of what he and the captain might try to do with me. Don't think I'm stupid, I know what this meant, it meant I might like it, it meant I almost wanted it, it meant I was afraid of my own base depths, that's where I was looking straight into hell, but I also knew I'd be safe, I knew it, if I could keep away from Marco's lovers and most of all the captain, who said to me laughing on the ride back from the evil inn, remember I rode behind him, that he wanted to take me overseas and sell me to a friend of his, a Turk general.

I'm not going to put it off any more, here's number <2>.

No, wait, I won't do it, I will not do it, I won't tell <2>, I'm putting a fist to my chin, I'll be strong, I'll stop this pen and bite my tongue till the blood comes and not give way to my great sinning need for words, I'll only tell you about how Marco tricked me this time, I mean into the evil of <2>.

He sometimes went to church with me not really to pray, I don't know if he ever prayed, but to keep an eye on me, or else our servants Daria and Giovanni were my watchdogs, so one evening when I planned to go to vespers at Santa Marina in the lower city, you must know it (I used to go there once in a while), Marco said he would accompany me because he didn't like me going down there not even with our servants. I put on a full veil before we went out as women from above always do when they go down to the under city. After the service when we left Santa Marina to go home Marco said he knew of a shorter way to the Grand Canal so we went that way and as we were going through a dark street, though there were lots of lanterns about, we passed a tall man standing at an open door and before I knew it I'd been pulled inside, the door was shut and Marco had his hands clapped over my mouth till they tied a cloth around it, then Marco swung me up on the stranger's shoulders, we went through dark rooms and then started to climb flights of stairs. You may know father Clemence that many ancient palaces in lower Venice have their high newer parts in the upper city and we were inside one of those climbing up and up from the lower to the upper city and the captain was waiting for us at the top. That two-part pile belonged to him for his own use, his wife and family lived in another palazzo. When he greeted us at the entry to a great chamber the stranger went away, I learned later he was a Turkish slave, and Marco took off the filthy rag from around my mouth and I was crying and sobbing. I knew I was lost, I knew it, that Judas had led me into a trap and put me into the hands of king swine but I swore to them both that I would tell my father, I insulted Marco most bitterly and I went on crying. The captain took me aside into another room and sat me down, telling Marco not to come in and then he reminded me of Big Hands and the three miscarriages, I was amazed. That Judas Marco again, he had told the captain everything about us, everything, and given out all the details. Why? I'll tell you why. To talk the captain into getting his evil paws on me or that man wouldn't have dared because he knew my father too well. Anyway the captain told me that if I said anything against him, senator and big hero of the seas that he was, who would believe me? And if anyone did believe me what about the disgrace to my father and all the Loredans and to all the Contarinis too because of Marco's doings, sodomy? First of all my father wouldn't believe me but if he did what could he do even considering his name and authority, kill the captain, demand a trial in front of the Ten, lock me up in a convent, kill me, kill himself? The whiff of the scandal would blow through the city and the Loredans would be in the mud, also the Contarinis, and the more the captain talked this way the more I saw that I could never go to my father. He was sitting on a bench beside me and after a while he went on to a different speech. He began to say, *Listen to me Loredana I'm nearly as old as your father, I know the world and you don't, next to me you're a mere child, a little girl, so stop crying and accept your lot, please stop crying and come over here to me . . .*

Enough. This is as much as I'll say about <2> because what came later was, well maybe there isn't even a word for it. Base isn't low enough. So nothing I did that night can be written down here. Wait, except one thing but it was not nothing I did.

Hours later on that night of <2> in the captain's house I was all alone and in one of the rooms I found a small picture on a table, I couldn't believe it and it almost made me want to throw myself from a high window. I pressed my candles close to it to see it better, then I turned it around to look at the back, there was Marco's name, he had given it to the captain, and someone had written there (but it wasn't Marco's writing) DEATH AND THE MAIDEN, just like that. Who painted it I don't know but on the front in one corner were the letters NM and the year 1509, and this is what it was. It was the picture of a most lovely young lady (who certainly wasn't a maiden) and of a skeleton looking like a devil. She was wearing floppy slashed sleeves, billowy skirts, a ribbon tied just under each knee, and you could see most of her breasts. This wasn't all, for the skeleton of the devil had one hand and arm around her while with the other he had pulled the front of her skirts up all the way, and the lady was helping that ugly hand of his with one of hers, she was pushing it into her place of lust so that you could see all her legs up to the top of her round thighs. And, she was also kissing that horrible skull on the mouth. God help me, I've never forgotten that picture because that was me, and Marco and the captain must have thought the same thing, that it was me in a disgusting lewd action with death and the devil, or why would they even have had such a frightening thing? I'll just add this, that picture was a help to my prayers against Marco and the captain.

But I've already told enough about <2>, as much as I needed to say and now it's out of me for ever and you're fleeing from me in disgust father Clemence because <2> happened, but at least I haven't put it in words, so maybe you'll think something even worse took place and I confess, it did, and you may as well believe my soul can only go to hell and I'm terrified because I think you may be right, but what should I have done, put this confession in the fire? Is my doom in what I did, in writing it down or in not writing the last part? I stopped to think about <2> and too much came back to me, it was too frightening, but please always remember the trap set for me by that traitor and Judas Iscariot my husband and by the smooth-talking captain who'd sniffed out the sin in me though I fought hard and truly against it and I hadn't wanted <2> to begin because if it did I knew I'd sink all the way to the bottom.

33. [Falier, SECRET CHRONICLE]:

[*Deletions: many pages on the political career of Loredana's father, brothers, their marriages and progeny*]

Often seen in the Doge's Council and Council of the Ten, Bernardo and Tommaso Loredan [*uncles to Loredana*] are also experts on mainland policy. They sit among the influential senators. Consequently, Antonio's lack of legitimate male heirs poses no dangers to the clan: his brothers and their five sons have shown themselves to be shrewd guardians of the Loredan place in the state. His two nephews, Jacopo and Pietro di Bernardo, already figure among the most active young noblemen in the Grand Council.

[*More deletions*]

Venetian noblemen sire a customary number of illegitimate children. This is understandable, for all our marriages are arranged; spouses are selected by parents and elders; and inevitably, therefore, certain couples find that they are not truly suited for one another. They perform the act of marriage, but with little interest for the male, and if he comes from the well-off nobility, he may then sow his seed in women of the lower city, in servants and household slaves [*usually Circassians and Saracens*], or in common women from the mainland. In promiscuity of this sort, the Loredans have been heavy sinners, despite the fact generally of being paired off in marriage with good-looking girls. Overabundance corrupts, wherefore they have had to learn more discretion than others. I have the particulars regarding four illegitimate Loredans, and each case reveals exceptional secrecy in the child's upbringing.

[*Deletions*]

My third instance concerns Sier Antonio's brother, the austere but once wayward Bernardo. I take the particulars from baptismal records, the papers of trust funds, and conversations with the surviving relatives of a girl from the village of Rana.

In about 1500 Bernardo Loredan and his wife visited Rana, in search of a thirteen-year-old named Maria Brenta, a local beauty born to a family of farm labourers. They found her and elected to take her on as a servant. After paying the family a sum of ten to fourteen ducats – the accounts vary – they led Maria off to Venice. In June 1501 she gave birth to a son and died two days later. Baptised in the lower city, in the parish of San Martino, the infant, named Bernardo Brenta, was put out to the family of a wet nurse in the village of Montebelluna, above Castelfranco. Having been, it seems, extremely fond of Maria, Bernardo set up a trust for the child in 1507, providing a generous income, to be administered by Vittore Maffei, a leading notary domiciled in the lower city. The boy was then whisked away to be educated . . . I also come on a curious notice which brings out the furtive style of the Loredans. I find a near-illegible entry (Appendix xxii), cryptically noting that Sier Bernardo's natural son, Bernardo Brenta, has always been known by another name . . . These are the strategems of powerful families.

34. [Orso, CONFESSION]:

Death came on the fourth day of her deep sleep. I hurried to X's house and walked into the murmur of a score of women, relatives of the sisters. They had already washed and wrapped the body. The servants moved among them, offering plates and food and glasses. Later, I led the mourners in prayers for the departed soul. Not a single word passed between X and me: all speech was in our eyes. Her father came home to kneel and pray for an hour, then returned to his occupations at the Palace. X was not oppressed by the death, persuaded, as I was, that her sister, a celibate and third-order [*lay*] nun, was destined to see the Light. She had made the funeral arrangements days before, when tradesmen and others had been called to the house. I observed her as she dealt with a chandler and stone carver. As she spoke to them, her glance moved between their chest and shoulders, never higher – that curious habit of hers.

Having no further reason to visit the house, I did not see X again for two days, a tristful time. But on the day of her sister's death, when taking me to the door to see me out, she simply said in a barely audible voice, *I'll know how to find you in a day or two.* As promised, she came to me at San Domenico di Castello, where I heard confession daily. Veiled and dressed as always in black, she was accompanied by a servant who waited just inside the church door. I trembled as I saw her, enfolded in the blacks of her silk and linens. Only she could make black unmournful, only she could lighten it, only she could shine through it. She was so uncomplaining. And though our tears had to be held back, it was a moment for tears, knowing, as we did, that almost every meeting from now on would be like this, a scene of infinite self-control. We were forced at once to learn new ways.

There and then, in the space of minutes, I began to take joy from her eyes, those eyes now so luminous in my memory that I want to think they threaten the presence of everything else there. If all my memory is possessed by X's eyes, what am I but an envelope for them. I turn into her. But no, for then I return to myself and I go slowly through all the places in memory that are reserved for Luca, messer Lanfredino, Robert of Paris, Gismonda, Ibrahim, Picchina and the eyes of the Damascene beggar. I have put all of them on the great stage of the Third City.

Madonna X and I agreed that from this time on she would come to San Domenico di Castello as my penitent. In this way we managed to talk briefly almost daily, while her maid waited nearby, though out of earshot, in the belief that I was offering religious guidance to her mistress, as I had to the dead sister. Now and again we were able miraculously to meet secretly, where we could live in one another's arms, but these were rare and perilous meetings. Had we been discovered, her father would at once have sought her immurement in a nunnery and then, perhaps, my mutilation or quiet murder. Being a priest, a bastard and half a commoner at least, I could never in Loredan eyes restore her honour or theirs.

We saw each other, as I said, nearly every weekday, but seldom for more than a few minutes at a time. Those minutes, seized at the place where I was meant to hear confession, had to be enough for our famished eyes and words. The words became whole embassies to the body and soul. There was no touching, no tribute in our faces, no generous movement of the body. Action was banished. Only the rhythms of our breathing changed, and often I could hear the beating of my heart, the thumping, in my ears. Can you grasp the life in those minutes, the discipline of speech, and the cargo spirited into the power of sight? You learn to rise out of the flesh. You begin to live on feeling itself. You transform seeing and being-seen into an art of love. You discover a new language in bare flickers of the face, eye and lip, in the mouth's shaping of words and the blink of teeth. Yearning turns into wonder, then into a mode of pleasure. Anything more than this – the least bit physical – is dangerous. And so a new alchemy is born. You come to love with so much care the little you have that the tiny sum is transformed into an argosy. Those inflamed meetings between make-believe penitent and confessor gave light to each day for me, and thus I was able happily to carry out all daily tasks. Even my part of the weight of things in the Third City became more bearable.

It is certain that you would not want testimony here of the few times when she and I were together as one flesh and one soul. What, as husband and wife, one flesh? Yes I say, for we took this vow, despite my ordination and in so far as such a pledge is admissible in the eyes of God. You and I know that marriage among priests was common in the early Church, and that nowadays the rare dispensation may be occasionally granted, giving a priest the right to renounce his vows and leave religious orders. In the worst of cases, priests go off, they vanish, and the Church maintains a wise, self-protecting silence. Together as one soul? A figure of speech, since every man and woman must answer for the soul allotted them. The individual sense cannot be forsaken. Yet when we were together in the flesh, she and I were so joined in spirit, in thinking and in feeling, that we believed ourselves to be one person who could not be sundered. In this claim and feeling, I am ready to believe that I was mad. But the leap from reason to faith is also mad: one vaults over a chasm.

Since I am seeking your absolution and blessing, I must feel repentence for the sins committed with madonna X. Having confessed my deeds, I say that in so far as I broke the laws of God, my lot is a deep contrition and the need to make amends. I would not live in a world where divine law is freely flouted. That is no world but a dark wood and a thieves' den for the likes of Cain and brute animals. However, in so far as I broke the laws of man in the pursuit of what I know to be right, no contrition is due and I have none to offer. My vow of chastity . . .

Father Clemence, I have just received a notice which forces me to break the flow of this confession.

The Third City again.

To guard their lives and safety, the members of this secret society were broken up into a scatter of small groups. I have just learned that all the men I knew in this confraternity, including those from abroad, have either taken flight or are dead. A few have fallen into the hands of the Ten. I know my source and the report is reliable. This means that I am able to tell you more about us. But since I may be seized at any moment and need an extra hour to think about what I have confessed, I am going to follow a strict outline of culpability. Your own grievous suffering at the hands of Venetian justice assures me that you have hard, particular reasons for maintaining your sacred vow of silence regarding all confessions made to you.

The men of the Third City tried for years to shut their eyes to the fact that converting the two cities back into one cannot be done without force, no matter how peaceful any approach or plan for such a change. The leaders of the nobility would never agree to it. When I came back to Venice from the desert, the Third City had finally resolved to act, although resistance continued, and I myself did not hesitate to take up the pleas for action.

Insurrection in the cities under Venetian rule was to be the moment for our entry into the piazza. We proposed:

To arrest the leading patricians, some seventy men in all, and to hold them hostage in order to keep Venice's foreign soldiery, a bloody and barbarous lot, away from the lagoon.

To arouse the people of lower Venice and get them to dismantle parts of the lower and upper tiers, particularly around government buildings, the main churches, the main squares and bridges, and the main points of trade. All these had been carefully charted.

Next, to connect the now opened or perforated tiers by means of great ramps, stairways and arching spans, to make for a skyline of harmonious up-and-down movement.

To remove all structures placed flatly over habitations and shops, so that all main roofs shall be directly under the skies.

To release the seventy patricians as soon as ever they took oaths to abide by our plan for a single city, or once the labour of reconstruction had passed into its final stage. The binding oaths were to be guaranteed by the rotating house arrest of select family members.

To work closely with all noblemen who support the purposes of the Third City. We looked for the particular help of the poor and shame-faced nobility, the *barnabotti*.

To act in the name of Christian brotherhood, and therefore to show mercy and compassion at all times.

Finally, the proud construction of the upper tier had required eight decades in the 1300s. Our labour of dismantlement and rebuilding would take not more than twenty years, with most of the city working, including certainly ourselves.

My part in the seizure of authority was to be limited to our arrest of the principal patricians. We all knew that this would be necessary, but few of us dared to insist on it. I did not see how the reconstitution of the new city was otherwise possible. Despite my Dominican habit, I was and am ready to lead armed men to the arrest of the Ten, the ducal councillors and the chief senators.

As a priest, I have no right to meddle in worldly affairs, though our bishops, cardinals and popes do so every day and are masters at the art of such meddling. May I, in a more noble cause, draw no example from my superiors?

As a priest, I have no right to spill blood and I have no intention of doing so. But I do have the right to defend the life of the spirit, and what pray is this if not the spiritual life of the faithful? Denial of the sun to Christians, or to any people, is a denial of God's light and warmth, of divine mercy, of a natural right and of the image of God in all men. I say that these denials maim the victims in spirit and in their perceptions, hence in their capacity to approach God and to take hold of moral precepts. And I am ready to use my teeth and nails, as a last resort, on those who build such murderous denials into the structure of cities and man-made laws.

As a priest and a Venetian, I feel no regret about my words and actions in the Third City. I would do the same again. Yet if innocent blood – innocent, I say – had been spilled in our cause, I would have been stricken with remorse and driven to redirect the course of action. I do not say that I could or would have retreated from the need to build the Third City.

From public affairs I now pass back to private matters, to the mystery of my identity. Not for years have I cared to know who my father was, although I know that he lived in the Venice of the upper tier. My allegiance to the Third City removes any suspicion that I may give a scrap of importance to noble rank. In this connection, there is the persisting enigma of the forty ducats per annum, kept in trust or paid out for me to the Bardi family, to the convent of Santa Maria Novella, and to Dominican houses at Bologna and here in Venice. This income gave me exceptional freedom of movement as a cleric. Who administers it? Why was I picked to be a Dominican? Am I meant to make up for the sins of my father? Why had he never the curiosity to meet me? Why was my abode in the desert tolerated? How did the Third City find me in Bologna, and whence their first report regarding my Venetian birth? My benefactors, were they used by the Third City, or is there no link between them?

I have the means to end my life. Every member of the Third City carries a powerful poison. We wanted at all costs to keep ourselves from falling into the hands of the Ten, with their grim instruments of torture and their piked stage. In the clasp of horrible pain, any one of us might give away the names of the men in his quintet. Knowing that the early Church tolerated suicide, as in many instances of self-martyrdom, we thought it better to die by our own hands, though this go against Church law, than to take the lives of our confrères through unwilling betrayal. But I shall not take my life, Father Clemence. I want to go on troubling my lords of the upper city. And I will not betray my associates, even if I should ever stand before the Ten. May I never hear their ten voices. But if I must, I pray God that I shall have the spirit to endure their barbarities.

I come to the closing words of my confession. How can they not be about X? I fear I am about to lose her. The dreaded hour has come. I must flee. My throat is knotted rope and I am overwhelmed with misery. How can this be so, this shocking admission? What about the reasons for the life I have lived — all my toil and prayers for the sick and terrified, the wretched and the humiliated? Can I put behind me, for all times, the familiar faces from the lower city? La Tromba, poor thing, who as a servant lost a leg in the upper city, victim of a savage family row? Nason and Recion, the idiots? Volutta, Cesca Gamba, and Birichina, twelve-year-old prostitutes, though they pass as fifteen-year-olds, whose tearful voices did not know how to confess? Squarcia, Uccellaccio, Marin Storto and il Fico, each with stumps as hands, cut off for snatching a purse in the tier above? Giovenco, an ex-servant, whose skeletal fingers reach out to your knees? Or Trini Tron, Stefano Brutto, il Gran Giorgio and the twisted Bulghero – Venetian sailors for more than forty years, though now they crawl around for alms and crusts of bread? And hideously ugly Angelo, branded all over the face for having seduced a virgin from the upper city?

I know the eyes, rags and humbled voices of them all. My defining belief was that I lived to serve them, *quorum nomina in corde fixa ante Deum porto*. How then can I be strangling with a spasm of illogic, with the feeling that I have no wish to live without X? All my thinking, as I write, is an incoherent clobber; I reason one way and feel another. Something at the centre of my spirit has turned and gone wrong. The claims of charity for the lower city are larger and primary. This is incontrovertibly the case. Reason tells me so. Yet my body runs cold, my stomach quails, my arms go dead, I am stricken with gloom and I want to cry out against the whole empire of my old devotions. We are on this earth to try to live unselfish lives, to reach out for what is good, to seek our salvation. We cannot both turn away from others and save our souls. Then how can I put my selfish desires and my beloved X above the Third City and the keening needs of the wretched? Are these truly in opposition, or is it only that my own life puts them pitilessly at war? Could I not be with her and also do the work of my city? Everything about her is dear to me. Father Clemence . . . I'm breaking up . . .

Can I put her blessed flesh above the thousands of bodies in the lower city? No, I cannot, I must not, or I spurn all meaning: God, humanity, the law and reason.

Who am I anyway? I shall be myself, and doing so means that I must give up all thought of being with her, although I was not half-alive until I looked into her face. In another life I would have taken her in holy marriage and we should now be one body, a single self. May I not take my case to Rome, to plead for a release from my vows, to leave the Dominicans, to be with her in marriage, to teach new ways in the dark city? I do not want to kill. If need be, flight and concealment could be our lot, mine and X's. Christ, how I fear my exile from her. No wrong was done by us as one, we have wronged no one. In paradise we shall be one and look upon the true light.

Father Clemence, I plead for your absolution in all actions corrupted by my pride. May God forgive me. In Venice. xix-xxiv September, 1529.

Yours in visceribus Jesu Christi, Orso

35. [Loredana, CONFESSION]:

Well all that, all that part was a dark corner and we never looked that way, Marco and I never talked about our lewd actions, *never*, it was just as if they never happened, but two mornings after the deeds of number <2> Marco came into my rooms to say that the captain was going overseas in four days and that tomorrow we would be going to his house to a supper and a little party and right away and even before the words were out of his mouth I said *No* that I wasn't going. For the past day I'd been thinking about nothing but the dark acts of <2>, sordid is the word, and that frightening picture (remember?) of death and the girl. I was the most afraid that I'd ever been in my life and I was in the clutches of clawing shame, I was disgusted by my woman's parts, I had to rescue myself or strangle in sin, so I told Marco that I wasn't stepping out of our house and I also said that I was going to do something different for a change, I was going to have my sister Quirina spend the next three days with me. Marco blew up like a cannon and came up to me with fire in his face and said that after what he'd seen two nights ago I had no bloody right to say no, that if the captain was lecherous I was far worse, I could even give him lessons, and with that, without any warning or anything, he wasn't even moving, suddenly he shot a hand out against my skirts and pushed the fingers up hard between my thighs, and just then too I heard a thump – I'd hit him in the face with a fist in that same instant, like that, I wasn't even thinking. Afterwards the hand hurt, that's how hard I hit him. Well but wait, it's unheard of in the upper city and for all I know in all the world for a woman to hit a man with her fist, so Marco paid me back with interest and many blows, a swollen cheek, a bloody nose, a blackened eye, and he pulled and dragged me across my bedchamber floor by the hair of my head, calling me every kind of whore and said I was cunt for dog licking, but I gave him back his insults and didn't care how far he pulled me or picked me up by the hair, I called him a horned pig, a cuckold, a pretty girl, an enemy to his backside, a tart and a stinking sodomitical pervert (words I'd heard in a sermon). I also told him that the captain lived for his lechery and maybe Marco did too but I hated mine, I was horribly ashamed of it and I'd soon wash it out of me for ever.

That deadly violent fight and those evil words were the end, I had to get away from Marco or die, I had to find a way of telling my father. The captain was going off to sea for five months but he'd be back and Marco would pull me down, Marco would find other captains, Marco would always pull me down and soon I'd want nothing else, I'd run away to look for strange pleasures or I'd just go to the captain one day and beg him to steal me away from that pretty girl and sell me to a Turk in Alexandria or anywhere, and I had no doubt he'd do it, he was that sort, a villain to the very eyes of his soul. So right away without really thinking about it I started to do one thing at a time, one after the other slowly, I had no plan because if I got one up I knew I'd never get away from Marco, I'd find reasons to wait and change my mind and do nothing.

Late that day, the day of our evil fight, I went to Marco and told him I was feeling too ashamed and unclean and almost ready to die, and I begged him to let me hear mass the next morning, I'd go to some little church and veil myself so no one would see my battered face, and he said that then he couldn't possibly go with me because such a veil in his company would look too strange, that Giovanni and Daria would attend me. Well so it was, but when we came out of mass instead of turning for home I told the pair that I had to make a stop at Polissena's convent, they tried to argue but of course they couldn't stop me even though Marco had ordered us to get back to the house as soon as mass was done. They came along and at the convent I made them wait outside when I went in to see Polissena and that was my salvation. I did not come out. Polissena when she saw me was shocked and couldn't believe what she was seeing, so we talked to the abbess (who had seen such things before) and I said I wouldn't leave the convent till I saw sier Antonio my father. A messenger was sent to him, then Marco arrived and tried to quarrel but heard that my father was on his way so he went back to the house to wait. Seeing who we were, the abbess knew that everything had to be kept a tight secret and when my father came (he was amazed by what he saw on my face) we were shown down to a cell, down in the lowest part of the lower city and there I talked to him but I didn't mention the captain, that name didn't cross my mouth, I knew it couldn't. Anyway this is what I said through my crying and sobbing the whole time, I told my father that he could choke me to death but that I would not go back to Marco, I said that Marco loved men, that he'd never so much as touched me that way, that he'd got one of his lovers to take my virginity but that I wouldn't give out the man's name, what good would that do, that I had said nothing till now because I was ashamed and afraid of scandal, and also that the three times I was with child were not Marco's doing because his only interest in me was to use me to catch others for his own vices.

My father cried, I'd never seen a man cry that way before except Big Agostino when he was losing Marco, then he embraced me and remembered that I had tried to tell him once, I suppose he had to admit that, and after a little he said he knew that Marco liked men but couldn't ever have thought he would go that far, that he'd never heard the like before. He also said, *Daana in all honour I should kill you now and then myself but I can't force my hands to do what they will not do. I can't put these hands on your throat.* He said that the injury to me was anyway done and could not be undone, and if he killed me and himself the scandal of two killings on top of the stories about scandalous Marco would be too horrific. That way the Loredans would be disgraced for ever and they might as well go and hide their faces for a thousand years. Then he told me he had to go off and think about what he must do and would come back to see me before vespers, also that in the meantime he'd get word to that swine Marco telling him to keep away from the convent and keep his mouth shut, that I was running a religious fever. My father returned at vespers and we made this agreement, he called it a compact, that I would go back home to Marco if he swore to keep all his friends away from the house, to let me visit my family every day, to let me bring in a maid of my own, never to insult or strike or hurt me again, not so much as a hair on my head, and last that Quirina and one of my widowed aunts would spend summers with me out at Asolo. That night Marco agreed to these points, my father did all this by sealed letter and trusted messenger because he was afraid that if he got close to Marco he'd kill him on the spot, then there'd be murder as well as all the gossip about Marco and vice and me. But there was none of this, we all guarded the secret and nothing reached the ears of the Council of Ten.

Next morning Giovanni and Daria came to fetch me, I brought in a maid from my father's house and Quirina spent a few weeks with me. From then on my relations with Marco were calm but cold as ice and we rarely sat down to a meal together, but when we did I'd look across the table to his beauty and wonder what God had done there, it didn't seem right, but after all who was I to think that, the Lord has his ways. And besides, Marco would look across to me and who knows what he was thinking for we were two mortal enemies living side by side, though once he did say (catching me quite by surprise) that he kept seeing me sitting on the captain's lap. I left the table, it was like a violent slap on the face but I deserved it and I have to say that he kept the agreement with my father and never again insulted me or brought men into the house, and now he would sometimes stay out all night.

Then came the great change in my life, about half a year after our horrible fight Marco drowned one night in the Grand Canal and nobody knew how it happened but everyone asked if it was murder or by his own hand. The Ten of course came into the case, they combed over things for many weeks and three of them came to the house to question me, they came twice and the questioning lasted a long time, they even asked about Agostino and the captain but they couldn't find anything criminal and Marco's brothers and uncles were very cross. It was a smear on their family name for anyone to think he killed himself. If you ask me I'd say it didn't happen by his own hand, I never saw him weighed down with gloom, I think he was drunk that night, he must have made enemies and was maybe killed by someone paid to do it, very well paid, but I wouldn't want to prove it and that's all I'll say. They did find enough red wine but no food in his stomach. Something else I have to admit for which God help me, I was not too sad about his death, I dressed in black at once and it was more a sign of quiet feasting than mourning but at the same time I also made up for my stony heart by praying truly for his dark soul, he was so bizarre and wicked and cruel to me. He was like a demon who looked for every way to make my lust come bursting out and I think that if he hadn't done this it wouldn't have been there, by this I mean that if he'd been my true husband and had wanted to have children, maybe I'd have liked being in bed with him too much, who can say, but this is allowed in holy marriage when there is love, the sign of God. I've heard priests say in sermons that wanting to be with child in marriage removes lust, that's why I wanted to think of Agostino Barbarigo as my secret and real husband. Poor Agostino, I'm deeply ashamed of all the things I did with him, I repent those deeds and actions with all my heart and may his poor poor soul rest in peace for ever. Even now sister Polissena arranges to have masses said for him. The captain was something else, a creeping animal in human form, he terrifed me and to this day I loathe him. He did kill a boy in Alexandria with his own member and he had a hellish dog and servants and vices, and I consider that we are donkeys to heap him with honours this disgusting and evil old senator and goat with his grand ways and fancy paintings for altars. Enough of him.

I need to rest a while to think of the last part of my confession.

The day after Marco's death the servants Giovanni and Daria were put out of the house, my father called them accomplices in crime and scared them with having hot irons stamped on their faces if they ever so much as dared open their beaks about Marco and me. They went off cringing and terrified. I moved back to father's house and by legal rights got all my dowry back, also so I could marry again but I wasn't going to, I saw to that. I had turned against men, I considered most of them base and I wanted nothing to do with them, I took a vow to myself and in God's name that I'd never look at men in the eyes again, not in the eyes, the soul's place.

All that first year after Marco died when I was supposed to be in mourning my father tried to talk to me about another marriage for the sake of the family, our name, our position, my dowry, our property and all that kind of thing, especially considering Quirina's disgrace, but I got my sister on my side and we'd simply repeat Convent! Convent! And that meant I'd rather go into a convent. Or I'd get into crying fits and say I preferred to die, and my father would have to tell me not to clench my hands and make fists, doing that was disrespectful to him. He also said what a pity it was for me not to marry again as I was still the best-looking young woman in the city but when I was alone and I turned to considering things I often wondered what he really thought (though naturally I didn't ask) when he looked at me and remembered my violated parts. Heavens if he had a picture of that in his head how could he even bear to look at me? That has to be hard for a father, even frightening and maybe this was why he took a new turn and started saying that with my looks and magnificent dowry he could easily marry me into an honoured old family from Vicenza or Padua. Or what about a man from one of the courts, Ferrara or even Milan? Years before he'd often gone to those cities on embassies and knew many people there. But I prayed to him to get rid of such marriage thoughts, I stopped the tears, I held my ground as they say, I reminded him that his brothers had lots of sons and grandsons which meant the family properties would be safe and in the meantime I made myself useful at home, I brought order into the household, I looked to the servants and marketing and meals, I watched over all the linens and sier Antonio's shirts (I have few peers when it comes to needlework), and I took over all the accounts for the farms and houses, shop rents and open-air market rights. He soon started to see what a good thing it was to have me at home, my practical bent made up for the too-pious Quirina and he could now leave the house daily without any household worries and give all of himself to his affairs at the Palace. *Insomma* I won and I've been in the house ever since (nearly seventeen years now) and if people thought it was queer for me not to remarry I think they changed their minds when they saw that I didn't go out much, I never once went to a party or a great wedding, I was always well-covered and swathed in black, I seemed a pious sort like Quirina.

I'm telling you all these things father Clemence because they're on the way to my telling the truth about Orso.

After a year or two I settled into a new life with my sister and our father. No more lurking dangers, no more of Marco's big men, no more looking at myself in the large glass with shame and surprise, no more sly glances at my breasts and other parts, no more listening to the gurgle of low thoughts, no more spending too many hours thinking about my linens hair dresses frocks sleeves stockings bodices shoes jewellery, no more being locked up with a tormented woman in the body of a man, no more strange fears. I came to feel fresh again and light and as if I could walk straight across all Italy and back again and not be weary. Heavens the new strength! Summers we used to go to the country to Castelfranco but only for a week or two each time, we always went back and forth like that because our father had to be near the Palace, he loved it, I mean the Palace, and of course I saw much more of my aunts, cousins and uncles but still not that much because they were not too pleased with Quirina and I knew they talked about me, I felt it and I hated it, I hated the feeling of being watched through their pretending that I wasn't being watched. I felt as if I wanted to hide all the important parts of me, I wanted to look as if I'd quit the world and like someone with no interest in the things around, so I always wore widow's black and as much of a veil as people would put up with. My aunts for years tried to make me wear a little colour but I wouldn't do it, I was firm about that for I knew colour was a step back into the world and I didn't want to go back because at the end of that there'd be men and lust but first there'd have to be a husband and I'd made a decision about that. No. I was not ever again going to be under the thumb and forefinger of a lord and master. I was my own lord. How easy and natural getting up every morning to be mistress in the house, to obey my own commands, and many mornings I wanted to shout with pleasure, the day is mine! I wonder if I should confess that I started reading more books, I used to get my father to bring them home to me, mostly by Petrarch, Boiardo, Dante and a Florentine named Pulci. He also gave me a special book written by hand, a lexicon it's called, for the meanings of Florentine words and there were many of these.

And now I have to confess father Clemence, it happened again, only this time it was connected with the poetry and getting stirred up. After I came back to Ca'Loredan I started to touch myself again but not too much, truly not much, maybe only a few times a year and I'd feel very ashamed of it afterwards, but with time I got quite over that temptation, how? With the help of prayers and especially by keeping busy and just always trying to be strong that way. I also had to stop reading poetry romances but that wasn't hard, it wasn't a big sacrifice because those romances added up mostly to rather silly stuff, to tell the truth Petrarch was more dangerous because he was sly and talked grandly about common things like just a touch maybe or clear water or Laura's eyes, so I gave him up too for a long time. I went to confession regularly in those years but I never confessed to touching myself so I make a full confession of that here and now with every shame and true deep repentance. I repented it very much at the time but I couldn't confess it because of our priests, you know that. Too many of them are the true shame and obstacle. How can you confess such a thing to them, especially if you're a widow? Widows don't do such things, they're supposed to be more than half-dead. Do you know how coarse stupid idiotic and lecherous some of our priests are? I changed churches ten or twelve times over the years unless I went with Quirina to hers. When I went alone with just one of our servants sometimes I'd pull the veil right down to my nose to hide the eyes, or I'd hunch up a little to look older, or I'd even slow down my walk a lot as if my legs weren't well. This may seem amazing to you but it's the truth. Any widow under thirty is fair game because some people want to believe that the houses of widows have no lords and masters. Doing my old woman's tricks was the only way to keep some of those men of God a step or two away from me and the plainer they were with their grizzled matted hair and hairy ears and noses the worse they could be. Anyhow you don't confess the low sin of touching yourself to men like that. A few times I had to use words of the sort that made their faces go as red as scarlet cloth, or else I'd stop their lewd words and signs by telling them to apply first to my father the Saint Mark's Procurator sier Antonio Loredan. That silenced them.

Now a last item goes here like something added later with an arrow next to it in one of my account books. In wanting to seem religious I went to church too much for my own good, especially when I'd go with Quirina and could really sometimes smell her piety. Then my thoughts would peel away from prayer and stray off to a poet or to a task at home or to

my dark time with Marco. Those hours in church were badly
spent and I repent the waste, may God forgive me please for
all those many lapses.

I keep mentioning Quirina. Listen father Clemence my
doings with her were never easy, she being so pious, the older
sister, the good one, already at home when I moved back,
and all that. She should have been the abbess of a closed and
strict convent, I mean it, but she always said she wanted to
be a comfort to our father and help him around the house
since he didn't marry again, and so she stayed at home but
I think she also wanted to punish him, surely that, and he
put up with it because he thought she'd fetch down some
heavenly grace for him and because she kept to her own part
of the house as I did to mine later on except at mealtimes.
When I went back home after Marco's drowning Quirina
tried to get me to obey her and be always crossing myself
and start being as pious as she was. For her we were two
women in the world but not of it, these were her words and
for a while I pretended to obey her to keep peace in the
house but I couldn't be like her in all those religious exercises of hers, like getting up before daybreak, early mass every
morning, two hours daily of prayer, days at a time on bread
and water with a drop or two of wine and even whipping
herself hard enough to leave bruises. How with all this she
could be a comfort to my father I never knew. She used a
scourge on herself once a month. I saw the dark welts on
her back one hot summer day and they were serious even if
not big and ugly.

Naturally I loved Quirina, let this be said, but I can't say
I liked her, not truly, she was too lean and dour and never
laughed, she lived for the next world. Anyway we had quar-
rels about my not following her in her exercises and I had

to get father to talk to her to stop her from demanding that I fast more, pray more, cross myself more and go to church twice every day. The other thing was that though she was older than me by more than a year, I'd been married and out of the house and had the Contarini name so this gave me a place of some kind above her. Remember this too, I soon ran that entire household and Quirina had nothing to do but her pious exercises, put all this together and you'll understand that after a year or so she had to accept that I would not take commands from her, if anything I gave them. God forgive me for what I did. As I write these things down here I see that I used Quirina's ways to hide myself, this is why I was seen with her so often in church and in the streets, even when we'd had a quarrel of some sort, I'd stick to her as Marco had stuck to me, I'd go out with her to seem like her and sometimes I was even ready to cross myself every time a bird flew overhead but I did it to keep gossip and the eyes of others away from me. Let them say I was drunk with God as they did about Quirina, I didn't care about that as long as it wasn't tell-tale talk about me. Polissena once heard a nasty two-liner about us and here it is.

> The crucifixion of Quirina's saintly parts
> Was quite undone by Loredana's lower arts.

My God the shame of it, I wanted to hide myself for weeks but how could I if the jingles of those nasty twopenny poets were in mouths all around? I was horrified, by heavens they talked, the bad mouths talked, I wasn't just imagining things. Behind all my worries I was afraid people thought that in carnal deeds I was no better than an animal. Some nights I dreamed I carried the signs of lust on my face and hands so here was another reason for me to cover up with folds and veils. People had their carnival masks, I had my daily mask, Quirina's piety was there for my use and I learned to use it.

My father wasn't fooled I think, he must have heard that two-liner but I was maybe even less pious than he thought. I do repent all this now father Clemence, I mean my hiding behind Quirina, and I beg your forgiveness but at that time I couldn't be more honest, I couldn't show myself to be of the world (yes I loved it) because my father and aunts would have pulled me into another marriage. I was too happy being my own lord but I couldn't say that to anyone, could I, because it didn't count as a good reason against marriage. You know that. Young women are supposed to be under the strict rule of husbands. All right then for seventeen years I looked at no man, I had no need of one and no need of the colours of the world and I believed I'd never look at a man again. I was always busy racing up and down stairs, sewing, marketing with the servants, helping to cook, I liked lifting heavy things, taking long walks with our servants or with father and so I got myself into good spirits and the best health of my life.

36. [Orso, codicil to his CONFESSION]:

Esteemed Father Clemence, I have been stricken by shame over the past two days, since completing my confession; therefore I am making this addition, which madonna X will not see, because I cannot get it to her. It will be delivered to you at your usual place, I know not when.

I am astounded by what I wrote concerning the Third City. Since you and X are to be the sole readers of the document, I shamelessly bound you both in a conspiracy, and I pray that you will forgive me. I was caught in a tangle of fear and fierce contradiction, but it was all unwilled. My own frailty overwhelmed me.

With every route out of this city now under the eyes of the Ten, I look for some secret exit, but by the time you get these words I shall certainly be away. So let me again vow, I hereby forsake X in order that she and I may rightfully hope for heaven's grace. And I also forsake her so that I may give the whole of myself to what remains of the Third City. That city, this city, shall be rebuilt. I tried for some days to pick apart and undo the knowledge that I must break all ties with X. In so doing, I was beating against the face of reason; but if we batter reason, what remains of us?

Now that blood has been spilled, ours all of it, I see that I was a fool to think that the Third City could ever have its beginnings in anything but strife and fire. Yes, of course, I was flat up against danger every day and I knew there would be bloodshed, but all such knowing was theory, an abstraction, words. Now the knowledge is in the pit of my stomach, and this changes what I see and am.

The ruling families will fight to the death to keep us from stealing back what is also ours – the sun. My office is the right care of souls, but I am charged with it in a site which is squalor for the soul, a site that wants a crusade for light, warmth and hope. The ancient world knew how to murder tyrants. The Ten mean to kill all men sworn to the Third City. We are forced to defend ourselves by doing to them what they would do to us; and bear in mind that they, for all their iniquity, have the full weight and dignity of government on their side. We must also bring every claim, theirs and ours, out into the open. I regret the need to take this route. May God forgive me. My love in Christ to you. Venice, xxvi September. Orso

37. [Loredana, CONFESSION]:

My sinning with fra Orso.

You've had Orso's confession, you know the story, now I'll tell my sinning part and I'll call him Orso because that's the name I know him by and I mustn't pretend to call him fra Orso or father Orso, that would be a lie here.

Orso has a connection with our Loredan parish church and my father or someone else may have put in a call for him to come and give comfort to my dying sister Quirina, that's the way we met, and though he'd been coming to the house for a week or two I didn't know what he looked like really because as I told you I don't look at men, not in the face, that was my vow, but Quirina made me look at him because one night when she had fever and started seeing things she began to say he was one of us, that he looked like our uncles and cousin Leonardo. I took no notice of her wild talk but she went on saying it and every time I showed him into her bedchamber she'd have her feverish eyes on him, not taking them off, it was amazing, and she'd want to touch him, straining, they even got to where they were holding hands, so when I opened the door to him one day something came over me, I decided to look hard at him and Quirina was right, I saw a strong likeness, the melancholy eyes and strong chin of our men (had he been sent by God?) but his young looks surprised me because I'd heard him talk to Quirina and the voice was deep or maybe too confident, not a young man's voice. Listen father Clemence something happened then which I can't explain and I'd better not try. An earthquake? When his innocent eyes looked at me and I looked back I was, I can't say, as though pulled up out of myself and that made me look even more and I felt a spirit between us that got stronger every time I saw him. I don't know why I felt sorry for him but I did, it was a strong sorrow, I wanted to protect him even if he was a priest, I sensed a wound there all around, and then his face passed over into my spirit, took hold of me, a face I already knew, there isn't another way to say it. I'd made a vow against men but not against him, that's how I felt suddenly and one afternoon when he came out of Quirina's bedchamber and he had his great slow eyes on me I felt I had to touch his face, put my hands on his cheeks, don't please want me to explain, I can't, I had to do it, I also knew he wouldn't reject the touch, I'd seen it in his eyes (can you understand?), and it was almost as though he wasn't a man for me, he wasn't vile and carnal.

I know you can't believe this but I'm telling it in a confession and I must tell the truth or my soul will be in worse danger. Which I can't afford can I? So I want to say it again, that day, the day I first touched him, I didn't feel or think of Orso as a man, I thought of him as I don't know what, he was someone who made me feel kind, he brought out my good and best feelings and as I went to touch him, there was no warning, it was all surprise, I thought of Marco and my evil days as his wife and of the face there right in front of me and my eyes filled with tears and I touched that face. What do I know of this world? I come and go, I get up mornings, I do nearly the same things every day, I slip around in my different thoughts, then something queer happens and I can't stop it, I don't want to stop it, it's like a strange new day, but when that happens to us (which is almost never) we like it, and when I touched Orso it was a new day, my heart was in that touch and all of me was in my heart, and that changed the touch. I want to go off to one side here and say what the touch wasn't. Can I say it wasn't real, not like flesh touching flesh? I have to use the word love, that was there, it came as fast as light in a dark room when you open the shutters, and that word says as much as I can say about what happened and what I feel, it was love and it doesn't matter how I turn or pull or pinch my conscience, it is love. I know the feeling from what priests say, and what I feel about Orso comes next to my feelings for Christ and Mary, I mean that it is close by, very close because it is tender and high and good. I don't know how to describe it another way and if this is blasphemy (is it?) I beg forgiveness, I am but saying that what I feel about Orso I put under the banner of my prayers. I know I'm in trouble, I know I mustn't love a Dominican, I know he's one of God's knights, this is what I need to talk about. Heaven help me.

I wanted to stop here but I'll go on. The sinning first. A day after I touched Orso's face, that was the beginning, we did the act of marriage in my father's house and there was no shame, there was deep joy. These words write themselves in me first and then I put them down here. In my heart Orso and I were held together by the feeling that belongs to wives and husbands but you'll tell me this was a sin because of Orso's vows and my unchastity, and I don't know how to answer with reasons to say that it wasn't a sin. You call it fornication, yet I can say it was a hundred times less sinful for me than just being in the same room with my husband Marco, not to mention his touching me.

Let me start again, I don't cause my own feelings, they come. Of course I don't do what all my feelings press me on to do, nobody does that, or I'd have killed Marco and Agostino and the captain. I didn't look for Orso, I looked for no one, he came to our house, he stood at our door, he walked up and down our great staircase, he moved through the same rooms where I grew up, the same light and shadows fell on his face, I saw his profile against our walls, his youth pressed against me like a gentle wind, heavens he even looked like us as Quirina said, a lot like us, not just his face, his shoulders too and all his manner. So was he sent by God? Listen, through him I saw the young me, oh but not wasted, it was a bitter and tender feeling, and when I put my arms around him I felt I was fading and fading till I'd not be there. More happened. He thought I was near to him in years but when he told me his age, I said I was old enough nearly to be his mother which is true, and he clung to me all the same. This made me happy, I almost wanted him to be my child so I could protect him. I've moved off the line I should be on here, I know, and also I think I'm not answering your questions, the ones you'd be asking if you were here before me but I'll get to them.

After Quirina died Orso couldn't go on coming to the house, he had no reason to, had he, and I can't tell you the giant sadness of that, about as great as the seas for me, I say for me because he has many other cares and duties mostly in the lower city but I have only him to think about and the house. I confess I look and wait for him with every possible tender passion, without him I'm a body without a soul. Now you see why I had to pretend he was my confessor, why I used to meet him in church on most days for a miserly few minutes and in those minutes we talked in whispers because there'd be others nearby waiting to see him, sometimes a little crowd. We talked and talked but never touched, not once, our talking was a fever, our eyes meeting was life itself, and I found out about his foreign Florentine speech, his two years in the holy land, Bologna, the hot desert, the cisterns and his care for people and those on their way to die. Even so, though he'd seen and done more than me, much more, and gone very far and read a thousand books, though I've been only in Venice and close by, at the bottom of feeling I felt like a mother to him and like some mothers, I'm sure, I think I wanted to put him back inside me or by my breasts for ever where I could nurse him. This is what I tried to do when we were in the act of marriage, I confess it, I confess it. Also, all the talking we did took us more and more into each other, that's the way we talked, that was the soul, you truly get to know others through the soul, that's what lives and the body dies and is more like the cart trailing behind, though a dear cart. I began to understand the fire and sadness in his eyes, the first lines on his face and his up-and-down rush of words. I know his rushing words have a lot to do in some foreign way with his Third City but he never talks about that, I think because he doesn't want to scare me or lead me into troubles, it's all too dangerous.

Anyway the small crowd of people often waiting to confess to him were much of the time you know not really there to confess, they came to talk to him to get his help or advice, they wanted him to pray with them and I would see him touch them and they touched him, as though something precious was passed on in those touches, I know all this because I saw it. After my talks with him I'd stand over to one side of the church and watch him for a while but I couldn't stay too long because people would start to stare at me in my black veiling, they could tell I wasn't from the lower city. Listen father Clemence I talked to Orso about my evil marriage though I was sick with worry about it, I was afraid he'd be disgusted and angry and turn against vile me and not be able to set eyes on me, but he didn't. I told him about Marco and Agostino and the criminal captain, about the brute deflowering and Marco's Judas tricks and sodomy, also about the way I was pulled downwards violently towards sin and the lewd wanting to be base, but I didn't give any of the shameful details, good heavens, how could I and who'd want to hear such things anyway unless he had to as a priest? Well but what do you think he said after I told him? He took pity on me, he put his arms around me, he cried more than my father, he sobbed, he covered his face for a long time, I couldn't believe it, then he praised my courage and said he loved me and told me that suffering could raise people if they can be taken through it in thinking. I'm not sure I understood this. He talked about Marco too saying that more than anyone I ever knew Marco deserved my pity and prayers because he was the unhappiest of men and I was shaken. He said that lust is a kind of suffering, a terrible downward fall from God, more slippery and full of deceit than almost any other sin except pride. The blind beggar is better off because he can see God, whereas the flesh beggar blacks out all things but the lust, a misery worse than blindness. He also made me see some evil things about the upper city though nobody talks or thinks about them.

Next I'll tell you where we came together in the act of marriage after poor Quirina died, I want to remember those places even if you think I'm remembering sin though I vow to you it didn't feel like sin, I didn't turn away from God, so it wasn't sin in that sense, sin in the dark. I know what sin feels like, it rakes your skin with frightening pleasure, it fills and excites your lower parts, it pulls you down, it comes with a filthy shameful thrill, all of you turns into nothing but desire for it, and I had no feeling of any such sort with Orso, never once. The feeling I had was that I went out of the cart of my body.

I said I'd tell you where we came together, the places. Of course I know my father's movements, also I rule those of the servants, so two times I got Orso into our house and into my bedchamber, I hid him there. How reckless that was I needn't tell you but you can see that we had to be together no matter what, for in our city (did you know this?) strangers caught in houses can be cut to pieces, that's the law and in a passion my father might have killed me too. Orso spent those two nights and part of the two days clasped in my arms, I never let him go and he didn't want to be let go, and I'm not ashamed of this father Clemence though I know you'd find words to prove me wrong and make me see the sin, but all the same I trust my feelings because they've always known right from wrong and never once in the days of Big Agostino or the captain did they trick me into thinking that black was white, I knew my actions then were evil even when I wanted the baby and tried to think of Agostino as my husband, and my feelings about Orso tell me this now, that where love is there is no sin or depravity, no death of the soul. With the captain any glance was a vile and dirty action, with Orso any action is an act of love so how can it be anything but good? I'll go on. Three times by secret means Orso went out to the country where I had farm business for my father, I didn't send for the servants and the local ones were kept out of the house on a string of jobs. We remained indoors for a day or two each time and burned no candles at night and we were one as I think few married people ever are. Those days and nights gave me a picture of heaven's choirs and when my last hour comes may it bring that picture to my closed eyes. Then last of all the boldest of our love meetings were in lower Venice, we were together there two times, I dressed up as a man and went out of father's house at night through one of my windows, keeping to the shadows and feeling my way through the dark and down a stairway to the lower city to meet Orso. My heart raced. We went to a house and spent the night there but I was back in upper Venice and in my bedchamber before daybreak. What were my feelings during those night hours? That I weighed less than a feather and had risen up out of my body, that I could see straight into the skies, that I was somebody else and I was not afraid. I also saw that I would risk my life for Orso and do it again and again without even thinking about it because I had to be with him, and God forgive me for saying this but it's true, I would jump over my father sier Antonio's face to be with Orso, and I mean no harm to him.

There it is then, that was all, we were together by ourselves only seven times after Quirina died though a few were for two days each. Were they too many times, too many as sin? They were too little for love. From your books and penitents but maybe also from your own heart too you'll know about love, the poets are full of it, the songs are full of it, and you must know that what we did can be forgiven, this must be so. I've heard of popes who were with the sisters of cardinals and of bishops who have concubines, still I'm sure they hope to deserve heaven. Why can't we hope for the same? Jesus didn't condemn the adulteress.

I have to rest my hand, I press down too hard, I must stop writing now, I think I've said all.

Why am I thrashing around in this confession? What am I going to do? I'm a sensible woman and even so here I am spinning out all these words, spinning them out against what I see, as if words were actions and shields, I'm choking with words and I must put a stop to them. Loredana, look at things in the face, as they truly are, this is what I must tell myself. Orso is to come and find me only one more time because he's in hiding to save his life. I'm more than afraid, I'm terrified he'll be arrested and killed, I know the likes of my father, I know about the Ten, I know what they do, I've been hearing about them all my life, Orso and his Third City friends say they want sunlight for the lower city but that cannot be, can it, without soldiers and blood? Christ and Mary help Orso, even now he could be under arrest though my father would have told me if a Dominican had fallen into their hands, as he told me about fra Dolfin Falier and the others who poisoned themselves. Anyway here I sit raving in a confession like a crazy woman, as if I'll see Orso easily again tomorrow and the next day, but I don't know, it won't be easy.

And here's the last thing, I didn't tell Orso about it because first it was too soon and then everything rushed along and it was too late. I am with child these two months and in a month or two it'll be noticed and I want Orso to know. Maybe we can steal away together and go to some far secret place and take another name and live there quietly.

Father Clemence please come into Venice and talk to me. If Orso doesn't see me or send word by tomorrow night I will go out and scour the city for him though I don't know where I'll begin, my feelings are all turning into desperation. I repent all my sins and I beg you for your absolution and blessing. In Christ I commend myself to you. Venice, 26-28 September [1529].

Loredana Loredan Contarini

38. [Bernardo Loredan to Pandolfo, in code, LETTER]:
Pandolfo. In dei nomine.
The hour has come. We are to make an arrest at Castelfranco, in the Loredan villa. You know the site. Your

debts you know. Now at last is the time for payment. The instant you get this notice, you will have just enough time to gather your men and rush out to Castelfranco. Rescue the friar, or if our guardsmen have already arrived – there will be eight – snatch him from their hands. Fail and we are lost. Christ keep you. i octobris [1529].

Bernardo

39. [Loredana, fragment of CONFESSION]:

. . . also that this last bit is to say goodbye and God be with you father Clemence because I'm in the country near Castelfranco and I'm going to quit Italy with Orso, we leave tomorrow so I must push this quill as fast as it'll go, there's no time at all . . . After I finished my confession to you and gave it to sister Polissena together with Orso's tied in a bundle I went down to the lower city to look for him and couldn't find a trace but he sent word to me through one of those old women who sell fancy combs and ribbons in upper Venice, she was clever and knew how to talk in parables around her message. He got two fishermen to take himself and me to a place near Chioggia but he was in the water and nearly under the boat most of the way, he was holding on to a net and the worst thing was that we set out before daybreak, the time to go out for duck you know and there were groups of men everywhere in their little boats shooting out at the ducks, arrows [from crossbows] fell not far from us, our bad luck, and with all those sharp eyes around Orso had to keep pulling his head down under the water, sweet Mary I thought he'd drown, and halfway to Chioggia we had to drag him out of the water under cover of a sheet of canvas because he was too cold and almost blue and I had to lie on top of him to warm him up. That's when I told him, I whispered it into his ear, *I'm going to have a baby,* and it was like pouring warm water over his body he was so happy and soon he got back into the cold water. I was in that boat with clothes for a merchant and my heart was in my throat every minute of that long journey, we kept an eye on everyone and every-thing, then we landed and Orso changed dress to look like a merchant and I like his wife and it was all a trickle of sweated fear when we heard voices. Next from there winding round toward Castelfranco we went by horse to the house of a widow, a woman who's almost my creature and can be trusted, I love her, we spent one night in her deserted moun-tain cottage. Going by horse brought up strange and wonderful feelings because either I rode behind Orso clutching, I buried my arms in him, or as I rode he walked beside me holding me with one hand. My feelings then were – no, nothing from this quill can give them a name, all these scratchy marks and words are such poor things, good enough for telling about sin and twisted deeds but misers when it comes to talking about what is good. Glory is not for words.

Listen father Clemence I left a note for my father sier Antonio telling him that I was going away, not to look for me, that he'd never find me and I didn't confess anything to him, he'll find out for himself soon enough, I'm sorry about this but there was no other way to flee, just think about it. Though it's quite dangerous we're going to stay in the Castelfranco villa tonight but only this one night because we can't leave without a chest of jewels and ducats that I have hidden there or I wouldn't go anywhere near Castelfranco. Tomorrow and the next day we'll be on our way back to Chioggia to join a caravan of merchants on their way East, we leap with plans. Orso is saying please hurry. Father Clemence I pray you'll forgive me for running away with

him, I can't be different, I can't change, no power in the world
can hold me back, so my going must be right, my conscience
does not trouble me, the flesh is not evil when love and God
shine through, which is why I'm happy and why I'm writing
this last part to you. Sometimes I feel that Orso is close to
being my own body, his hair mine and his hands and feet
too, his bony feet, the scars on his hand and arms, the teeth
in his dear mouth and the way his Florentine tongue says
words like compassion heart and glory, and I . . . but he tells
me I must absolutely stop now, the sand in the rounded glass
has run out. You'll get this last part somehow, I yearn for you
to have it, I want you to know. God be with you father
Clemence, pray for me bless me forgive me.

Loredana

40. [Falier, SECRET CHRONICLE]:

When I learned of Fra Orso's arrest, I hurried out to the
Palace landing in time to observe his arrival. Therefore I offer
direct testimony, for I saw him as he got out of a gondola to
be led to the Palace by the guardsmen of the Council of Ten;
and he was not, contrary to reports, in his Dominican garb.
Looking back, I note that he had the characteristic haughti-
ness of the Loredans. His step was light; he stood tall; he had
an easy manner; his large eyes surveyed the surroundings but
fixed on no man or detail. I was struck by the notion that
he was not there in spirit, and it came to me that he had no
sense of the enormity of his crime.

[*Deletions*]

There is something perversely grand about the conspiracy,
even in its crafty name, the Third City. Think of it, they
proposed to make one city out of two by means of insurrection and colossal reconstruction; and some of them had

the lunacy to hope that this might be possible with little or no bloodletting. I associate such energy and overreach with the crazed ambitions of the Loredans; hence I can more easily see Fra Orso at the head of the conspiracy, despite his youth, than my poor deluded cousin, Fra Dolfin Falier.

41. [Vendramin, DIARY]:

iii October [1529]. Before midnight. More arrests. The Ten tighten the ropes. If only this were all!

But I have to report a shocking event, the more painful because Bernardo [*Loredan*] is one of the Ten. I don't want to believe it. I don't want to think it. I don't want to record it. I don't want to know it. Yet how suppress it?

The Ten yesterday made a spectacular arrest out at Castelfranco. They struck by night. Seized a Florentine priest in Antonio's [*the Loredan*] villa. Grabbed him and one of my cousins-german. It shames me to name her. The widow Loredana Loredan Contarini. Of all people! But all at once her disappearance is explained. We were astounded, silenced really. Such a church mouse. Though she once inspired sonnets, long ago. That's how wonderful-looking she was. The priest is a Dominican, a certain Orso Veneto. How can a Dominican be party to a bloody plot against the upper city? And Loredana involved with him? Mystifying.

Later still. I got some particulars from the ashen and shaken Bernardo. Half the story I already knew. She vanished from Venice three days before the arrest, fled in disguise. Somewhere the priest joined her, or she joined him. Worse was to come. They made their way to Castelfranco and she let the blackguard hide in the villa. No one knows what business they had there. Her father and others, myself included, had spent three days looking for her. Frantic with worry, we alerted the Ten through Bernardo. They got the assistance of the night constabulary. Their agents went to work. But who could have imagined the outcome? Who knew there could be a link with the priest?

After her arrest she was not taken to the Palace. Not until nightfall. First they held her in a convent for several hours. The renegade priest they say was traced by his Florentine speech. Naturally the Ten have agents everywhere. When guardsmen arrested him at the villa, Loredana threw herself into their midst to protect him. She quarrelled with them. First she insisted they had the wrong man. He was innocent. Then she announced that they must arrest her too, that she was an accomplice. So they also had to take her away. The priest kept denying her. He claimed that she had nothing to do with him, that she was too agitated to know what she was saying.

Venice talks about nothing else. Nor do we. With Loredana in the custody of the Ten we expected that Bernardo would know what to do. But not at all. He had to hold his tongue. The ties of blood disqualify him. And really, by the rules, he should not even be there. Facing Loredana [*his own niece*], what on earth could he say? What could he do? What else but look on in horror! So Antonio [*Loredana's father*], some cousins and many others, including Cardinal Pisani and myself, went to the Ten. We argued that her reason and common sense had been occluded. How could the daughter of a Saint Mark's Procurator be an accomplice? What, in a most hideous conspiracy against the republic, and she a Loredan? Discussion was fierce. The Ten split apart. Bernardo had to sit there like a deaf mute or risk exclusion from office. Doubtless he should have resigned. One councillor taunted him. At any rate, the ruling group is now split. The Loredans have cunning enemies in high office, set to strike fatally. Set to repay the years of defeats and injuries. After some hours the Ten released Loredana. We prevailed. But only on condition that she be confined in the Convent of Saint Margaret of Antioch. It's a strictly cloistered house.

Antonio's daughters have been dogged by ill luck. First there was the cursed scandal of Quirina's impediment. The thing, whatever it was, made her an impenetrable virgin. It sounds killingly funny. And that was the curse, the buffoonery of it. What could the crucified Quirina do? I thought people would never stop talking and laughing about it. Nor about her dissolved marriage with Marcantonio Mocenigo. The whole affair naturally was a costly business for us at the Palace. We lost face and support. The Mocenigos were furious for years. They felt ridiculous and humiliated. Then it was the beautiful Loredana's turn. Her turn to be on the altar of tales and scandal. I knew her then. She was so beguiling. We all yearned for her. I used to stand and wait for her to come out of church. I loved to watch her as she stepped out with that quick, courtly, round sweep of hers. The servants bounced along behind her.

Fra Orso is being questioned. Can the Dominicans disown him? They say he was Loredana's spiritual advisor. If so then I believe in the mad work of the stars.

Bernardo lives in silence and stays away from people. What's wrong with him? Meantime Antonio is in despair, all but overwhelmed. His enemies crow in private. And he a Saint Mark's Procurator, the likely next doge. Or he was! They would not dare crow in public.

Antonio spoke to Loredana and came away astounded. About one thing however he is serene. She knew nothing of the demented plot, absolutely nothing. How could she? Yet he fears that she verges on a disorder of agitation. She talks to herself and spends hours praying.

iv October. The Palace is rent in two. Fortunately most of the Ten and main senators side with us. A tiny group want Loredana removed from the convent. Want her questioned again. They sail under the pretext of the law and customary procedure. Allege that she must have got important particulars from Fra Orso. Among her most venemous critics are two beasts. We know them. The sort who have sometimes dared hint at an unnatural tie between Loredana and her father. An ancient scrap of evil scurrility. But the beasts have been defeated. Yesterday it looked as if the Contarini clan were mostly on their side. That would have been dangerous. They still smart over what happened to their lady Marco. But we made them see that any worse scandal would spatter them too. They passed back to our side. Antonio touched delicately on the matter of Marco's sodomy. If they made anything of Loredana's supposed carnal relations with Fra Orso, her marriage to Marco would surface and be talked about. They should beware. Tongues would wag. So what? Well, what about the new suspicion that Marco was murdered by a male lover from lower Venice?

42. [Council of Ten, PROCEEDINGS]:
   [*The three* capi *of the Ten conduct the cross-examination:*]
   Fra Orso Veneto. The Third City.
   Session of 3 October. Anno domini nostri 1529.
   Ten: Secretary, see to it that your clerks get down every word of this morning's proceedings. If the prisoner so much as sighs, note that down too.

Now Fra Orso, we come back to you. Let us note the few facts that you have offered us thus far. And once again, we suppose you to be a sensible man. We expect truthful testimony, above all because, as you have seen by now, we sit here before you with heaps of facts and particulars, already provided us by members of your sect.

So then, you were born about twenty-eight years ago, you think, out of wedlock and in Venice. You grew up in Florence and later went to Bologna to study in the University. But before you quit Florence, a papal court in Rome rectified, shall we say, the conditions of your illegitimate birth, so as to make way for your honourable entry into the Dominican Order. Is all this so?

Fra Orso: Yes, my lords.

Ten: And at Bologna, friar, did you study canon law?

Orso: No, my lords. My subjects were theology and philosophy.

Ten: Then we must be dealing with a learned man, eh?

Orso: I don't think I'm learned, my lords.

Ten: To tell you the truth, we have our doubts too, or you would not be in this . . . this sewage calling itself the Third City. What makes you think you were born a bastard in Venice?

Orso: I didn't say bastard . . .

Ten: No, no, don't quibble. Is it not the word for you? Never mind about the legalities of legitimation. The things of lawyers are mere niceties and of no interest to us here. After all, if you were born in Venice and don't know who your mother and father were, what else can you be but a bastard? That's logical, isn't it, *philosophiae doctor*? Now tell us, how do you know you were born a bastard here?

Orso: I was told many times that I was born here, my lords. The people who looked after me as a boy always called me a Venetian and I assumed they knew – the Bardi family in Florence and my superiors in the Florentine Convent of Santa Maria Novella.

Ten: We are searching through all parish registers here, both in the lower and upper cities, and have yet to find the facts of your birth anywhere. Do you realise that to have been born a Venetian doubles your treachery?

Orso: Yes, my lords.

Ten: And that if you are misleading us to protect others, we may have to take you through a journey of awesome pain?

Orso: My lords, there is a trust fund of some sort for me here in Venice. The income is paid out through the Dominican Order.

Ten: Secretary, look into this *quam primum*. Contact the Order here and get messengers out to the Dominicans in Florence and Bologna. See if you can verify the prisoner's claim . . . Guards, why is the prisoner so spry? We think he's not frightened. You're not doing your job. [*They pull him down to his knees*] . . . That's better. Now Fra Orso, when were you first in touch with your secret society?

Orso: About seven years ago. Fra Alessandro Basegio, a Dominican, came to see me in Bologna. He was on his way to Rome. But I think you know, he died last winter.

Ten: Don't anticipate our questions . . . And this Basegio, was he from the noble family here, do you happen to know? Yes? Well, and why did he visit you in Bologna?

Orso: That I don't know, my lords. I knew no one from Venice at that time, I mean apart from two or three Venetian students in Bologna. But Fra Alessandro seemed to know me, or anyway about me.

Ten: That's curious. How could he know the least thing about you?

Orso: I suppose he'd heard things through the Order. One does.

Ten: Aren't you impugning the Dominicans?

Orso: No, my lords, I would never hold them responsible for my actions.

Ten: Go back to Basegio.

Orso: He knew somehow – but it must have been through the Order – that I'd worked in hospitals for the poor in Bologna and Florence, and he knew about my zeal for the work of the confraternities that bring solace to condemned men and women, to those who are about to die. He admired this and later on he told me that his group admired it.

Ten: Indeed! His group, did you say?

Orso: Yes, my lords, and that was my first contact with the Third City, although I didn't know it at the time.

Ten: And what did they find to admire in what you did?

Orso: They thought I was doing works of mercy and charity, they thought . . .

Ten: Stop there, Fra Orso. You understand, surely, that you are not here to sing your own praises . . . You want us to believe, do you, that you knew nothing about them, a group in Venice, while they knew all about you?

Orso: Yes, my lords, that's the way it was. They even knew that I was born in Venice.

Ten: Well, well, you are building up a nice mystery here. They teach you to be clever at Bologna, don't they? We're going to see how clever you are. You're suggesting that shadowy presences in Venice had their eyes on precious you. Is that so?

Orso: No, my lords. If I may be allowed to say it, your tone is not mine. But yes, they did seem shadowy to me. The word is fitting.

Ten: Guards, get this talkative priest out of this chamber until we are ready for him again.

[*Deletions*]

Ten: Prisoner, tell us more about the poison you carried. You had ample time before our guardsmen arrested you. Why did you not swallow it, as some of your sworn associates have done? Were you . . . not brave enough?

Orso: Maybe I was too cowardly, my lords, as you suggest . . . There was also another barrier. Suicide is the casting away of a supreme gift, unless there be ineffable suffering. It is also condemned by the Church, although the early Church praised it in martyrs.

Ten: Get to the point!

Orso: To keep the men of the Third City from falling into the hands of the Council of Ten, I approved of suicide. I approved. But when I had to face it myself, I couldn't go through with it. I had time to pray, and the moment I was arrested, everything in me changed. I . . . I wanted a meeting with the Ten.

Ten: One moment, please. What's this you wanted? You say you wanted a meeting with us?

Orso: When the Third City was betrayed and my confrères began to die, I was tormented by the desire to flee and the desire to stay. I was in a fever to hide or to rush forth and be arrested so that I could represent our views. I believed the Ten might be interested. After all, what is this interrogation all about?

Ten: Where, friar, did you learn to be so shameless, in bombastic Bologna or braggart Florence? . . . Answer us!

Orso: My lords, I am here to answer questions and I am answering. This is also why I put forth my views in the letter found on me.

[*From Fra Orso's letter to the Ten*]:

[*Deletions*] . . . so it happened that your forebears had the bravery to build a new city directly on top of the old one, thereby separating the nobility from the commoners. They took the upper city and the sun for themselves and put the common people into the lower city and darkness. The feat was astonishing, it dazzled everyone: themselves, their neighbours and the rest of Italy. But no other city, I note, has imitated their brutal assault on equity and the natural law, the law as inscribed into the free distribution of the earth's natural goods: air, light, water and the warmth of the sun. The wide outer margins of the lower city have the sunlight, to be sure, but those parts are reserved for rich commoners of the better sort. For lesser tradesmen, artisans, workers, labouring women and all the rest of the poor, to these the tenebrous, humid, reeking inner core of lower Venice. There the light is dim or non-existent, and the wellwater is bad because the best of it is routed first to the upper city. There, since we front on canals, the air is often damp and full of stench; and there, too, sickness and misshapen bodies abound. My lords, it is time to tear down parts of both the lower and upper cities, and to have a new third city on a single, uneven plane.

[*Deletions* . . .]

Ten: Where did you and your Third-City accomplices hold your meetings and hatch your plots?

Orso: My lords, out in the open. In the streets, in market places, on the Grand Canal, out fishing. We did not hide.

Ten: What about certain inns and houses in the lower city?

Orso: Never. That would have been dangerous.

Ten: So you say, but we say that you're protecting a pack of traitors down there.

Orso: No, my lords. We were safer in the open. Sometimes we went into parish churches, San Martino and San Daniele for instance, but only to pray.

Ten: And since your Dominican habit was a mask for the others, you looked like a good little prayer group, didn't you?

Orso: Yes, my lords. It was a secrecy best kept in public. Our preferred meeting place was not far from this chamber. The Piazza di San Marco. We used to walk there because it attracted the least suspicion. My Dominican robes and the one nobleman who was in my circle permitted the other three to be with us in that grounded part of the upper city.

Ten: You take an insolent pleasure, don't you Friar Orso, from telling us about your walks around San Marco?

Orso: No, my lords. I am your prisoner, I'm answering your questions as best I can.

Ten: No, Sir Orso of the brooding eyes. You also think that you can pull our beards, and we're generous enough for the time being to let you do it, but only because we have you by the well-fed testicles of a friar and know that in a day or two you'll have nothing there but red paste.

Orso: My lords, will removing my manhood attest to yours?

Ten: Very well, big mouth. The job can be done now. Guards, take this criminal out of here and . . .

Mask I: No, my lords. Not yet. Let him talk. He's surely one of the *capi*. He knows too much. His manner be damned.

Mask II: This man is an impenitent monster, my lords. You see it and hear it. So I say, let his punishment proceed now.

Mask I: No, my lords. We'll lose a whole day if we take that route, more than a day. And what useless, petty revenge at this point. The procedure, bear it in mind. He'll be doubled over in pain, agonising. He won't be able to hear or talk, and we need more facts now, not tomorrow. Therefore, I call for a vote.

[*NOTE: the vote on proposals in the Ten was by secret ballot. Motions were carried by a simple majority of the ten votes. Ties*

(5/5) were broken by the head of the six ducal councillors, who were nearly always present]

RESULT: 7 against castration, 3 in favour. Proposal defeated.

Ten: Fra Orso, be thankful for the results of our vote. You need not say your prayers yet – this will come. The punishment for your insolence is deferred, but take note. Note that unlike you and your Third City, we do things here by the rules. Be warned therefore, and learn to control your tongue. Three votes have already gone against you. You can be certain that this number will rise.

Confess that you joined the conspirators out of a ravening envy. You hate the nobility.

Orso: Forgive me, my lords, but I must say no. I took the oath of the Third City because their merciful and benign purposes appealed to my compassion.

Ten: Considering that your aims were to butcher the nobility, that's a squalid reply.

Orso: My lords, the complete answer is in my letter to you.

Mask II: That letter is an outrage.

Mask III: By heavens let him speak!

43. [Bernardo Loredan's PRAYER]:

[NOTE: *in an elliptical aside at the top of this prayer, salvaged from among his papers, Bernardo notes that his confessor had urged him to work on a single supplication, to write it out, and to repeat it over and over again*]

Heavenly Father, on my kneees I plead with you, in the name of your sacred blood I beg, take this cup and these dregs from my lips. Break my bones, impale me, let me die, only let him live and let me not see his [*Orso's*] flesh bloodied and broken. Let me not look upon him in his howling and suffering.

Out of the mercy won by your crucified wounds, throw me
into a dungheap of shrieking devils. I will fear none of them,
if you but keep the light in his eyes and his limbs straight.

Father, what am I to do? How will my jaws grasp at the
air to breathe? How can I go on in this sordid vase, this
stinking body of mine, and see him die? Take me in his place,
rip my body open, batter my face, make me pay before you
make him pay. I am older, wiser, more cruel, and all corrupt.
Have you so soon forgotten the unspeakable sins of my youth?

I wanted a new city, but not this way, never this way, not
in agony and urine, not in the face and noise of smashed
teeth and torn tongues, not by violent handfuls of hair, not
at the cost of screams and burned flesh, not in a shower of
blood, not on the horns of wrath, not in a cesspool of humiliation and shame.

Dear God, my God, in all my days I have never prayed out
of such a well of pain and fever, out of such burning truth
and need. Take the Loredan money – gold, farms, forests,
boats and houses – and give it all to the lower city now, up
to the last of pennies. Do but grant me this grace: transfer
all his horror to me and keep him alive. Put his lot into my
flesh and make me pay. I am the one who deserves to pay.

Down on my face I implore you. Crush me. I led that
young friar on. Omnipotent Father, you saw it all. Forgive
me, I conjure you, by punishing me with the highest and last
violence. And forgive him by giving all his pain to me. Amen.

44. [Council of Ten, PROCEEDINGS, 3 October]:

[*Deletions*]

Ten: Listen to us, disreputable priest. You talk and you
talk, but talking for you is the art of telling lies. Did all
members of your secret church love talking this way? What

were you, a pack of jabbering housewives? Certainly not. You were, are, scheming knaves and enemies of the Venetian republic, yet you have the face to come in here and present yourself as a man who wants nothing but the sun and light of God for the lower city, when in fact you were ready to murder all our best men, to lay hands on our property, to rape our women and to move your rabble of underlings up into our city, in violation of the laws of Venice and your sacred vows.

Orso: No, my lords!

Ten: Yes, Sir Friar of the elevated airs, as if you were too fine and clever for the honourable men in this chamber. We're going to see about that. Let's get down to essentials. Up to this point we have been toying with you, but we have also been counting your tricks. We want you now to describe the composition of the Third City. Who are the officers, what are their names, and how many are you? These are the only questions that interest us. Reply!

Orso: My lords, having every reason under the sun to fear the Council of Ten, we had to shield ourselves against all easy detection. Therefore we erected barriers inside the Third City itself, the better to protect our *capi* and the group as a whole. But I myself never met our officers and I can put no faces on them. The Confraternity of the Third City was broken up into clusters of five men. Only one man in each quintet knew a member outside the group. Directions went out or were received through him and him alone. I assume that at some point, when reaching a certain level, this arrangement stopped and that everything was then drawn together into the hands of those who governed us.

Mask II: Impossible, my lords. You couldn't possibly appoint a serious conspiracy along those lines and give it any coherence. If we believe the prisoner, then we believe that our enemies had no sure way of conveying orders. That's the first nonsense. Secondly, if most of the conspirators never met or saw their leaders, how could they even begin to trust them? Yet they were all of them risking their lives. Remember the poison. The friar is being eloquent again.

Mask III: One minute, my lords, please. The prisoner may be telling the truth. I see it all clearly, I mean the order and arrangement of the Third City. I could almost sketch it for you. Listen carefully. Imagine a five-pointed star. That's their pentad. Take five, ten, or any number of stars on a plane. Extend upwards, up to another plane, one of the legs of each star. That vertical leg is your key man, the one with that star's outside connections. Now, either the one vertical of each star touches a central point above, and that's your supreme head, or, each vertical touches all the other vertical legs on an upper plane and that's your Third City's governing council. Think about it, the structure makes sense.

[*Deletions. There was a muted consultation*]

Ten: Very well, let's suppose that we now see their demonic organisation. In this case, it follows that with all his doings and many ties as a Dominican, Fra Orso was the head of his pentad. So either he is in the Third City's ruling council or, yes, he has been in touch with the supreme rector.

Guards, let the prisoner stand up for a few minutes.

Fra Orso, is it not the case that this conventicle of yours reached all the way to Bologna to make you one of them? In other words, they marked you for a special place in the conspiracy. And considering what you said about their quintets, we believe that there you singled yourself out. You know how the Third City is assembled. You understand it. Your villainous ease with words and books also points to you as one of the prime conspirators. This means that you are familiar with all the others too, all of them. You heard the business about the arrangement of stars – that told us everything.

Orso: No, my lords, I have never seen the faces of the men who captain the Third City. Or if I have, I didn't know it. I vow to you – it might as well have been one of you.

Ten: Make no vows to us, friar, please. You treat vows like figs. And again, control your tongue. Did you not travel abroad for the Third City?

Orso: I went to Vicenza and Padua and other towns, but not for my secret society.

Ten: You have just condemned yourself, Fra Orso, for now we know that you are lying again. In a few minutes, we're going to confront you with the evidence and the bloody reasons for your trips to neighbouring cities. But first tell us when you met the friars Pietro Ziani and Lorenzo Tiepolo.

Orso: I met only one of them, my lords. Fra Alessandro Basegio once talked about them by name. He told me that they were the first to have the idea of the Third City, but his words were general. He gave no particulars. I took for granted that the two men, the founders, were deeply unhappy about the lower city. The Dominican Tiepolo was killed in the Holy Land, I think a long time ago. I was still in Bologna. The other man, the Franciscan Fra Pietro, was very old and died about two years ago. I met him once, but the meeting was brief. I was extremely curious of course about both men, but our express rule was to stay away from matters that were meant to remain a mystery.

Ten: What can you tell us about Fra Dolfin Falier?

Orso: Dolfin Falier? Nothing, my lords. I know no such man.

Ten: That's curious, he must have known you. He knew all about you.

Orso: Then by your reasoning, my lords, he must be the one in his star who knows all about the Third City's internal arrangements.

Ten: He did, Fra Orso, he did. He does no more.

[*Cuts . . . Later the same day*]

Orso: As you say, my lords, I have blackened my soul with all sorts of sins. And you ask, then how can I hope for salvation? I can only hope in the force of contrition. The early Church recognised public confession only, and this inflicts searing shame and humiliation. But we have only the private sort. For us, therefore, true contrition has to be painful. It has to be a violent beating of the dirty wool, or it's no good.

Mask IV: The only thing you're going to be contrite about is having been lofty with us.

Ten: Let the friar speak.

Orso: But contrition is hard, except for poor folk, who have not had the sweet time to develop the round and refined sins of the rich and powerful.

Mask II: Gentlemen, I beg you, stop his tongue now. How much longer are we going to suffer this insolent sermon? And anyway, what a stupid claim! Has the friar never heard of the hardened criminals who come from among his beloved poor folk in the inferior city?

[*Deletions*]

Ten: A Dominican? You are riddled with heresy! When you say that God is as near to you as your own veins, and suggest that He is in you in fact and nearly so in substance, not only in spirit, your doctrine is – every man his own God! Pagan! Philosopher and master theologian! You ought to know better than that and you deserve to be burned alive for such doctrine, so be happy with our promise of an instant death on a bed of pikes.

You were saying about the desert . . .? What are you waiting for? Speak up.

Orso: My lords, I can't go on.

Ten: In Christ's name, friar, though you insult the name of Christ, we are indulging you, indulging you! And listening to all your rot. So carry on now.

Orso: . . . My lords, the desert was the final home of the old pagan gods and demons. The demons now are in ourselves. I was sent into the desert to purge myself of them. There is nothing more to fear now. There is only the Cross.

Ten: Yes, the Cross and the Council of Ten.

Orso: I fear Christ but not the Ten.

Ten: Yet you know that we can inflict infernal pain on you.

Orso: You can indeed, my lords . . . But even the Ten must draw up last wills and testaments.

[*The clerks recorded 'murmuring' in the chamber*]

Ten: Listen, Fra Orso, take this promise to be a contract. Before you embrace the pikes, you're going to pay dearly for your insolent tongue.

Orso: My lords, please take off your masks and let me see your brave faces.

[*The clerks recorded 'gasps' and 'anger' in the chamber*]

Ten: Guards, take the prisoner out of here and have Doctor Bortolo blind him. We want the eyes pierced. Wait . . . One of our colleagues will certainly demand a vote, so let's have it. We call for his blinding now.

RESULT: 5 in favour. 5 opposed.

Resolution: the ducal advisors voted against Fra Orso's blinding at this time.

Mask V: In God's name, why do we go on coddling this murderous priest? He wants us all dead. He seeks the destruction of this city. He deserves torture and the fires of hell now!

Ten: Silence, councillor! You heard the result of the vote. Let us keep to the rules.

Mask I: My lords, please. Please give me a minute or two. Before we resume the cross-examination, allow me to address a few words to the prisoner. I will of course avoid all your questions and line of inquiry . . .

Fra Orso, hear me now. Forget my visage. Listen to the voice, listen to it. You are caught up in a delirium of pride and folly. Calm down. Pull yourself together. For your own good – if you know your own good – take my advice. Put aside your antics. There is more on the anvil here than your life and dignity. You believe, don't you, that every man in this chamber is evil. Does it follow that you alone are good here? Are you without sin? We are performing the tasks of office, and some of us – although you surely don't deserve it – some of us are trying to make things a little less grievous for you. Have we not just kept you from being blinded, and have we not already saved you today, three times as it happens, from the hammers and pincers? Well, but we cannot go on this way. Take heed. You seem determined to have yourself skinned before you die. What is it you seek, the pride and prize of martyrdom?

Try to be reasonable. In you, yes in you, we are looking at a mortal enemy. You know this and you know it well. You know that your conspiracy sweeps aside our authority and cuts to the very innards of what we, the Venetian nobility, are. What you don't know . . . what you do not know is that there are other men present here who also deplore the condition of parts of lower Venice and who would like to see . . .

Mask II: My lords, no, no, no, no! We cannot have this! It's a disgrace. Our esteemed colleague – and how dare he! – is offering public comfort to a man who has earned our horror and hatred and deserves the fires of hell not tonight or tomorrow but now, today, this very instant. Nor is it our custom in the Ten – let me remind us all – to flourish our disagreements in front of others, least of all, good God, in the face of our capital enemies . . .

Ten: The gentleman is quite right, of course. Guards, take the prisoner out, but stand by.

[*When Fra Orso was taken out, masks were removed and the debate continued*]

Mask I. Andrea Dandolo: My lords, since the friar faces execution, nothing I said in his presence will be of any consequence. I was saying it to draw him out, to move him into talking more freely. As I said in the earlier course of the interrogation, his proud manner be damned! His facts, his secrets, this is what counts and what we must have at all costs, with the help of torture as well, to be sure. But we want him clear-headed and cooperative. Clear-headed, and so we ourselves should also be composed. Which is why I recommend that we exhaust all moderate means first. The use of torture is, remember, under the rule of law, a medium of last resort.

Every man in this chamber knows about the foul conditions of the under city's inner parts. Yes? But we prefer not to bend our minds that way because the prospect is too grim. Fra Orso is forcing us to bend. Without those conditions – and we do all know this – there would be no Third City, no plots, no insidious friars. And therefore I argue that we should strive to understand our enemies, not just execute them so as to remove their bodies from the scene, in the mad hope that this will trick the sun into shining on lower Venice.

Mask II. Pietro Mocenigo: My lords, what a fine speech that
was – I almost said sermon – and done with a fine touch of
human kindness. But I cannot help feeling that it both coddles
the enemy and has no earthly use. There's nothing practical in
it. We the Ten are not here for theories and kindness. We are
practical men. That's our job. We face an immediate mortal
threat. We have armed enemies on the mainland too. The health
and well-being of the lower city do not belong to the concerns
of the Ten. Not for an instant! We leave these matters to the
Senate and Grand Council. Our office, our only office, is to
safeguard the state: to foil conspiracy, to squash dissent, to punish
all crime against public order. We are – yes we are – soldiers,
spies, guardsmen, prosecutors, harsh judges, hangmen and
keepers of the peace. We are not philosophers. We are not sisters
of mercy. This renegade priest is a demon and more cunning
than any of us. Make no mistake about this. So we do not
want him with a clear head – we want him terrified – and
nor can we trick or seduce or coax him into talking. Trickery
is *his* vocation. He will only talk with the help of our hammers
and tongs. He has led us around by the nose. He has waded
around in his mystic bilge for the better part of two hours,
and we still know almost nothing about the plans and leaders
of the sect.

Mask III. Bartolomeo Gradenigo: My lords, allow me please.
On the contrary, we know a great deal. We have the names
of thirty-five noblemen, merchants, clerics, lawyers, a *condot-
tiere*, and several patricians from the mainland. We have also
had more particulars about the procedures of the Third City
from this friar – even if we have had no names – than from
any other prisoner. The Franciscan, that first friar, Dolfin
Falier, blabbed endlessly but contradicted himself at every step
along the way. I wanted to slap his face and shake him up.

Fra Orso is young, perhaps too young, but Mocenigo has called him a clever demon. Why has it not occurred to us that he himself may be the Third City's ruling intelligence? [. . . *There was murmuring and much movement in the chamber*] If so, here is the more reason to delay the use of irons and fire. As Dandolo says, there may be more to be got out of this man by measured means.

Mocenigo is perfectly right to insist that we are the arms and teeth, not the reformers, of this Serene Republic. All the same, let us not forget that we are also counsellors to the Senate, and the truth is that we carry enormous weight there. In the next day or two, I shall recommend that we urge the whole body of senators to take up the question of holding consultations on the ills of the lower city.

Mask IV. Andrea Barbarigo: My lords, please. We have come to a point, I believe, where a compromise is necessary and possible. Let me point the way.

Forgive my repeating it, but I must say again that we have been shamefully reluctant as yet to question the prisoner about his relations with Lady Loredana Contarini. Every man here knows why. Now, my lords, you know that I am not one to mince words. So, are we to go on putting private interests and fears above the common good? Have we forgotten that we are the Ten? In the present circumstances, we have the pressing obligation to get to the core of this bloody conspiracy. Fra Orso's link with Lady Loredana is a point of inflamma-tion — for him, I mean. Therefore, if we now fix the eye of our investigation on that link, I have no doubt that more facts and details will come tumbling out.

[*Deletions*]

Ten: Fra Orso Veneto, when and where did you first meet Lady Loredana Loredan Contarini?

Orso: My lords, I met the lady last April when I was called to attend her sister, who was very ill. My office was to pray with the dying woman, to try to comfort her.

Ten: Since most of your engagements are in lower Venice, who summoned you to the Loredan house?

Orso: The summons came through my convent. I was told we had an obligation there, but I cannot say that the call was meant for me or anyone in particular.

Ten: How often did you go to the house and for how long?

Orso: I went almost every day over a span of some three weeks, until the lady died. I would spend a half-hour or so with her.

Ten: With whom?

Orso: With the dying woman, of course, Mistress Quirina.

Ten: Not with Lady Loredana of course . . . but what relations had you with this lady, the younger sister?

Orso: She was usually at the house. She or the servants would open the door to me and then see me out.

Ten: We asked about relations, friar, not about who let you in and out of doors.

Orso: My lords, I became an acquaintance of the lady. We exchanged words almost daily about Mistress Quirina's condition.

Mask II: Did he ever see the Procurator at the house, Sier Antonio?

Ten: Well, prisoner?

Orso: Yes, my lords, I saw him four or five times, and heard his voice on several other occasions.

Mask II: Did the Procurator ever give him any instructions?

Orso: None, my lords. He spoke to me only once, to thank me for my services.

Ten: What happened after Mistress Quirina died? Did you go on, by any chance, seeing Lady Loredana? . . . Did you hear the question?

Orso: Yes, my lords. I became Lady Loredana's confessor. She came to see me at San Domenico di Castello.

Ten: Her confessor? That was quite a change on the lady's part, wasn't it? What made her give up her previous confessor and turn to you?

Orso: Having seen me attend her sister, I suppose she had some faith in my moral guidance and felt that she could talk to me.

Ten: What delicate matters, eh, Fra Orso? Conscience is a prickly business, isn't it? And tell us, after Mistress Quirina's death, how often did Lady Loredana come to you . . . to confess?

Orso: Reasonably often, I would say, even several times a week.

Ten: Let us jog your memory a bit, Sir Friar. Wasn't it more like every day?

Orso: Yes, my lords, but never for more than a few minutes. I had too many other obligations.

Ten: Come now, a few minutes of daily confession? Isn't that so unusual as to be downright – what shall we say – bizarre?

Orso: There are always the exceptional cases.

Ten: You have an answer for everything, don't you? Then give us an answer to this question. Is it common to scratch at insignificant sins every day? Is it? And in the case of such an esteemed lady, what little sins could there have been for her to scratch at and confess so often?

Orso: My lords, you know that I am not allowed to break the seal of confession.

Ten: Nor are you allowed to break other seals and get into places where you don't belong, and yet you do. Listen, Fra Orso, as you may well imagine, we have made our inquiries, we have counted things up, and this is what we throw in your face. One, confession is not an everyday affair. Two, what were those intense, daily conversations about, if not about sin and illicit endearments? Three, if you and Lady Loredana were mere confessor and penitent, what were you doing in her bed out at the Villa Castelfranco? Four, were you not also hiding from us out there, under her warm protection? Five, was her flight from Venice, three days earlier, an act of mere benevolence for you or the wild action of a lover? And six, why did she first plead for your innocence, knowing nothing about it, then turn right around and plead to be arrested with you? There is only one answer to all these questions. You and your widow were carnal lovers. You were plunged in sin, Saint Orso.

Orso: No, we were not lovers. She's wholly honourable. We were friends, we . . .

Ten: Friends you say? What, and kindred spirits? Unholy priest, hold your tongue. Don't befoul your soul with more lies. How can a young friar and a handsome widow, a noblewoman to boot, be friends? That's a thing unheard of. And not only friends but sly, passionate, secret friends both in town and country? Lecherous sinners and lovers, Saint Orso, a beast with two backs, that's what you were, not friends. There's a flaming difference, and we need no buggering philosophy to draw the distinction. The stream of lies in this part of your testimony runs right through the whole of what you have said here today, so we should have your lying tongue ripped out, and I would put this to a vote now, but for one thing. We need that tongue of yours to go on spitting out words until we have you impaled.

But let us hear you do some honest talking for a change. We want to know what you said to Lady Loredana about the Third City over the long period of your relations with her.

Orso: Nothing!

45. [Vendramin, DIARY]:

iv October [1529]. I rush around for news. Renew old ties. I even talk to men I don't like. Result, I have almost no time for this diary, damn it. But my sons will like having it. My father left a diary for me. One missed day leaves a gap, so I force myself.

Our friends in the Ten could not quash that shameful business, the flesh eternal. I mean the friar's relations with my cousin Loredana. Oh the whore. Fra Orso was cornered by the chief inquisitor. The carnal tangle between those two passes all belief. A curse on it all and on them! The friar is young and handsome but she's nearly forty. Where have I seen her in recent years? Mostly in church or moving past people in the streets. Always half-veiled, and in black as befits a widow. I saw a strong walk. And I saw the eyes, ever-wonderful. Still, after all these years, could she have been inflamed again? Age is supposed to snuff it out in women. Anyhow, what did he see in her? But of course widows are notorious. First they've had it, then the husband dies and they must do without it. Except that Loredana didn't get it from madonna Marco. She got it from others they say. I've tortured my wits about it. Where could she and the friar have met to slake their passion? In a church? How? In Antonio's house? Too dangerous. Out at Castelfranco? Possible but still dangerous and too close to scandal. All those inquisitive eyes in neighbouring villas. Then where? In the lower city? Good Lord, did Loredana steal out alone? How could she even dare? My friend Livio says that love is a malady, desire is crafty, and lovers are ingenious. The friar was also her confessor. What an unholy, messy, murky business. I see why so many priests have a reputation for lechery.

I am gossiping like an old crone, but cousin Loredana's beastly carnality touches us all. It dishonours her father, uncles and even the Contarinis. Then add the shame and treachery of Fra Orso's conspiracy. He will be executed, making the scandal worse. She lay with a traitor, it will be said. She opened her legs to a common bastard and friar. And who knows what else she did? No wonder we keep a keen eye on women. All it takes is being once caught in an act of lechery. The dishonour spatters everyone around, like dung. Three years ago it was the wife of Marcantonio Zorzi, that painted strumpet Veronica Trevisan. Got herself convicted of adultery and exiled for five years. He wanted her back, the buffoon. And wept for her in public! If she'd had a bastard, would he have taken it in as his own? People have always said he loved her. Yes and dearly did he pay for that. The next time he came up for a place in the Senate, check! Try as he might, he couldn't get the votes in council. Little boys hooted at him in the streets. And men laughed behind his back. An honourable man has no business loving his wife. Not that way. It makes her disobedient.

iv [*October*]. Much later. Alberto [*Giustiniani*] was present at Fra Orso's interrogation. And has just given me a description. He was shaken. Yesterday the friar was remarkable. An unusual spirit. He stood straight, a mane of dark hair over his wide forehead despite the tonsure. Brooding or fierce eyes – they seemed to change. Strong bones. A sharp Florentine diction. And all the while he brought in a stream of Venetian words and phrases. After a little he was made to kneel down but seemed unafraid. The stream of words continued.

Then, in the watches of the night, he was broken. This morning he was blind, his eyes punctured. Each was a reddish egg. His face, all streaked with blood. Hair had been torn from his head. His hands were bloody, also his lips. Some of his teeth had been knocked out. His shirt was in tatters. He couldn't walk. They carried him on a stretcher. His ankles were disjoined. In frightful pain, he could not make sense of questions. His execution is delayed because the Ten think he has more secrets. Two doctors were called in to ease the pain, to help get him to talk. They used ointments and special waters on his swollen limbs. One of the Ten conducting the inquiry leaned into his face to taunt him with an insult. The unheard of happened. Fra Orso spat into his white mask, spattering it with blood. Gasps sounded through the chamber. A guardsman slapped his face but was immediately stopped. The Ten want no further injury done to him. Of all the conspirators he has provided the best account of the plot, yet he gives no names.

v October. I got hold of Alberto. Again he treated me to a description. I noted down his words. Late last night there was bitter disagreement in the Ten. They shouted at each other. Insults were hurled, threats made. The Doge himself bellowed at one point. Bernardo [*Loredan*] was the only quiet one.

This morning's session opened with a hint of the quarrel. Some of them see Fra Orso's case as a matter of simple revenge through pain. Anger blinds them. They demanded that he again be tortured, then quickly thrown to the pikes. Others instead wanted him questioned at length. The first insisted that they had suffered too much insolence. The others replied that too many of the conspirators are still free. That the Ten have the bounden duty to listen to Fra Orso, to learn as much as possible.

At nones today the Ten again tried to make him talk. His groans filled the chamber. To pull him through the pain they gave him a dose of opium. Instead of calming him, at first it plucked him up. Maybe it wasn't opium. To everyone's astonishment he started to make an incoherent speech. Out came remarks about cowards, pagans and beasts of the upper city. About illegitimate children. About how the Ten should tear off their craven masks. About how every one of them would have to render an account to God. The Ten were curious and listened. He burbled something about their pagan prayers having the value of cow dung. No true contrition, he kept saying, so they could not but end in the lower city of hell. His lips foamed with blood. His punctured eyes seemed to get redder. His fingers seemed to claw at himself. Alberto saw one of the Ten cross himself. They let Fra Orso babble on. Someone laughingly said that he had bought his moonstruck ideas from a pedlar in the Damascus bazaar.

v Oct. Later. Fra Orso is still gibbering. The Ten think his reason impaired. He made a vigorous effort to sit up in his pallet but fell back again. Three members of the Ten and four ducal councillors curse the extent of his injuries. They say the lack of fresh facts is delaying the investigation. And they strain to make out the friar's laboured words. Today he half-muttered that the conspiracy was in the bellies of the down-at-heel nobility. A curious remark. Then crazily shouting it out, he claimed that his mother was bought with squalid ducats. No one knows the meaning of that.

46. [Bernardo Loredan to Pandolfo, in code, LETTER]:
Pandolfo.
Let this warning suffice. To be rash was never our way. If you make the least move, I expose the lot of you and die. He must

go to the pikes. Not with a hundred or a thousand men could you rescue him. Have you said adieu to your reason? Conceal yourselves in the lower city? How then would you get out of Venice? Every one of you would be butchered. In God's name, listen. The friar is blind, out of his wits, and will never walk again. What would you be rescuing? A sack of miserable flesh. The best of him is already in flight and no longer belongs to us. He belongs to God. Embrace your men and pray for a new day. Bern.

47. [Council of Ten, PROCEEDINGS]:
  Interim report on the Third-City Conspiracy [*selections*]
  7 October. Anno domini nostri 1529.
  Over the course of the past three weeks, we have unmasked and undone a conspiratorial sect, hellishly constituted and coyly known as the Third City. There is reason to think that it was first spawned about a dozen years ago. Its origins are obscure . . .
  The purpose of the sect, a secret confraternity, was to demolish the upper city and bring all residents, Venetians as well as foreigners, down to the same ground level. To achieve this end, they were ready to massacre the nobility. They claimed that in taking the sunlight from the under city, we violate the laws of God and nature. Of God because light is a sign of His presence. Of nature for two reasons: because all animals on the earth's surface [*etc.*] . . .
  We say that there are natural and inevitable divisions in peoples and cities: male and female, old and young, rich and poor, lords and servants, rulers and subjects, intelligent and stupid . . . Wherefore our ancestors built a second city [*etc.*] . . . However, the layout of the lower city is such that all its people are free to walk out to the sunny perimeters or to their several open squares.

The plan of the conspirators was to incite disturbances in our mainland cities, to have our soldiers rushed out and engaged there, to seize and murder [*etc.*] . . .

The conspirators claimed that the Third City began as a mystical religious sect . . . That claim was a poisoned hook in their web of intrigue. Their sole reason for being was to eliminate the upper city by means of cannons and prayer, and prayer was a pretext . . . Controlled by a shadowy council at the centre of a spiderweb of grouplets, all decisions were routed through a single man in each group . . . every member carried an instant poison, to be swallowed at the moment of his arrest . . . a few of them were in holy orders. They were a clumsy, ill-constituted lot, but enigmatic at the centre and top, hence exceedingly dangerous . . . The principal conspirator, Fra Orso Veneto, was executed this morning.

A complete report will be drafted tomorrow.

48. [Vendramin, DIARY]:

vii October. Fra Orso Veneto, conspirator. Impaled at sunrise. The Ten departed from custom. Yesterday two heralds went up the Grand Canal and coursed through the lower and upper cities. We were surprised. Trumpet blasts sounded their stops along the way. They announced that an arch traitor was to be impaled at dawn today. Fra Orso. I was there. The execution of a Dominican is not seen every day. Besides, I could not rid myself of this inner picture. The sight of Loredana's religious copulation with him, and I don't know why I write religious. So I was up before daybreak and betook myself to the platform. Only about two hundred witnesses were allowed to get close. I counted them: seven members of the Ten, three ducal councillors, two procurators, many senators, as well as Contarinis, Loredans, Morosinis, and men from the Mocenigo,

Dandolo, Grimani, Barbarigo, Pesaro, Venier, Giustiniani and Pisani families. A crowd of gawking, minor noblemen also stood by.

Fra Orso arrived in a cart drawn by two black horses. The sun was breaking. Distant bells pealed. No one spoke. Nobody shouted insults. He was not hooded, having been blinded three days before. His eyes were patches of black blood. This was his hood. His face had been washed. There was still some rich straggly hair around his tonsure. His hands were tied together in prayer. His battered lips moved. He knew what was happening. I saw five or six men cross themselves. Two of them, wearing masks, kneeled. A rag-tag gentleman spat in the friar's direction, an ugly action somehow that, but Alvise Venier rebuked the idiot. I confess I felt a moment of sorrow for Fra Orso, though he had wanted to murder us. Even in his broken state I could see that he had been a fine-looking man. An illegitimate bastard, but still learned and a good speaker, I was told. They also say that at nineteen he taught philosophy at Bologna. What then befell him? The gullible, and there are many, believe he was seduced by the devil.

The impalement. Fra Orso's shattered legs were loosely bound. The executioner and his assistant, two brawny men, took him up. He did not resist. They carried him to the edge of the balustered platform. I was standing close by. His sounds rose in prayer. I pressed in to listen. His last words were astonishing. I record them here. Perhaps he had prayed enough. As the executioners lifted him up above their heads to hurl him down on the piked stage, unbelief came over me. Was I the only one who heard him? He was intoning a barely audible chant. Repeating a name: Lo-re-daa-na, Lo-re-daa-na. I fixed my eyes on him as he plummeted down and down. There was a nasty crunch and an eruption of cries. Still looking down, I saw a crowd of underlings collected around the railing. They were staring at the impaled body and looking up at us. I heard his name called out. A murmuring of muted cries and prayers floated up. Scattered fists, brazen, were raised up high. Some of us drew away and took the nearest stairway down to the lower city and its sombre stage. For a minute I gazed at the horrid sight, a grotesque silence. The legs had snapped their bindings. How contorted our bodies can be. And so strange the face. I think hell will have no new inventions for us. Guardsmen dispersed the crowd of underlings. Too many of them kept mouthing Fra Orso's name. They had known him. This was clear. They said he had worked among them, among the poor. A few were not afraid to come and tell us that they knew nothing about his doings in upper Venice. In the lower city he had been a man most gentle and kind. This made me very cross, but I said nothing. Alberto Giustiniani turned on them in a fury. Fra Orso had been a criminal of the bloodiest stripe, he told them. And the head of a pack of outlaws who plotted to murder all the city's best men. They listened grudgingly and muttered as they drew away. I could see that they didn't believe Alberto. Or didn't care.

Later the same day. The Ten were forced to post guards near Fra Orso's body. Despite all the blood there and bone fragments, underlings wanted to touch the corpse. Dig their hands into it. Explain that! Worse still, several had the impudence to declare that they wanted a piece of his frock. A few said they would like some hair or another part of him. This pricked others on and they began to call him a saint. A saint! Such is the bovine faith and ignorance of the common people. The Ten had to send out soldiers. The bawling crowd was finally broken up. Guardsmen remain there.

I forgot to say. Fra Orso fell to his death in a new Dominican frock. The fresh black and white stood out. This was the Ten's doing. They chose to flaunt the colours of the Order. And there was reason for this. They want to teach those cowardly two-faced friars a lesson. The Dominicans have done all they can to put a great distance between themselves and Fra Orso. Of course. Yet they refused to answer the questions put to them by the Ten. For this they blamed Rome. Then they had the face to assert that they alone were fit to judge the treacherous friar. Are these the intellects of the Church? Heaven help us.

49. [Council of Ten, PROCEEDINGS]:

9 October. Anno domini nostri 1529.

WARNING. For our successors in office.

Magnifici domini observandissimi, looking ahead to the next few years, we are here forwarding a prudent notice.

There are the beginings of a schism in the nobility. The division gathers around the claims of the Third City and the figure of Fra Orso. Who does not know that cities and empires often reach a summit and then decline? That we live in the streaming waters of time? What happened to the Persians, Athens, Alexander and Rome? Are not the Jews scattered to the four winds? Where is Hannibal now, and what of Tamberlane? Our forefathers built upper Venice in triumph. We were the Queen of the Mediterranean: our fleets went everywhere; the East held no fears for us; and our sailors, workers and tradesmen did as we commanded. Has all this changed?

Some of our noble peers contend that the present age has whipped up new and extraordinary needs. They point to the flood of heresy in Germany, to the Sack of Rome [1527], and to the barbarous foreign armies ensconced in the body of Italy.

Granted, we are facing a time of novelty. Nevertheless, we want to remind these gentlemen, contrary to their allegations, that the Ten are their best peace and comfort. If it be true that the dark core of our under city is little better than a reeking cistern and a hell on earth, then we should most assuredly begin to consider changes there. Careful inquiry will be necessary. Our heads of state will need to develop a practical policy. Let us not, however, get carried away. Nothing can be done overnight; and any changes, if approved, will require many years, much courage, and more wealth, far more, than is now in our coffers. But all such thinking and planning – mark this well – must proceed from the Doge, the Senate and the Grand Council. That is Venetian law. Since when has reform ever been the business of the Council of Ten?

Secretly, our critics among the nobility accuse us of ignorance, cruelty and a fanatical devotion to decrepit ideas. Have they eyes? Can they not see that the first charge of every government is to maintain the civil order and to protect the life and property of its citizens? Is this not what the Council of Ten is all about? The Third City had knives at our throats and armed men abroad. The danger continues. Hence our current, overwhelming need remains the same: to disarm and execute the would-be assassins still hiding in the dark. And this would be the worst of all possible times to hesitate, or to seem eager and ready to engage in a debate over our rights as noblemen. What an idea! In the present circumstances, only a traitor or a fool would seek negotiation.

50. [Falier, SECRET CHRONICLE]:

Two days after Fra Orso was impaled, the Loredans were again the beating heart of gossip in the city, in a story concerning their lady of carnal fame. The facts are these.

On 9 October 1529, in the watches of the night, Lady Loredana escaped from the convent to which she had been confined by the Council of Ten and ran through the upper and lower cities. First she was espied near the ghastly platform, far above the pikes, where she appeared to want to throw herself down on top of the punctured body of her dead lover. What manner of loving congress would that have been? Then she found her way down to the corpse and somehow got at it. She was seeking frantically to free it from the pikes but was arrested by a special unit of guardsmen. They reported that she seemed possessed. When I spoke to their captain in confidence, he told me that she had offered so much resistance that they were compelled to use force, in the course of which her legs were exposed. The sight so aroused two Romagnol soldiers that he had to defend her *armata manu* from a carnal assault. Later on, the two broke out into a song about her comely backside. They were fortunate to have gone no further, for the Loredans and the Council of Ten would have demanded their heads. Mad she may be, but she is still a Loredan.

Afterwards, under sustained questioning, she told the Ten – quietly but insanely – that she had been secretly married to her Dominican friar and wished to die with him. She asked to be hurled down on the very pikes poking through his remains. Everyone present was aghast as they looked upon that ruined woman with her flicking hands and unlooking eyes.

[*Deletions*] . . .

I ought to love Lady Loredana Contarini for helping me to wreak my vengeance on the Loredans. Her lower orifice belongs, as a new device, on their proud coat of arms. Let them brandish that around.

51. [Vendramin, DIARY]:

ix October. Bugger this cursed diary! Yet another shaming incident.

Cousin Loredana broke out of her nunnery last night. No one knows how. Her part of the convent is always locked. High walls, with a drop of fourteen feet, enclose it. The great outer door was barred. Yet she got out, clad in an unfamiliar cloak. Her escape required careful outside help. It could only have been the work of our enemies. Anyway, once out she stole down to the lower city. That was easy enough. But then she got as far as the piked dais and Fra Orso's body. The guards heard and saw nothing. Suddenly she darted out between them. Next, got up to the pikes and began leaping up to grab at a lifeless hand and tatters of cloth. What she got was caked blood all over herself. The guards had trouble subduing her so gave the alarm. They also smeared themselves with drying blood. She was in a crazed state. A detachment of soldiers soon arrived at the scene to arrest her. She was not concealing her identity. On the contrary. So they got word at once to the three heads of the Ten. In the space of just over an hour the full council was assembled. Loredana calmed down. They questioned her. She insisted that she was Fra Orso's wife, that they had been secretly married. This entitled her to collect his body for burial. The Ten reminded her that the friar's vows put him for ever outside the possibility of marriage. No she replied. The love of God could break any vow and allow such a marriage. Curiously, one of the ducal councillors said there were precedents for her claim. The Ten ignored this remark. Loredana's madness was only too visible. But she clung to her argument. If they would not release Orso's body to her (Orso is what she said), they ought then to impale her too. And let it be alongside his corpse.

For she was an accomplice. She had hidden him from the Ten. Being one flesh with him, she even had a part in his crimes – obviously a demented claim. She ended by saying, the more I think about his poor body out there, still on the pikes, the more I want to die there, I belong beside him.

Loredana had made a speech. Astoundingly. I can't believe it. The facts however I have from Jacopo [*Loredan, one of Bernardo's sons, thus a first cousin to Loredana*]. He was there with a special summons as an observer. Bernardo is still a wall of silence. He has to be, in view of the scandal. Yet he manages to hold on to his place in the Ten. Miraculously.

Jacopo had other particulars. There was blood on her cloak, face and hands. She was smeared with it. When talking, she never hesitated. The words streamed from her mouth. Her hood at one point fell with a sudden shake of her head. Whereupon the abundant hair billowed forth. Another sign of her insanity. In public our women always cover their heads and keep the hair well bound up. Her tears flowed continually. And her eyes – these were fixed, Jacopo said, on the table in front of the Ten. She never looked at them. A hand jerked about now and again. Her face moved and worked with a troubled spirit. Jacopo was horrified. Then what must Bernardo have felt? How could he bear the shame?

She was taken back to her convent this morning. With only three dissenting votes, the Ten ruled that they could not hold her criminally responsible. She is after all mad. Bernardo did not vote.

I wonder, was there a stray meaning in her outburst about a secret marriage? Had she got so close to that young friar as to feel a queer bond? Priests do sometimes run away with women. Run away and are never seen again. Venice has a few fathers and husbands who could say bitter things about this. Merchants report that priests from Italy live in the lands of the Saracens. The renegades keep concubines and call them wives.

Antonio [*Loredana's father*] pins her escape to a Franciscan friar. The evidence rests on circumstance. But others accuse our bitter enemies in the Senate. Being a prisoner in the convent, how did she learn of Fra Orso's impalement? Through spirits? Yes, the spirits of those who hate us. Antonio verged on denouncing her Franciscan confessor to the Ten, then held back. That would only fire up the scandal. So now he will himself face the rogue. And Loredana is to have a different confessor. The whole Loredan clan chokes with the shame of her demented actions.

Antonio is going to retire from public life. Our ancient enemies gloat. My own rise in office will now be slow or even held back. The wisdom of the old proverb comes back to haunt us: women, vice and luxury are the ruin of great families. But luckily, most of our first houses toil to conceal one horror or another.

NOTE. *Throughout Europe in the early sixteenth century, Church and state assumed that blood ties between first cousins were too close for marriage. Hence any such bond was seen as illegal and immoral on grounds of incest.*

52. [Council of Ten, PROCEEDINGS]:

29 October. Anno domini nostri 1529.

Ten: My lords and colleagues. We have just spent the night in an extraordinary session and summon you here this morning, because we have grave findings and a dolorous sentence to advertise.

We return to the accursed case of the Dominican friar, Orso Veneto, the clandestine head of the conspiracy [*sic*] . . .

You will remember that we were perplexed by his claim to be both a Venetian and the illegitimate son of a gentleman from the upper city. We greatly doubted this at the time, not only because of his treachery but also because we could find no trace of his birth in these parts . . . He also claimed to benefit from a Venetian trust . . . On this matter too we could find nothing in Venice . . . When we applied to the Dominicans for assistance, they replied with their customary arrogance . . .

Yet this republic has its resources and external friends, owing to which we can now shed light on the mystery in question – we might almost say too much light, for the finding is cruel . . . It touches people of such weight among us that we must shield the identity of our original inform- ants and seek to keep the finding as confidential as is humanly possible. We therefore issue the first warning now. Any man here present who, after leaving these chambers today, dares to speak of the particulars that we are about to divulge concerning the late Fra Orso, or his father, incurs a fine ipso facto of 750 ducats for the first offence. The penalty for the second offence will be . . . exile.

Fra Orso was born in Venice, in the upper city, on the 22nd day of June, 1501, and spent his infant years in a hamlet near Castelfranco. He was baptised in the lower city, in the parish of San Martino, but the name given him was Bernardo Brenta. This explains why we could not find him in Venetian parish registers: we had the wrong name. His mother, Maria Brenta, came from the village of Rana. She was a servant in the house of Bernardo di Francesco Loredan, and died two days after giving birth to a son who would later be known as Orso. She was thirteen or fourteen years of age at the time. Bernardo Loredan, our friend and trusted colleague in office, was the father of Bernardo Brenta, id est Fra Orso Veneto. The infant's name was changed almost at once in actual usage and later legally confirmed in Florence. When the boy was sent to that city at the age of six, Bernardo established a trust for him in the name of Orso Veneto, to be fully and freely administered by his friend, Vittore Maffei, one of our distinguished secretaries, as you all know. The baptismal name, the new name and the details of the trust all appear in the acts (xiii, 4) of the Florentine notary Ser Lando di Ser Lando Landi, for the years 1505-1509. The Roman writ of Fra Orso's legitimation also carries the two names. We have transcripts of all these papers, but we also have more: namely, the testimony of Bernardo Loredan, whom we arrested late yesterday and questioned during the night. There are clearly, now, some disturbing questions about this case.

Bernardo has told us that an aversion to gossip and the possibility of future challenges to the boy's estate moved him, twenty-eight years ago, to change the infant's name soon after his birth. Nor, for family reasons, did he wish the youth to know anything about his parents . . . A few generalities reached Fra Orso regarding his parentage, but he died knowing nothing about his baptismal name and nothing, really, about his mother and father.

After Bernardo resolved that the youth should take holy orders, he relinquished all other decisions to Vittore Maffei, and while having no strong objections to Fra Orso's ultimate residence in Venice, his first desire was that the friar live abroad. Bernardo knew nothing of the man's presence in Venice until his catastrophic circumstances came to light. There had never been any contact between father and son, for after Fra Orso's mother died, Bernardo vowed never to set eyes on the infant again. God and *fortuna* now administered their punishment by forcing him to look upon the visage of the grown man.

When Bernardo's niece, Mistress Quirina, lay dying and Fra Orso was called to minister to her spiritual needs, who made that summons? Bernardo could throw no light on this question, and nor could his brother, the illustrious Sier Antonio, for whom the friar was simply another Dominican . . . behind the summons there seems to have been some hint about a link between Fra Orso and the Loredans. Yet who knew this, apart from Bernardo and his trustee, Vittore Maffei? Having dispatched Fra Orso to the assistance of Mistress Quirina, the friars at San Domenico di Castello could tell us something, but they remain silent . . .

We considered the friar's claim that his evil cohorts in the Third City knew about his Venetian birth and noble blood. Our judgment is that he was lying about this, to enhance the mystery around himself. But if any truth attached to the claim, we have yet to discover how the early rectors of the Third City could be privy to facts that we ourselves were able to ascertain only after painstaking inquiry. The circumstantial particulars point to someone with access to papers in the possession of Bernardo and his appointed trustee, Maffei. Can we say, therefore, that these two men must be seen as suspects? That they themselves may be participants in the demonic Third City? And that they connived to send Fra Orso on an unholy trip to the Holy Land, with an eye to preparing his conscience for butchery? God forbid! For then none of us could be above suspicion, and we should have to fear the presence now of murderous enemies in these very chambers. We might as well stop sleeping at night and arm ourselves against our dearest friends and relatives.

We come to the most grievous part of today's business: the arrest of our own colleague, Bernardo di Francesco Loredan. The name and treason of Fra Orso Veneto first came to the attention of the Ten six weeks ago. None of us remembers Bernardo's face on his learning, as by a stroke of lightning, that his natural son was in Venice and at the heart of the conspiracy. At the time, there was no earthly reason for us to store away such a memory. He has however reminded us that a sharp illness, produced by the sudden knowledge, drove him out of these chambers within the hour. In the event, the days passed and he clung darkly to his secret. He was present at all our cross-examinations. He heard us pointedly inquire into the friar's birthplace and saw that we were determined to track it down. Our plain purpose was to deepen our understanding of the plot against the republic. But Bernardo did not come to us, nor to the defence of Venice, with the needed facts. Instead, as he confessed a few hours ago, overwhelmed by Fra Orso's deeds and the infamy of his incestuous bond with Lady Loredana, nothing could make him let go of his terrible secret, and he prayed that it should for ever go undiscovered ... We are therefore banishing Bernardo Loredan to the island of Corfu for five years. Since he has already reached his sixty-eighth year, this is a heavy sentence. The rich trust established for Fra Orso is naturally herewith confiscated.

You shall want to know what we propose to do about Vittore Maffei, Bernardo's trustee. Our investigations proceed. We are looking into all Vittore's friends, acquaintances and personal ties, reaching back over the past fifteen years. His neighbours and servants, past and present, are being questioned. Nothing suspicious will escape our notice. But the task is proving to be difficult because, as some of you know, Maffei, who is seventy-six

years of age, had a crippling seizure last June. We have had him
thoroughly examined by three physicians. They find that he has
lost the faculty of speech and that the whole of his right side,
from cheek to toes, is completely immobile.

53. [Falier, SECRET CHRONICLE]:

The disgrace and exile of Bernardo Loredan has been
hushed up in a manner which verges on a crime of state
. . . the Loredans retain their authority; for blood ties,
patronage, marriages and ancient arrangements bind them
to the city's prepotent families; and oh the many cousins
with hands on the helm of this great republic! Few other
lineages could have survived such a sinister connection with
Fra Orso. Even if unknown to himself, Bernardo's money
underpinned the education, plans and criminal pilgrimage
of the most insidious traitor in the whole sweep of our
history. His niece was mounted for months by the traitor,
her own first cousin and his bastard son. Not satisfied with
all this, and though himself a member of the Ten amid their
struggle against high treason, he concealed fundamental
particulars from them for nearly seven weeks. Yet the same
Ten exiled him for five years to neighbouring Corfu, a ludi-
crous and scandalous sentence . . .

As a Falier who loves this earthly Venice more than is good
for his soul, I am duty-bound to speak out against the Council
of Ten and the other heads of the republic. In their efforts to
root out the Third City, they have been confronted by suicides,
well-timed deaths, an odd seizure and curious conduits of
knowledge. All this they have brushed aside because they are
afraid. They fear the bitter resentment of the poor part of the
nobility, the shadowy links between the two cities, and the
devious, mystical voice of men in holy orders.

54. [Bernardo Loredan to Antonio Loredan, LETTER]:

In the name of God.

Distinguished brother. Moments before I board ship for the island, when you and I embrace in the crowd of family and friends, I will put this letter into one of your sleeves. Once you read it, you will rush to burn it, and rightly so.

Dare I put down here the name of my unspeakable Fra Orso? Yes, I kept the secret from the Ten, from you, from everybody. Can you believe that it was anything but a cross? For seven weeks now, every minute of my waking day has been a panting nightmare – the sort in which you race, strangle, cower, hide, plummet fearfully, or die. You wake up in a soup of sweat, terrified, a mess, your heart galloping, and your eyes blind with tears. Only I do not wake up, Antonio, I am always there, choking, dying, running. So consider this letter a wonder of God. To pray does, after all, help. Besides, what else is there but prayer for a man like me?

Once my exile's boat is out in the deep and it is night, I pray that I will not rush out and throw myself into those waters to seek deliverance. I don't deserve such peace, even off the coasts of barbarous Dalmatia. On this account, I will ask the captain to tie me up at night. I cannot aim another blow of disgrace at the family. We seem a cursed generation.

Of all people you, Antonio, even better than I, know why I tore hands and nails to hold on to my secret: you, quite simply, the likely next doge, and us, the family, the Loredans. These were my reasons. Has it ever occurred to you that this is our true evil and blackest sin, the family? We serve the devil. For the sake of the Loredans we would make the sign of the fig at Jesus. Sometimes I loathe us, but the loathing never goes down deep enough, because I am polluted by us through and through.

By the time I knew that Orso was in Venice, it was all horror. He had been exposed and worse still, he and Loredana had taken flight. All the hideous doing had been done. Their arrest was only a matter of time – that voice of his. My confession then could only have thickened our cargo of disgrace and shame. Therefore I chewed and mashed and ate my secret. I would rather have eaten the devil's dung. Instead of which I made the most sensible and rational decision in the world: to be silent. I made it first in the slim hope (I confess it to you) that Orso might elude our guardsmen; and then, once he was caught, in the desperate expectation that his baptismal name and circumstances would never come to light.

From the moment Orso and his plight came to our attention in the Ten, I fell ill and quit the Palace to go home and hang myself. Why then did I hold back? Every time I went to do it, I heard Christ's voice. Convenient, you will say. Don't think that, Antonio. Christ is not convenient. And there was also another horrendous restraint. I had to wait for the outcome of the friar's misfortunes. I had to wait and see what would happen to him. I could not die in ignorance of that. Then came the story of his ties and incest with Loredana, and I was nailed to the proceedings. My Christ, those days. I could not sleep. Every sinew in my body erupted with pain. My eyes and ears took fire. Half the time I was drugged. Ask Doctor Padovan. This too, the sheer hellish pain, is why I held my tongue in Council, why I avoided people, why I would not see you, why I was not human. I was scraping the ground like a wounded dog. And can you imagine what I felt, when Orso came under our inquisition? When I saw that head of his, how could I desire anything but life for him? How could I not want him for the Loredans? How could I wish to see that body bloodied and punctured? It took every drop of my will's blood to keep me from screeching. To keep me from throwing myself on him like a crazed father. To keep me from shrieking out accusations against myself. I had loved that girl, Orso's mother, and I had blamed him for her death.

This has been my life for seven weeks, and it is so now. If I should be overwhelmed and do the dire thing, thank God for me, as I shall be delivered.

I have your letter. You say that you have abandoned public life, never more to return. Antonio, let me conjure you; and let me touch, for the last time, the most bitter of all things between us. Go back to the Palace. Go back. The upper city holds many decent men. We all know that. It is also known that you are not one of them. I think you know what I mean. For once in your life, listen to me, Antonio. You are an old man. You cannot have more than a few years, if any, in front of you, and too soon we shall both be standing before the true judge. Nevertheless, there is time to save yourself, even now, after all the horror. Go back to the Palace. Force yourself to work with the decent men. Look to the lower city. Bring in new laws. Use your final days to do what is good and what is just. Let the work take years but make a start. Let it at least begin. We cannot have the evil of lower Venice and particularly not of the black inner core. It is a smear of leprosy on our humanity and conscience. And Christ will not have it.

You see why you must burn this letter, unless you want to bring me back to Venice in chains. But then I will not come back.

God sever you from evil. Bernardo

55. [Vendramin, DIARY]:

xxxi October . . . The family all knew that Bernardo had an illegitimate son. A few old aunts and uncles even remembered the pretty mother, Maria Brenta. But who could even dream then that the child would turn into a Fra Orso? He was given too much learning . . . a few things suddenly make sense, even his allure for Loredana. This morning we all went to see Bernardo set sail. The women carried flowers. Our family banners were borne by the children. Masses were said for his safe voyage out, and masses too for his return. This, perhaps, in only three years' time with an amnesty. Everyone cried. His sons Jacopo and Pietro, and his brother Tommaso, are already at work in the Grand Council. Brokering future marriages, offering blocs of votes, making low-interest loans.

56. [Sister Polissena Giustiniani, LETTER]:

To the Most Reverend and Esteemed Father Clemence, Order of Friars Minor. God be with you.

Here at once is the letter, and so you see, I keep my promises. Now that I am head of my convent I can do things with more speed and silence. How this letter will reach you I only know, though it's to be by a route so private that I could put all the secrets of the world into it.

What a grand surprise to run into you yesterday, a grace and a pleasure, for I know how much you cherished the good of my dear cousin, madonna Loredana Contarini. She so admired you. In the dark days after her arrest, you alone were her help, and she still claims that death itself would have been her spouse, had it not been for your hail of words and prayers. Such was her desolation.

It was also then, I dare say, that you were banished and forbidden to see her, because your authority with her was too great. And I thank God you were absent from Venice, proofs in hand, on that horrid night now going on to five years ago, when Loredana rushed into the square of pikes. For there were people here ready to arrest you, and you'd have been in stormy waters. After many private enquiries, I was unable to find where you'd gone. But now at last we have you, safe and sound in Padua. Teaching perhaps? Never mind. The joy is that with God's will we found you, or how make sense of my nearly knocking you down as I turned into that quiet alley? Had you hoped to catch sight of me near my convent? All the happier. When I see Loredana tomorrow before vespers and tell her about you, she will give way to joy and she will want to see you of course, but that would be dangerous still. I needn't remind you of the trap-like memories of those who rule the world.

Now let me tell you about Loredana, as I promised. You said you wanted a whole chronicle. Let it be a sketch, as the details would take me days and they're no good for a letter. Sometime soon you must come back to Venice for the day and I'll tell you more. We can arrange a meeting in my great parlour, with two or three sisters knitting in one corner, while you and I sit in another, chatting quietly. You can even have a sip of dark Candia wine and some honeyed pastries from our choice local confectioner.

Soon after the horrendous events, Loredana passed into agitations and silence, tilting back and forth between these. And I believe that her being with child, thinking about nothing else and wanting it, was what kept her alive – this and the words you left with her. She detested food but was eager not to lose weight, so she forced herself to eat. That child had to be born and born healthy. She and I prayed for this as we'd never prayed for anything. I used to visit her nearly every day, and for a long time, apart from her father, I was her only visitor. No one else could see her. The mighty [*the Council of Ten*] were strict about this. I can't tell you what a hard winter that was, but it was all to be much worse. The miracle is that she and the child are alive today. But to get there, good heavens, I sometimes feared that I myself would fold under the weight of so much effort and worry. Her father was unbending, and I can't decide whether he was punishing her or trying still to keep things so quiet that he might yet become our doge one day, as if by a miraculous stroke. I won't say more about this.

The scandal of Loredana's deeds at the Palace slowly died away. She was after all out of her wits, and this too is why her pregnancy escaped all the beady eyes and wagging tongues. When Sier Antonio made a swift and large donation to the convent, she was given her own chambers and the abbess was ready to do almost anything for her – anything. Then in February I think, about four months after her arrest and the ghastly events, and after another turn of the mighty [*a new Council of Ten took office*], Loredana was free to leave the cloister. But her father kept her on there till one night, as the time for her parturition approached, she was moved secretly to a tiny convent near Motta and there gave birth to Orsino. This is her name for him, though he was baptised Bernardo Maria Motta, after his grandfather and place of birth. Maria? For Loredana's devotion to Our Lady.

Now all the most horrific troubles began, first with a fight between father and daughter. The infant was taken away from her and put out to a wet-nurse for adoption. How could she, a widow and a Loredan, keep or recognise it? And what choice had we if Loredana was ever to live in Venice again? Well, but even the lords of the earth can't always have things as they wish. Loredana desperately desired the infant and fought bitterly, even fiercely, to have it brought back. She attacked her father with her own hands. She wanted to nurse the child herself, and without it – it had been torn away from her – something in her shivered into fragments. It might as well have been a demon. The parts went in a dozen directions. She screeched and howled and raged and in truth became a beast. Don't even try to imagine the sight. Then this passed and she quit eating, she quit talking, she quit caring, she quit moving. In one corner of her rooms she sat and sat, and there she stared and stared, and occasionally she moaned or wailed as from a deep part of herself, so that the sounds were muted or only half came out. Some mornings she was found standing against a wall, her nose almost touching it, staring. Had she slept that night? Nobody knew. She had to be washed and fed by force. Overnight that still handsome woman changed. She became a creature. I can't tell you. We had been so close she and I, during all her years as a widow, even if she was in the world and I wasn't. She'd come to the convent once every three days or so, and we would spend an hour together, an hour which always began with a minute of prayer.

What were we to do then, her father and I? At first the question was all in his hands, since I couldn't see her more than once in a week – the trip to Motta was too far – and meantime she was falling more silent. After a month of that, I saw that either I moved in with her to try to pull her back into the world or we must lose her for ever. I'd known nuns who had shed their reason. So I went to her father and told him what I thought I could do, but I also said I wouldn't so much as touch my sleeves for him unless he took a solemn oath to bring back the infant to her, if I decided this was the only way to help fetch back her reason. He finally agreed. I made him vow, and with a few words from Cardinal Pisani I was given leave to be away from my convent for ten months, to be with Loredana. Her father had us moved, along with servants and everything else we needed, to a large secluded house near Cavarzere, where he himself visited only by night. And there I lived with her.

My story comes down to this. I was with her day and night. I talked endlessly to her. I soothed her. I recalled our childhood. I recited scenes, and I began to find minutes – often in the middle of the night – when the real Loredana emerged. Suddenly she was all there. What do you think of that? After some time she started now and again to fix her eyes on me, and more so after my discovery of those minutes when she was ready to know me, to call me by name, and to strain for her clarity, as I held on to her hands and strained with her in that fight. I would promise her the baby and go on repeating the promise, changing the words like a changing prayer. She always then fell back into her darkness, which she said was alive with a tangle of silent demons, though she wasn't afraid, she said, and maybe she preferred them. As soon as it seemed right to me, I sent for the wet-nurse and the infant and had them lodged in the house. Her father gave me no trouble about this. Every so often, day and night, I had the baby brought into the same room with her, but not, at first, in her moments of complete clarity. These moments grew slowly, then by leaps and bounds, till we began to have long minutes and even hours of bliss, and by now of course the baby was often with us.

We were not yet safe, far from it. My ten months were all but gone and Loredana was frightened. We saw that if her healing was to go on, she must be able to see me three or four times a week and this required her return to Venice. I had to be back in my convent. But with her attachment to Orsino, no one could see how this was possible. Then she herself saw the way. She and the child could be taken secretly into Venice and there, in her widow's weeds and under a new name, she could live as a retiring stranger in the lower city, in a house near to my convent, so that I could go down to see her. She would go forth into the streets well veiled and only during the quiet hours. Her father naturally rejected the idea at once – brutally. He was outraged. But if we wanted to rescue her from a terrible night, what else could we do? I couldn't leave my convent, and so I gave him no rest. No matter what he had been at the Palace, I swept all that aside and begged for Loredana's life. I wasn't overly courteous or kind with Sier Antonio. I made him see that he could not put his fear and family pride – I understand these things – above Loredana's good. I unfolded a plan and vowed to him that we could keep the secret, even from his brothers and the whole web of cousins. He stopped resisting, I got him to agree, and with the greatest secrecy in the world a house was found. Mother and child moved into the lower city, and there they have been these three years, under these foundations, very near to where I sit writing this letter.

There you have it, Father Clemence, the story of her recovery, all thanks to the Lord, for without our belief in Him through prayer, our pluck would have been impossible. I was there to help Loredana get Orsino back, but the rest was in God's grace and in her. I wish you had seen her battle against the returning spells of darkness. She was a brave soldier. Is this why she was best, to begin with, in the middle of the night? Had she more strength then?

Anyhow, her courage came back, she has it to this day, and what you see is a woman again gracious and pleasant. She still has departures into darkness – you may as well know it – but she always and sooner returns, and the little boy is her bell tower, the first face she looks for. That child has a bewitching laugh. He's four years old – beautiful, alert, quick, strong, and he has the large eyes of the Loredans without the rue. Maybe this will come but I pray not. You'll understand, I'm sure, that his grandfather detests the name Orsino and forbids its use. Loredana however knows him by no other name, though she avoids it whenever Sier Antonio pays one of his secret midnight visits. You will also understand when I tell you that she lives for the child. But knowing this, she has imposed a rule on herself and is much ashamed when she breaks it. Afraid to overindulge him, she permits herself to pick him up or play with him only once a day. Next autumn he begins his studies. A lay nun, well versed in Latin and numbers, is to be his preceptor. Loredana tells me that whenever her father visits, he cannot tear his eyes away from Orsino, and I would give a ducat to know what exactly he is thinking then. One day he announced that the child could never be a Venetian gentleman. Well, what did he expect?

Loredana's comings and goings in the lower city are guarded and disguised. She lives a very simple life and I have to laugh when I think of how well she plays her part. She even walks with a different gait now. I think she enjoys it, I mean passing herself off as an ordinary stranger. But I shouldn't make light of things. We live dangerously. She has to be a fine pattern of prudence and self-effacement. Since her house is on the fringes and gets a share of sunlight, she emerges only at odd hours or in the rain – naturally always veiled. She dresses plainly, to catch no one's attention, and since the lower city has many widows, when need be she can melt nicely into that throng.

This is as much as I'll tell you for now, Father Clemence. To learn more you'll have to come and visit me in Venice. But then we must have an exchange, for I shall want to hear all about you.

I commend myself in Christ and most humbly to your goodness. Venice, this 19th day of April, 1534. Suor Polissena Giustiniani

In the convent of San Zaccaria

Compiled by Benedict Loredan, Ordinis Praedicatorum, in the years 1697–1699.

AUTHOR'S NOTE

History and Fiction

Leonardo da Vinci's statement about a two-tiered city, quoted at the head of the novel, voices the High Renaissance search for a utopian upper-class world. Other thinkers held similar ideas. When imagining an ideal city, for example, the fifteenth-century humanist L. B. Alberti conceived of an inner urban circle for the nobility and an outer one for the common people, each to be fully walled-in and gated.

Although *Loredana* is a historical fantasy, its account of manners and mores, of sights, sounds, places and the condition of women seeks to reproduce the ways of daily life in Venice and Florence at the beginning of the sixteenth century. The Venetian Council of Ten was founded in 1310, and soon began to operate so secretly that its members might as well have worn masks.

I shall only add that the array and format of the novel's 'documents' is insidious. Drawing on my professional experience in Italian archives, I have sought to give every numbered entry the feel and ring of authenticity. But readers who wonder about the liberties that I may have taken with history will, I fear, do so in vain. Only historians of that time and place are likely to know, and even they may wonder about certain entries.